FRESH HELL

Also by Cameron Chaney

Autumncrow
featuring:
"Follow Me In," "Pumpkin Light,"
"Burnt Brownies," "Frost," "Saving Face,"
"I Have No Mouth and I Must Feed," "CRYP-TV,"
and the print debut of:
"There Are Monsters Here"

Available from Library Macabre Press

"Karakoncolos"
collected in:
Served Cold
edited by R. Saint Claire & Steve Donoghue

"At the End of the Rope"
collected in:
Local Haunts
edited by R. Saint Claire

"The Switch"
collected in:
Other Voices, Other Tombs
edited by John Brhel & Joe Sullivan

Available from Cemetery Gates Media

CAMERON CHANEY

AUTUMNCROW HIGH

Fresh Hell

A Library Macabre Press Book

To Benjamin,
for everything

A LIBRARY MACABRE PRESS Original

First paperback printing September 2023
First hardcover printing September 2023

10 9 8 7 6 5 4 3 2 1

Cover art by Cameron Roubique
Edited by Benjamin Brinner

Published by Library Macabre Press

PART I
ECHOES

CHAPTER 1

THE DREAM COMES AS IT ALWAYS DOES, oozing from the edges of sleep like blood from a gaping wound. There's no way to stop it, no way to stay safe and snug in my warm, cozy bed. I can fight all I want—and I usually do, just to say I tried—but the struggle only wears me down, leaving me weak and vulnerable.

The dream is stronger than me, and it shows no mercy.

"Come. Let me fix you . . ." the phantom voice says. The words are summer honey, sugar-sweet and sticky with tenderness, but they scratch along the insides of my skull like some undead thing clawing its way out of a casket.

No! Please, please, please! Not tonight. God, please! I cry in silence. But my pleading goes ignored as the peaceful nothingness of sleep is devoured by the all-too-familiar terror. It floods my vision completely, and within seconds I'm whisked away, yanked around my midriff by some unseen force as though a rope were knotted there. It hauls me up, up out of bed, toward my bedroom ceiling.

No, no, no!

I know what happens next. I've endured this torment many times before. Several nights a week, in fact. Sometimes every night for weeks on end. The dream comes and goes, but it's never gone for long.

My struggling body hits the ceiling with incredible force. Plaster crumbles on impact, raining chalky dust onto me. The dust lands in my eyes. It jockeys my panicked breaths, rides them up my nose and into my lungs. I cough and cry and plead in my head—*No, no, no, no, NO!*—but the relentless force continues to pull, indifferent to my cries of torment.

I feel the pain as though I were wide awake, feel each and every blow as the rope slackens and tugs upward again, slamming my helpless body over and over into the ceiling. My skull cracks. My vision brightens. I pass out and reawaken, still here. Still in the nightmare.

I can't fight anymore. My limbs slacken as every last bit of energy drains out of my being and trickles over my mattress onto my bedroom floor. I taste copper.

SLAM. SLAM. SLAM.

The house shakes. Paperbacks and trinkets tumble off the bookshelves across my room. My body snaps and caves under each blow until the ceiling breaks in half completely, forming a jagged crack from wall to wall.

The tension on the rope ceases, and I fall back onto my bed, bouncing a few times, springs squeaking. Then all is still. Silent. A nightly hush.

Anyone else would be relieved, thanking God that this terrible dream was finally over, but I know better.

The nightmare is just beginning.

The fracture in the ceiling glowers down at me. It twitches. It widens.

It smiles.

My lips part in a silent *O* of horror as a bellowing roar rumbles from the mouth in the ceiling, a dry, rasping wail that threatens to burst my eardrums.

Help me! Please, help! I cry out from the depths of my mind, but no one hears me.

The bedroom ceiling sinks. It drops so fast I'd hardly realize what I'm seeing had I not experienced this all before.

This is the part where the hungry jaws of hell eat me up.

The gap in the ceiling opens wider and swallows me whole, plunging me into darkness.

How did it come to this? Before the nightmares started, summer break had held such promise. Now everything has fallen apart. Hard to believe I once bubbled over with that summer-sunshine happiness teenagers get when months of freedom from school are on the horizon. Little did I know my days would be spent doing my best not to succumb to the nightmare that plagues my every waking moment.

Trying not to think of Dad.

Summer-sunshine happiness. Any bit of it I had before is eclipsed by the hot, gooey blackness of this dark wasteland, laden with a stench so vile I can feel it squirming on my tongue like starving larvae. I know that smell. The funk of rotting corpses. Thousands of them. Their flesh squelches beneath my feet, clotting the gaps between my toes.

"Help us? Help us?" the bodies chant in unison, not pleading but questioning, as if help were a permission to be granted.

"Help? Help us?"

Desperate hands claw at my legs, grasping with oily fingers as they pull me deeper and deeper into the abyss. I have no way to fight back, nothing to grab hold of.

Then that rope, that spectral vine, slides around my waist and hoists me up again. My feet—dripping with gore—leave the fetid tangle of putrefying bodies, and for once I am grateful for the rope, happy to be pulled from that hell filled with sufferers.

"Yes, I'll fix you," the voice repeats.

My body bursts through the roof of my house, and I am thrust into the sky, spinning up and away. A crescent moon shines silver in a sky littered with stars and small puffy clouds.

Upward I soar, on and on until I am miles above the earth. Then everything comes to a pause. I hover in the frigid night sky, anticipating the worst. The very worst.

The drop.

Tears pour down my cheeks.

It's only a matter of seconds before I plummet toward earth, and there's nothing I can do but accept the inevitable.

It's just a dream. I'll wake up soon, I reassure myself.

Sure, Bailey, sure, I counter. *You know this is no ordinary dream.*

I fall, crashing down from the sky like a meteor. Fast. Faster. The force of the fall seizes my chest, and I hope to die of suffocation before splattering on the ground like roadkill.

One thing is for certain, though: Autumncrow Valley looks beautiful from up here. Those foggy nighttime streets aglow with the soft light of old-fashioned streetlamps fill me with a kind of peace in this horrible dream. There's a flutter in my chest, not unlike the one that stirs inside me whenever I catch a glimpse of Bill Macklin and his bashful smile.

But Autumncrow was my true first love. This is the town that raised me, the town I spent my childhood exploring. Bicycle rides, flashlight tag, shopping sprees, scary stories in the cemetery, monster movies at the theater—I have a bird's-eye view of my entire life from up here, and my heart swells with wistful affection.

I guess that's what we all feel in the valley. Even the resident old-timers, better acquainted than any of us with the town's dreadful secrets, seem content to live out their days here. They could easily uproot themselves, move elsewhere. But they don't. Why is that?

It must be love. Falling in love, falling to your death— it all means the same thing in Autumncrow Valley.

My brief moment of peace fades when I realize how quickly Main Street is approaching. I hold my breath—not that I could breathe to begin with—and close my eyes as I await impact, the bone-crunching thud of meat against pavement.

The time it takes for my skull to split open like a smashed pumpkin depends on how long my eyes stay closed. If I keep them shut, I will fall forever. But when I finally tire of the endless skydive and part my eyelids, even just a crack, the ground will rush to meet me.

Best to get it over with.

I open my eyes and watch as Main Street pitches its fist. My head hits first, clashing with the cobblestone so hard I can hear the rupture of my skull and the slosh of my brains. I don't die, but the pain is so excruciating that I wish I would.

My eyes roll aimlessly in my head, taking in the many sights of downtown. The storefronts tower above me, each with its own cutesy Halloween display. The café stands off to my left, darkened except for the buzzing neon glow of a sign reading: "Spooky's Café: A Bite of Fright!" Purple and green light illuminates the phony spiderwebs stretched taut from one corner of the window to another, entangling two plastic skeletons enjoying their cappuccinos together at a small bistro table.

I helped with that display just yesterday during my shift, and now here it is, a brand-new addition to the dreamscape.

The gaps in the cobblestone brim with rivulets of something thick and crimson. Blood. My blood. I watch as it spreads to the pool of gore surrounding one of my arms lying a few feet away, all alone like a shy kid at recess.

Pieces of me are scattered all around Main Street, reminding me of the time my big brother snatched the Barbie dolls right out of my hands and hurled them from my second-story bedroom window. Each doll hit the ground in an explosion of limbs. Inconsolable, at the tender age of six, I could've sworn the dolls were bleeding. I refused to play with them after that, even after my mom stuck them back together with super glue. I couldn't look at the dolls without imagining miniscule human bones inside, each doll complete with its own teeny-tiny anatomy. Plastic torsos and painted smiles, holding within a bubbling brook of blood.

"Let me fix you . . ."

That whisper again. It sounds like my mother's voice this time, but I know it isn't.

The tightening sensation returns around my waist. I am dragged along once again like a broken puppet on strings. The growing puddle of blood dribbles along after me, trailed by my arm and other unattached limbs, each struggling to keep up.

Boutiques, gift shops, mom-and-pop restaurants—everything here is as in real life . . . with one big difference.

Autumncrow High.

The school stands in the center of Main Street as if it, too, had been dropped there from above. The familiar downtown landmarks—Undead Video, the secondhand bookshop where Dad used to work, Madame Tinkett's Sweets, and so many others—all flank the hulking giant, stretching around its dark brick and mortar like birthday party bouncy houses, making way for every inch of the towering school and its haunted grounds.

The old oak is there, otherwise known as the "choking oak" by my classmates. I cringe when I see it. Even in sleep, the tree haunts me.

Enshadowed by its long dark branches and surrounding its massive trunk are tombstones. Dozens of them. A small graveyard was developed decades ago to serve as a monument and final resting place for the students and teachers of Autumncrow High who had lost their lives. New additions are frequent.

Mine could be next.

"Come. Let me fix—"

The front doors of the school burst open with a *bang!* Fog pours from the gaping entry, rushing down the stone steps to mingle with the lingering haze. A lonely melody echoes from inside the school, somewhere deep and distant, as though from another era entirely. The plaintive sounds billow gracefully down the halls and among the cracked, mossy tombstones as if the music itself were waltzing to its own tinny harmony.

I recognize the song as an old standard my parents would hum along to. "What'll I Do" I think it's called. One lazy afternoon a few years ago, I watched from the kitchen doorway as Mom and Dad danced to the tune, holding each other close, totally unaware of their daughter's presence. They looked to me like a couple of teenagers at prom, lost in each other's loving gaze.

In this god-awful dream, the lyrics of heartfelt devotion sound more like an ominous threat.

"When I'm alone with only dreams of you that won't come true, what'll I do?"

Die-cut letters spelling "Autumncrow High" adorn the iron archway at the head of the schoolyard. I am pulled underneath them, through the open iron gates, and guided along the well-trodden dirt path that cuts through the tiny cemetery.

"Help us? Help us?"

Tears roll down my cheeks as the despairing voices plead from below ground. So many voices. Teachers young and old. Students from decades ago, students from *just this summer* whose funerals I attended. They are all trapped in the dirt forever, crying out to me—*me*—for help I can't provide.

I'm sorry, I want to say, but the words roll out of my mouth as a feeble moan. It's difficult to form words when your brain is no longer inside your skull.

"Help us, please? Help—"

Another voice takes over, cutting off the whispering dead. They hush one another, a soft *"shh..."* padding the air as a dark figure emerges from the school's open entryway, emerging from the music itself.

"Bailey... let me fix you."

God, it sounds like Dad now.

Leave me alone! Please, please leave me alone! I scream the words in my head, knowing full well it's a lost cause. The figure descends the stairs, taking each one nice and slow, prolonging my agony. Teasing me.

Moonlight graces the figure's soft, perfect skin as he steps out of the school's gray shadow, exposing a grin as sharp as a killer's blade. He is seventeen at most—no older than me—with thick black hair greased away from his face but for a single strand that curves along the left side of his forehead, stopping just below his brow. The boy is tall, well-built. Broad shoulders fill his orange-and-black varsity jacket perfectly.

Handsome. So handsome.

But that menacing smile. And the unmistakable flicker of something terrible behind those pale blue eyes...

"Let me fix you..." he repeats, stepping off the bottom step and crossing the foggy path toward me as I am pulled, still, toward him.

There is a strange contraption strapped over the boy's shoulders, a bulky wooden wheel with a lever attached to one side. A crank. He grips it in his right hand, turning it around and around like Vincent Price at the end of *House on Haunted Hill,* an old movie I've seen more times than I can count.

Each time the boy turns the crank, unseen strings pull me closer to him. This boy is the puppeteer, the conductor of my nightmares. He cranks the wheel again and again, stepping nearer, bringing me closer until my bloody body lies mangled at his feet.

The boy leans forward, his smile broadening as he draws close to my face, eyes crackling with icy fire. He smells of strong, musky cologne, so rich I can taste it in my throat.

"Follow me in," he says.

There's only one thing left for me to do.

I scream.

CHAPTER 2

I JOLT AWAKE to find the entire cast of *Saved by the Bell* looming over the foot of my bed, their dimpled smiles stretched from ear to ear, perfect teeth sparkling in the golden dawn.

Grinning.

I blink. I turn my head from side to side against the sweat-soaked pillow. I mutter, "Thank God that's over." My voice is a death rattle, perfectly at home with the raspy squawks of blackbirds outside my window.

I sit up and curve my back inward, feeling the stretch and pull of my achy muscles. You'd think I had done fifty push-ups last night . . . or gone skydiving without a parachute.

I fall back into bed, wishing I could sleep for another eight hours. I'd settle for fifteen minutes, anything to help ease the pounding in my skull. I move my fingers in circles on my temples, but my efforts to ease the pain are shot when my alarm clock blasts to life. Most mornings, my clock radio wakes me up with a Top 40 summer hit. But today is different.

"What'll I do when you are far away and I am blue?"

"NO!" I whack the snooze button and allow my arm to flop lifelessly over the edge of the mattress. I lie in the post-snooze silence, chills raking along my back despite the warm rays of sunshine beaming through my open bedroom window. Sheer white drapes exchange ghostly whispers in the soft breeze.

Mom always tells me I shouldn't leave my window open at night, but this old house isn't exactly state-of-the-art in the way of air-conditioning, so—weather permitting—the window stays open. I'm on the second floor anyway, so it isn't like someone could easily climb through and hatchet me to pieces in my sleep. Maybe in my nightmares, but not in real life.

A quick *tap-tap-tap* rattles my bedroom door, followed by: "You walking? Or am I driving?" Mom's morning voice sounds much like mine. It barely reaches my ears through the heavy wooden door.

"I'm walking with Melody," I shout in reply.

Mom doesn't say another word. Floorboards crack and whine under her feet as she shuffles to the kitchen for a cup of pitch-black coffee and her "daily plate of guilt," as she calls it, otherwise known as Eggo waffles. Mom is a health freak and likes to cook her meals from scratch, but she's also the furthest one can get from a morning person. She claims she doesn't have the motivation required to prepare a balanced breakfast every day.

That had been Dad's job . . .

I can't blame her. I'm no early bird either, especially not today. If it were any other morning, I'd try to persuade Mom to let me stay home sick, but this isn't just another school day.

The first day of senior year happens only once, Bailey, I tell myself. *Please don't miss it. Get up.*

Groaning, I disentangle my legs from the bedspread, relieved to discover my limbs intact. *Yes. Good. They're all still here.* I slide my aching feet into my fuzzy black slippers before slogging to the dresser across from my bed. My *Saved by the Bell* poster, pinned to the wall above it, greets me once again. I fulfill my daily ritual of wishing Zack Morris a good morning. He beams in response.

"Handsome devil," I say.

Retrieving my purple-and-teal Sassaby makeup case off the dresser top, I cross the room to the window, framed by white floor-to-ceiling bookcases spanning the entire length of the wall. The shelves create a pleasant reading nook below the windowsill. It is padded with multiple pillows, each encased in lacy fabric for "maximum coziness." Mom's words, not mine. The lace feels scratchy to me, but Mom likes it for whatever reason. I pretend to like it too.

Mom and I built the shelves together at the beginning of summer to hold my various books and trinkets. Slim volumes of *The Baby-Sitters Club,* the *Narnia* series, *Little House on the Prairie*, and dozens of Mom's old Nancy Drew and Judy Bolton mysteries line the shelves, neighbored by strategically placed knickknacks and framed photos of my family and friends.

Most of the photos are of Dad and me.

I never realized that until now. I guess I took it for granted.

I focus on one picture, taken nearly a decade ago during one of our fishing trips to the pond behind Uncle Pete's cabin. In the photo, Dad and I are sitting on the dock. I'm beaming at the camera, fishing pole in hand, flashing an awkward combination of straight baby teeth and jagged adult tusks. Thank goodness for braces.

Melody is there too, striking a *Charlie's Angels* pose in the background, hammy as ever.

Dad, the polar opposite of Melody, sits to my left in the photo, his silvery hair in perfect contrast to my fiery locks, grinning softly as his bare feet dangle off the dock, toes barely grazing the water's mossy surface. He isn't holding a pole. His empty hands are tucked between his knees, shoulders slumped forward in boredom.

I found out when I was much older that Dad hated fishing. He only taught me because I was so eager to learn. It was one of those weird childhood phases, I guess. Much to Dad's relief, I quickly discovered that fishing wasn't my thing.

Instead, books became my enduring hobby. Mom says it was only a matter of time. After all, I am the daughter of two bookworms.

Dad had worked off and on at The Little Bookshoppe of Curiosities on Main Street since he was a teenager. "Bringing home books instead of money again, I see," Mom would say every evening when Dad shuffled through the front door with a box full of paperbacks. She was only half serious; Dad and I would give each other "the look," knowing we would soon spy Mom sneaking a peek at the strays her husband had snagged for their ever-expanding collection.

The home library is down the hall. But the door stays shut these days. On the other side is an alien planet existing in a completely separate atmosphere.

An ache arises in my chest. I tell myself it's a side effect of last night's dream.

Pulling my attention away from the photograph, I plop down on the window seat and crack open my makeup case. In the built-in mirror, a weary face looks back at me. Her eyes are made of blown glass, their usual jade vibrancy dulled to a dirty olive. Dark water balloons hang below them, her weary lids struggling to remain open. Her lips are parched, her skin as pale as ash, and her cherry-red hair—normally thick and wavy—hangs low in oily strands.

I'm only seventeen. *How did this happen?*

It's true what they say: sleep is important. I just wish the boy in the letterman jacket would stop hijacking my attempts to get some rest.

Who is he? Why does he keep coming back? And more importantly, what does he want?

These questions have been plaguing me all summer. I'm continually having to remind myself that, while everything else in the dreamscape mirrors the Autumncrow I know in reality, I don't know of any boy like the puppeteer. He may be wearing Autumncrow High's signature jacket and colors, but I've checked my yearbooks again and again, searching for his face—those piercing blue eyes, the dangling strand of hair, that wide grin—to no avail. This isn't my subconscious telling me I should be wary of some boy

17

from school; the boy is nobody to me. He's just a figment of my imagination. Plain and simple.

But you don't believe that, do you? What about your radio this morning, huh? It played the song. What's up with that?

I exhale a shaky breath and watch as it fogs against the crisp morning air. It isn't even September yet, but autumn temperatures have already emerged, paving the way for the spookiest time of year.

Fall always arrives early in Autumncrow. Some theorize this is because the town is nestled deep in a valley, encircled by steep wooded hills that branch away from Autumncrow for miles and miles. I suppose this might explain the cooler temperatures—*hardly*—but it doesn't explain why the leaves change color only halfway through the summer months, shifting from deep jungle greens to glorious shades of burnt orange, red, and yellow. Most places don't witness this transition until mid-October or even November. The way I see it, the laws of science have no place in this town.

And neither does restful, dreamless sleep.

I'm rummaging in my makeup case for a brush and palette, something bright to hide my haggard appearance, when a voice calls from outside my window.

"Hey! You're supposed to be ready by now. Coffee, remember?"

Crap! I forgot.

I lean forward and press my face against the screen. My room is at the front of the house, providing a great view of the front yard and the rest of Abraham Street. Our yard is small, made even smaller by the large elm tree dominating most of the space. The grass is barely hanging on to its summer lushness, but that doesn't matter; the leaves from the elm have blanketed the lawn almost completely, the autumnal answer to a winter wonderland.

A classic white picket fence frames the yard, complete with a picturesque swinging gate and red brick walkway leading to the front porch steps. Melody stands outside the fence, leaning against the mailbox Dad mounted to a post beside the front gate years ago. Hanging from the mailbox by small chains is a sign with the words "HAGEN HOUSEHOLD" painted in neat bold letters.

Melody is looking up at me, a smile plastered on her face, wavy blond hair glistening in the daylight. So pretty.

Her smile quickly fades. "Oh God. You look . . . ill."

"Thanks?" I say, not knowing how else to respond. "I'm getting ready now. Come on up. Mom'll let you in."

"Cool." Melody rights herself and hoists her denim backpack off the sidewalk, throwing it over her shoulder.

As she makes her way through the gate and up the path toward the front door, I quickly apply foundation and soft pink blush to my face, adding color to my complexion before Melody can see me up close. I'm not scared of her judgment or anything—I'm used to her teasing. What I don't want is her unsolicited advice that I should tell my mom about the dreams.

I'm moving on from the blush—it's rough, but I'll fix it in a moment—and just getting started on my eye shadow when Melody bursts through the door, immediately closing in to study my face.

"Jesus, you work fast," she says, narrowing her eyes. Melody steps back and walks over to the white wicker chair angled in the corner where my bookcase meets the wall. She throws her bookbag on the hardwood floor and collapses in the seat. "Hide from me all you want. See if I care."

Melody pulls a random hardcover off my bookcase—*Maniac Magee* by Jerry Spinelli—and flips through it aimlessly. She always has to keep her hands busy.

"I'm not hiding," I say. "I'm just putting on my makeup. You're wearing plenty yourself."

She really is. Melody's face is made up to perfection. She's rocking an earthy color palette, ditching her usual bright blues and pinks for smoky blush and light brown lipstick. She looks amazing, as always. And I look—

"Do I really look ill?"

Melody laughs and returns the book to the shelf (in the wrong place, I can't help but note). "Nah, not really. Sorry. But you do look tired."

She's lying. She meant what she said.

"I am tired," I admit.

"Like I keep saying, you need to tell your mom."

I grimace. There it is, the dreaded suggestion that creates a wave pool of guilt in my chest every time I think about it.

"No." I put my makeup brush down a little too firmly and pick up my pink lip gloss. "I can handle it on my own."

"Famous last words," Melody says in a singsong tone.

I lower the gloss before I have a chance to apply it. "Mom doesn't need the extra stress," I say. "What good is it going to do? She can't climb inside my head and take my dreams away, so why bother her with it?"

My words are narrow and jagged. Melody reacts with a pained wince. "I just . . ." She shrugs. "I think she'd want to know. She might want you to see someone."

"We can't afford a doctor right now," I say. My blood pressure is rising at a vicious rate. I'm not usually quick to anger, but with each passing night my patience withers and my tongue sharpens. I'm literally vibrating. "Mom picks up extra shifts at the diner every chance she gets and still doesn't make enough money to support the three of us. That's why I took the job at the café."

"I know," Melody says defensively. Her eyebrows are quirked in concern, but I'm too heated to stop.

"Dad's job may not have brought in much, but it was better than what I can manage. I'm doing my best to help out, but it's hard. Another bill is the last thing we need. Mom's still trying to pay off my braces from three years ago."

My voice is trembling. The dam holding my tears at bay is about to break.

Melody is no longer relaxed. She sits upright, her hands held in a pose of surrender. "Bailey, relax. I just care about you, you know? I'm worried. These dreams have you all messed up, and the extra makeup will only go so far before your mom notices you aren't sleeping. I know she's been through a lot, but so have you. It's okay to need a little help. Especially after your dad—"

"This isn't about my dad!" That's when the dam bursts. The tears come flooding out.

"Hey, it's okay," Melody says, abandoning the chair and kneeling on the floor in front of me. She takes my hands in hers. "I get it. I'm sorry. I wasn't saying you need to see a doctor, but the school counselor might be a good idea. It doesn't cost a thing. I saw her last year after Grammy died. And I've . . ." She pauses and lowers her eyes. "I've been talking to her again since Tommy and I broke up. She even let me see her over the summer. It helps."

The noise of my stress fades into the background, and my heart rate slows. This information is news to me, creating a much-needed distraction. "Really?" I say with a sniffle. "I didn't know."

"Well, I mean . . ." Melody releases hold of my hands and runs her palms over her bleached Levi's. She laughs. "We're pretty alike, you know? I hide things from people too. Sometimes."

Her eyes meet mine again, and I can see how much she cares.

"Thank you," I say, wiping the tears from my cheeks. My makeup comes off on my fingertips. "I know you're trying to help. I just don't want Mom to think I'm . . . like . . ."

"Weak?" Melody says.

"No, not that. I just want her to see me as capable of taking care of us too. And I am. I don't want all the pressure to be on her. These dreams have nothing to do with Dad or the stress. They're something else."

"Ghostly echoes from beyond."

I give Melody a sideways glance and widen my eyes in mock terror. "I suppose that's a possibility."

"Well of course it is, dummy. This is Autumncrow!" Melody grabs my makeup brush from the window seat cushion. "Now let me help. We're running out of time to grab coffee before school, and trust me, I'll need to be caffeinated if I'm going to make it through today. Do you have dry shampoo?"

I nod.

"Good. You have Crypt Keeper hair." Melody leans forward and gets to work.

CHAPTER 3

ONCE MELODY HAS TRANSFORMED my face from "undead horror show host" into that of a mostly normal-looking teenage girl, we do the best we can with my hair. Then I slip into the outfit I assembled last night before bed: an oversized off-white turtleneck sweater paired with an emerald vest, faded jeans, and black-and-white high-tops, plus the pair of studded skull earrings I usually wear.

Melody stands back to size up my outfit. "Subtle, but nice," she says, biting her thumbnail, face scrunched in concentration. "But you should—here, let me."

She steps forward and tucks the front of my sweater into my jeans, then grabs a narrow black belt from my closet and loops it around my waist.

"I can do it on my own," I argue. "I'm not five years old."

Melody shushes me. "I'm working here."

Once she has finished adding her final touches, Melody steps back once more and grins. "Perfect. You look amazing! The green goes so well with your hair. Do you have Pop-Tarts?"

"Thanks—huh?"

"Pop-Tarts," Melody repeats.

"Oh yeah. Pop-Tarts." Melody tends to jump from subject to subject at warp speed, so it takes my brain a moment to catch up sometimes. I've known her my whole life and still haven't gotten used to it. "Pop-Tarts. Kitchen. Same cabinet as always."

"Good," Melody says, starting for the door. "I'm famished. I know it seems like this beauty stuff comes naturally to me, but it's hard work."

Melody exits my room and heads for the kitchen, her footsteps creaking as she descends to the first floor.

I take a quick inventory of my binders and supplies to make sure I have everything I need for the day, taking a moment to reshelve *Maniac Magee* in his proper place. As I do, something slips from its pages and flops at my feet—a Polaroid I must've been using as a bookmark. I pick it up and grin fondly. It's an image of Melody and me as middle schoolers at the annual Halloween Carnival, posing in front of the Ferris wheel. Dad took this picture, I recall.

My grin fades. *I wish things could be like they used to be.*

I slip the Polaroid into my bookbag before joining Melody and my family downstairs.

Melody has done an expert job of disguising my tired face for one more day. Mom, to my relief, still doesn't suspect a thing.

Resting her fork on her plate, Mom faces me head-on. "It isn't too late," she says in a low voice so Melody won't hear.

I give Mom one of those smiles that's more like a frown. "I know. I'll be okay. Promise."

"There's always Kilgore High," she presses.

Worry is etched deeply into Mom's features. This past summer has aged her many years beyond her fifty-two. If I look hard enough, I can see last night's late hours at the diner playing back in her eyes. I blink, afraid she'll glimpse the nightmares reflected in mine.

"I'll be okay," I repeat, giving her a kiss on the cheek. "I love you."

"I love you too, my girl," she says.

Mom wipes a tear from her cheek and immediately recovers when she sees my friend standing across the kitchen by the snack cabinet. She is shoving half a Pop-Tart into her mouth.

"Hungry, Melody?" Mom asks with a laugh.

"Always, Mrs. Hagen," Melody says, undeterred by her mouthful of toaster pastry.

"You know, I only buy Pop-Tarts because of you," Mom says. "Otherwise, those sugary things wouldn't be allowed in my house."

"Thank you, Mrs. Hagen." Crumbs tumble from Melody's mouth.

I shake my head in mock disapproval. "You're too much."

My little sister Rae is seated next to Mom at the kitchen table, plucking blueberries from the top of her yogurt parfait and thumbing through my copy of *Seventeen*, trying her damnedest to ignore us.

"Good morning, kid," I say, playfully ruffling her hair.

A few short months ago, Rae wouldn't have minded this in the slightest, but she has become very particular about her appearance since then, taking extra care with her wavy brown hair, the same color as Dad's before he went gray. Today she has it pulled back from her face with a pretty pink hairband.

"Hands off!" she says, pulling away from my hand and fleeing for the half bath off the living room to assess the damage.

"Sorry!" I call. I turn to Melody. "I keep forgetting the hair is off-limits now."

Melody takes another bite of her cold Pop-Tart and says, "They grow up so fast." Then she grabs hold of my hand and pulls me to the door, chanting, "Coffee! Coffee! Coffee!"

I give Mom one last wave before I am dragged into the chilly morning air, made even chillier when the sun darts behind a large gray cloud.

"Smells like rain," I say, looking up at the foreboding storm clouds in the distance. I wish I had thought to wear a jacket over my sweater. Now I know why Mom asked if I needed a ride.

"That's Ohio weather for you. We need to hurry," Melody mutters. "I spent way too much time on *both* of us to let our hair get ruined."

We push through the front gate and make our way together down Abraham Street toward town, passing dozens of traditional Victorian- and Tudor-style homes. Each house is beautiful in its own unique way. Many have been meticulously restored to their former glory, while others are less polished, swarmed by decades' worth of ivy, their most shadowed regions garnished with moss. I prefer it that way. Cracked shingles and sagging gutters add that spooky touch Autumncrow is known for.

My house is a Victorian stucco, but it's on the smaller side compared with most of the homes on my block. Part of me has always wanted to live in one of these giant mansions, the kind I could explore when night falls, donning a flowing black gown of silk with a candelabra in hand to light the inky halls. Like the damsels on the covers of those gothic romances Mom likes to read.

My house may not be as sprawling as certain others in Autumncrow, but it does have its advantages. Because it's small, it's less likely to be haunted by malevolent spirits. That's just common sense. It's also less expensive to heat in the wintertime. *And* it's only two short blocks from the center of town. With the high school located only a few more blocks from there, my walk to school is fifteen minutes, tops. That's important when you can't afford a car.

Feeling the weight of all my school supplies sinking into my lower back, I tuck my thumbs into the straps of my bookbag and tug it higher onto my shoulders. At the same moment, a gust of wind carrying the aroma of freshly fried eggs and bacon from open kitchen windows lifts the leaves from the pavement ahead and pitches them at us. I squeeze my eyes shut against the cool breeze while Melody issues a roar of frustration and agony.

"Just what I need," she says. "A head full of leaves on the first day of school."

"Shh, you're fine." I laugh. "Here, I got you." I pluck several leaves from her golden locks and wipe them from her varsity jacket, proudly displaying "AUTUMNCROW

HIGH" in bold burnt-orange letters across the back. It is identical to the jacket the nightmare boy wears.

"Since when do you care so much about your hair anyway?" I say, removing the last of the leaves.

Melody has always taken care of her appearance, but she never used to worry so much about her looks. Windswept hair? No big deal. Melody looks good no matter what, and she knows it. So why the sudden insecurity?

"Oh, you know," is Melody's non-response.

I roll my eyes.

We walk by Eleanor McGuffin's house, just a block down from my own. She's sitting on her front porch—same as every morning, if the weather allows—sipping a cup of tea and paging through a Harlequin romance. She's a beautiful woman who has aged gracefully, letting the gray take over in the most elegant way. Beats stressing out about it like Melody over here. I'll probably let my own hair do the same when I'm old enough.

Assuming you even live that long, I tell myself.

It may seem grim to think that way, but this is Autumncrow. Young people die here all the time. No one talks about it or even seems to recall just how many funerals we've all attended over the years, but I guess it's the price we pay to live in Autumncrow Valley, "The Spookiest Town on Earth." That's the town's slogan, and I would agree with it for more reasons than one.

Mostly, the point of the tagline is to advertise Autumncrow's passion for Halloween. Even now, with summer still weeks away from the finish line, Halloween decorations have begun to sprout up in every yard seemingly overnight, as though strung up by a hoard of festive goblins while we slept.

Styrofoam cemeteries whisper in the breeze. Bundled cornstalks crackle and snap. Blow-mold jack-o'-lanterns wink at passersby from front stoops. Glow-in-the-dark paper skeletons dance gleefully in living room windows framed by strands of purple and orange lights.

Even Mrs. McGuffin, long since widowed and without family to assist her, has already erected an elaborate Halloween display in her yard. A dozen scarecrows of all shapes, sizes, and personalities have been thrust onto spikes across Mrs. McGuffin's lawn, wearing expressions of anger, terror, and happiness. Extreme happiness, the kind I'd more expect from a deranged clown.

Creepy, I think with a shiver.

Starting at the foot of Mrs. McGuffin's front walk are rows of hay bales stacked four feet high, just tall enough for children to peek over if they were to stand on tiptoe and crane their necks. The bales twist and turn all around Eleanor McGuffin's yard and end at her front porch steps.

It's a Halloween maze haunted by monstrous scarecrows.

"Whoa . . . I love the display, Eleanor!" Melody shouts.

"You have the best display in town," I say in awe. This maze would have blown my mind as a kid. "You'll definitely win the décor contest this year."

The woman looks up from her paperback and gives us a warm smile. "Thank you, girls. The trick-or-treaters will have to solve the maze to get to their lollies and chocolates this year. I'm going to hire some teenagers to dress up as scarecrows and scare the living daylights out of those pipsqueaks."

Melody and I just about strangle on our laughter. We grew up knowing Mrs. McGuffin and even had her as an occasional babysitter, but her colorful way of expressing herself never fails to make us smile.

"You girls wanna help out this Halloween?" she asks.

"Depends," Melody says, wiping tears of laughter from her eyes. "How much are you paying?"

"I have a whole stack of Halloween coupon books for the Frisch's Big Boy with your names on them."

Melody and I trade glances. *Does two dollars off a burger and fries count as payment?*

"Umm . . . gee, that does sound tempting," I say. "We'll get back to you on that."

"Yeah, yeah. That's what they all say," the woman grumbles. "Well, go on. It's your first day of school, right?"

"Yep. Have a great day!" Melody says with a wave.

We continue on our way, exiting the neighborhood and turning a corner. A street sign informs us we have reached Main Street, but we don't need a sign to tell us that. Even Autumncrow newbies can see that this is where the magic happens.

Although it's a Wednesday morning, the town is a blazing bustle. Shopkeepers have flipped their signs to "OPEN" bright and early. Storefront displays have been freshly stocked to entice customers swept into town with the crisp morning breeze. Dozens of cars bump along the cobblestone roads. Other folks have ventured into the village by bicycle or on foot.

These people clearly don't mind the swiftly approaching rainstorm. Coffee, fudge, home-baked muffins—the pleasure of these delights far outweighs a bit of rain.

Much like the houses throughout Autumncrow, each storefront is decorated in tribute to everyone's favorite holiday. In front of Madame Tinkett's Sweets—newly opened for business this summer—is a display featuring dozens of ceramic jack-o'-lanterns perched precariously atop hay bales, just begging to be knocked to the ground by clumsy tourists.

The windows of various boutiques, costume shops, and eateries are fully decked out in every shade of autumn that you can imagine. In fact, despite the overcast skies, the air itself seems to have a warm orangey tint here in town, as though we were nothing more than actors plodding about on an artificially lit soundstage.

A couple of men from the town committee teeter on ladders, stringing your basic run-of-the-mill cheesecloth ghost on a zipline from rooftop to rooftop on opposite sides of the street. That zipline ghost has been an Autumncrow mainstay for as long as I've been alive. Some decorations change with each passing year, but there are a few cherished standbys: the ghost, the yet-to-be-erected pumpkin tower in the middle of town square, the scarecrows mounted to each of the old-fashioned streetlamps along Main. It wouldn't be Autumncrow without these wholesome touches.

A few other committee workers are assisting Miss Maggie, the town children's librarian, with the chore of stretching fake spiderwebs in the trees outside the library.

"That looks great," Maggie tells them. "A little more there, please. And some right—*oh!* I forgot the spider for the tree! I'll be right back. It's in the basement. *Oh!* I also have a mannequin we can wrap in webs. Every giant spider

31

needs a victim. Won't that look amazing?"

Melody and I share a knowing grin, having volunteered at the library many times in the past. Unless the coming rain spares them, those poor committee people will spend the better part of the day helping Miss Maggie with her notoriously extravagant Halloween spectacle. Miss Maggie keeps you busy.

Spooky's Café is just ahead. Its purple and green neon sign burns bright even in daylight.

"Oh yay!" Melody adds a hop to her step. "I'm *so* ready for my pumpkin latte float."

Ah, the pumpkin latte float. It's one of Spooky's most famous beverages: freshly brewed pumpkin spice coffee, chilled, with two scoops of vanilla–cinnamon ice cream. It's delicious but admittedly not the kind of drink I'd order first thing in the morning. The amount of sugar in those things is through the roof. Most people are blissfully unaware of this . . . unless they happen to be an employee of Spooky's.

Lucky me, I guess.

Entering Spooky's is like coming home. Horror film posters and coffin-shaped bookcases crammed to capacity with monster movie memorabilia occupy every square inch of Spooky's wall space. And it doesn't stop there. The ceiling itself is a neon mural of staggering proportions, featuring a graffitied cast of fiendish ghouls, toil-and-trouble witches, pumpkin-headed cornfield stalkers, and eight-legged beasties spilling forth from a dark vortex, as though the Hellmouth itself were located just above our heads.

This is what I originally wanted for my bedroom, a space in tribute to my favorite books and my love of spooky things. I am an Autumncrow kid, after all; I've been exposed to a steady diet of Halloween from the moment I was born.

Sadly, Mom had her own ideas when remodeling my room earlier this year, and I didn't have the heart to argue. She was so excited to have a project going with her daughter and desperately needed the distraction, so I let her have at it. While there are notably fewer skulls than I'd prefer, my bedroom isn't too bad, I guess.

Speaking of skulls, the skeleton display I helped install yesterday is in the front window. To any other set of eyes, I suppose the scene comes across as cutesy and wholesome, but with its inclusion in my nightmares, it has taken on a sinister quality for me.

It was there. A perfect reflection of the waking world. Of course, my subconscious could have inserted the display into the scenery. But if my mind can do that, why can't it pull me out of the dream when I'm so desperate to escape? Any other time, I'd have no problem waking up as soon as I realize I'm not in reality. What's so different about this dream? Why must I relive the same terror night after night?

"Earth to Bailey."

I start and turn to meet Melody's stare.

"Don't you want anything?" she asks.

Brian McKellen, the barista, stares at me in wait, tapping his pen on his notepad.

"Sorry. I got distracted," I say. "One sugar-free pumpkin latte, please."

Spooky's is the only café I know of that uses pumpkin as an ingredient in their coffee, but God, does it work! The owner, Ms. Sookie "Spooky" Wallman, says it will catch on in a few years, and I believe her.

"Coming right up," Brian says with a wink and a grin.

Melody glances back and forth from me to Brian and back again, a scandalous smile on her face.

I shake my head.

Brian is a handsome young Autumncrow University grad with wavy chestnut hair, a strong jaw, and a great tan. Honestly, when I first started working at Spooky's, I couldn't help but swoon whenever Brian was in my presence. That changed pretty quickly, though. Brian is more like a brother to me now, but Melody clearly has other ideas.

Brian gets started on our drinks. "So, Bailey, you working this weekend?"

"Aren't I always?"

"Yeah," Brian says. "But I could use the extra hours if you ever need someone to cover for you. In case you wanna do normal senior things." He raises his eyebrows at me.

"He has a point." Melody leans over the counter and says in a stage whisper, "I keep telling Bailey she needs to act her age. Her retirement fund must be overflowing by now."

Brian laughs. "If by 'retirement fund' you mean 'free coffee,' then yes."

Melody perks and faces me. "Hold on. You get free coffee?"

"Yeah. You can too, since you're with me. I'm on staff, remember?"

Her jaw drops. "You mean I could have been getting free drinks all summer long and you didn't think to tell me?"

"I mean, I can't hand out free drinks while I'm working," I say. "But I'm not working today, and you're with me, so . . . free coffee for Melody."

"Wow," Melody muses. "Sheesh. I need to get a job."

"You should. Then we can retire together when we're

34

old and wrinkly."

"Deal," Melody says, sticking out her pinky. I wrap mine around hers, and we use our spare hands to bump fists. As secret handshakes go, it may not be the most impressive, but it's something we've done since our playground days.

"Here you are, ladies." Brian sets our drinks on the counter. "And don't forget my offer, Bailey. Really. Take a little time to enjoy yourself this year. It'll be gone before you know it."

His eyes are earnest. Brian's mother passed away two years ago—on Christmas, no less—so he knows a thing or two about losing a parent. Knows what it does to you.

"Thanks. I'll keep that in mind," I say with a half smile.

I turn to follow Melody toward the exit. Just as she is about to push through the door, a boy pulls it open and steps inside the café.

"Oh, excuse me," he says, sidestepping out of Melody's path. He grabs the door and holds it open for us.

"Thanks," Melody says.

Or at least that's what I assume she says. I can barely hear anything around me. It's like all sound has been sucked out of the air by a giant vacuum, leaving behind a high-pitched frequency that only I can hear.

Melody walks through the door, beaming at the boy and then looking back at me. "Come on," she says, motioning for me to follow, but her voice is thick and muddled, and I can't move my feet. All I can do is stand still, wide-eyed and petrified, as chills claw at my skin.

It's him.

The boy holding the door for me.

The boy from my nightmares.

CHAPTER 4

"OVER THERE! That table is open."

Even with Melody shouting over her shoulder at me, I can barely hear her voice. High school cafeterias are noisy as it is, but Autumncrow High's lunchroom is a tall and cavernous thing with insanely massive granite columns supporting the vaulted ceilings. A single shout in this room is as subtle as a nuclear bomb on karaoke night. Multiply that by the entire student body, and you risk the wrath of Godzilla.

We take a seat in the center of the chaos, not far from a table claimed exclusively by the Autumncrow varsity football team and cheerleading squad. The jocks are making their own contributions to the racket, releasing deep whooping sounds of encouragement to one of their own as he chugs a chocolate milk.

"How impressive," Melody says with an eye roll.

I shove a straw into my juice box and stare at the contents of my lunch tray: a PB&J and a Granny Smith apple. I went for the most basic meal I could find—much to the dismay of Ms. Peabody, our beehive-sporting lunch lady—but I still have no appetite. My stomach has been in knots since the encounter at the café.

My nightmare boy is real.

It has been eating at me all morning. Every word spoken to me by my teachers and classmates has somersaulted over my head. "Huh?" I keep saying every few minutes. "Huh?"

God. Everyone must think I became a complete airhead over summer break. A total space cadet. But I'm doing the best I can under intense anxiety.

What is going on? What is he doing here? Where did he come from? Who is he?

It's not like I could have asked him who the hell he was right there in the café as he held the door for me. Everyone would've thought I'd lost my mind, especially Melody.

Besides, I couldn't have spoken even if I had wanted to. I couldn't even move. I probably stood there for a good thirty seconds before Melody grabbed my hand and pulled me out onto the busy sidewalk.

"What is wrong with you?" she grumbled at me, clearly embarrassed.

I couldn't even begin to explain.

All I know is that he's here. The nightmare boy is an actual living and breathing person who has found his way to Autumncrow.

"Follow me in . . ."

A chill skitters down my back. It's enough to pull me out of my churning thoughts. I see Melody is distracted as well, staring intently over her shoulder. I follow her line of vision, coming to rest on Tommy Burke.

Last year, Tommy had a designated seat with the rest of the Autumncrow Scarecrows, but he quit the football team this year. It came as a shock to everybody, especially Melody. Yet his drop in social status has done nothing to deter Kristi Crowley. She has her arms wrapped around Tommy's broad shoulders, hanging on to him like a zoo monkey as she nibbles his ear.

Tommy doesn't seem to notice or care about Kristi's displays of affection. Instead, he is staring at Melody. His eyes are deep black wells of spiraling emotions: anger, sadness, confusion, despair—dozens of others I can't even pinpoint.

He looks like a madman.

Melody stands to her feet and books it for the cafeteria exit, leaving her burger and fries in the dust.

"Mel—" I start, but she is already too far away to hear, lost in the havoc of lunch period.

I know exactly where she is heading.

Abandoning my own lunch tray, I grab Melody's and scurry as fast as I can to catch up.

Entering Autumncrow High's great hall, I glance to my left out of instinct and—sure enough—Melody is rushing into the girl's restroom.

The usual spot.

I hurry down the hall, made dark and gloomy on account of the thunderstorm that barreled in earlier this morning. Melody and I made it inside just as the clouds burst, unleashing torrents of daggers onto the school. The rain hasn't eased since. It roars against the rooftop, beats furiously at the stained glass windows spaced evenly along the expansive corridor. Lightning flashes, bathing my surroundings in white before quickly fading to muted grays.

This place looks more like a church than a school, but instead of religious iconography, these windows depict scenes of farmers tending to crops and pumpkin patches, villagers making their rounds in a town that has changed very little since those long-ago days captured in glass.

Another scene depicts two lovers, a man in a white robe and a woman in a flowing black gown, coming together in a re-creation of the Two of Cups. I've been told this couple represents Abraham and Autumn Crow, the husband and wife who founded the town in the early 1800s. Autumn was the town's namesake.

The street where I live is named after Abraham himself and runs parallel with Autumn Street on the other side of the block. I'd find this to be romantic if not for the dark and grisly rumors that persist to this day and the unsettling circumstances of Autumn's death. So much of the Crows' story is shrouded in mystery, and whether it amounts to a bittersweet tragedy or an outright horror story depends on what you're willing to believe.

The stained glass captures the Crows gazing lovingly into each other's eyes, reminding me of how things used to be between Melody and Tommy before it all went to hell.

The two broke up at the end of our junior year. Scratch that—Tommy broke up with Melody. It crushed her, and I have to admit, it surprised me. They were completely inseparable and as in love as any two high school sweethearts could be. Or so I thought.

One day, Melody was telling me she could see herself marrying Tommy after college. The next, she was crying onto my pleated skirt, shocked and bewildered that Tommy would dump her so callously.

I thought there had to be some kind of explanation. Maybe Tommy developed superhuman powers after a freak accident and broke up with Melody to protect her from his new archnemesis. Or maybe he was secretly dying and thought a swift breakup might spare Melody the pain of his passing. Guys can be pretty dumb like that, after all.

It wasn't until a week later in junior hall when I saw Kristi Crowley locking lips with Tommy that the boy's true life-threatening condition became clear: Tommy Burke was a stone-cold jerk.

Bursting through the restroom door, I find Melody staring at her reflection in the mirror that runs the width of the wall above several old porcelain sinks. She is wiping tears from her eyes with a wad of toilet paper, fighting to keep her makeup from running.

Melody looks at me and frowns.

I prop her lunch tray on a sink corner and wrap my arms around her, letting her cry on my shoulder for several minutes until her breathing finally slows.

Melody pulls away, wiping her eyes again, but she is visibly calmer. "Thanks," she says.

"Don't mention it," I say. "You did the same for me this morning."

"True. I guess you owed me."

"That, or I'm just an amazing friend," I say, lightly punching her on the shoulder.

Melody laughs, then sniffles.

"What's that scumbag's deal, anyway?" I ask. "Tommy was looking at you like—"

"Like I'm wearing his jacket," Melody says.

I step back, realizing for the first time that the Autumncrow letterman jacket Melody is wearing isn't actually hers. "Oh."

"I should have known better." Melody tosses her arms in the air and lets them flop to her sides. "What did I expect when I put it on this morning? That he'd leave Kristi 'Creepy-Crawly' and come crawling back to me?"

"I . . . I don't know," I stammer.

Melody's face turns somber. "He's going to ask for this jacket back today, I just know it. Then he's going to give it to Kristi, who'll flash it all over the school. And if anybody doesn't already know I got dumped by Tommy Burke, there will be no denying it after that."

"I thought you bought that jacket last year," I say. "This whole time, I thought it was yours."

"Of course not! It's tradition for guys on the team to give their girlfriends their jackets. You know that."

I didn't know that. I'm not the one who dated a football jock. I've never even had a boyfriend.

As an uneasy silence passes between us, I see how defeated Melody is. How heartbroken. Now it all makes sense. The constant worry about her appearance has been because of Tommy. Melody was hoping he'd come back to her.

"Please don't judge me," Melody says, her voice pinched and tight.

I frown. "I'm not."

Melody dabs at her eyes again, smearing the toilet paper

with her mascara. "I know it must seem silly, but you have no idea how much this hurts. It really, *really* sucks."

I bite my tongue, afraid I might say the wrong thing.

Being the supportive best friend has only become trickier as we've gotten older. With her larger-than-life personality and growing popularity, Melody has changed plenty these last few years. Meanwhile, I'm still the weird, monster-loving girl I've always been. Try as I might to keep up with her, I often feel a bit like a fraud. Like I'm pretending to be someone I'm not.

And I guess I do think the whole thing is a bit silly, but I love Melody, and I hate to see her in so much pain. I secretly wish I could just snap her out of it and get my old friend back.

Before I know what I'm saying, I blurt out, "You know what? Screw Tommy Burke."

Melody blanches. "I already did, and look where that got me."

I pause, trying to hide my surprise. Does that mean she and Tommy had sex? She never told me that.

"That's . . . not what I meant," I stammer. "Just . . . don't worry about him, okay? Tommy will be Tommy. You just need to focus on being Melody, and the Melody I know doesn't fall to pieces over a boy whose peak achievement in life is receiving a cheap jacket." I flick a finger against the burnt-orange sleeve.

"It isn't a cheap jacket," Melody says. "These things are expensive."

"Take it off," I say.

"What?"

"The jacket. Take it off."

"What are you going to do?"

"Just trust me."

Melody sighs and obliges, pulling off Tommy's prized varsity jacket. She holds it for a moment, cradling it in her arms like the corpse of a loved one. Then she sighs again. "Don't make me regret this." She rests the burden in my hands.

I roll the jacket into a ball and stuff it into the nearest trash bin.

"I knew you were going to do that," Melody says, staring into the garbage. The jacket rests among a dozen or so to-go cups from Spooky's Café—at least one of them with a few lipstick-stained cigarette butts floating inside—and a half-eaten caramel apple.

"Then why didn't you stop me?" I ask.

"Because I was hoping you would do it. I wouldn't have been able to myself."

"That's what friends are for," I say with a shrug. Melody's cafeteria tray still rests atop one of the restroom sinks. "Want to finish lunch in here?"

Melody considers this for a moment. "No," she says. "I want Tommy to wonder where his jacket is. Good luck giving it to Kristi now."

"Atta girl."

Melody retrieves her lunch tray and hooks her other arm in mine, giving me a warm smile of gratitude.

I am just as grateful to Melody for the distraction from my own dark thoughts. But as we walk down the shadowy corridor back to the cafeteria, the mysterious boy returns to my mind once again, grinning down at me with those icy eyes.

Did the boy at the café have blue eyes? I can't remember. Now that I think about it, I can't recall whether he was wearing a letterman jacket, or whether his hair was slicked back like it was in my dream.

What made me so sure it was him?

Had I made the whole thing up?

When we return to our table, my lunch is gone, most likely swiped by a hungry student or tossed into the trash by Ms. Peabody. I see her scrambling from table to table, clearing trays and wiping up spilled milk. Since Mr. Greendale passed away this summer, I guess it's up to Ms. Peabody now to keep the cafeteria tidy, at least until the school finds a new janitor to replace him.

As much as I hate to see the poor woman doing double duty like that, I'm relieved Mr. Greendale won't be limping around the school anymore, staring at me like he hates my guts. The old creep had a chip on his shoulder when it came to young people. Why he chose to be a high school janitor, no one will ever know. But he's gone now, so it doesn't matter.

Immediately, a heavy feeling of guilt rests in my gut. How could I think of the dead that way?

Melody and I take our seats. Tommy is still in the same position, ignoring Kristi's desperate bids for his attention while keeping his dark, troubled eyes fixed on Melody's back.

Like the trouper I've always known Melody to be, she ignores him, no longer giving him the time of day.

That's more like it.

"So," Melody says, putting on a smile, "any plans for tonight?"

I'm about to tell her I'm free if she wants to hang—we could rent a scary movie from Undead Video—when somebody sets his lunch tray down at our table and takes a seat.

Melody and I look up at the same time to see a boy our age with messy jet-black hair and a square jaw, blue with five o'clock shadow.

The boy raises his gaze, locking eyes with me.

My heart stops beating.

"Hey," he says with a grin. "Didn't I see you girls at the café earlier?"

CHAPTER 5

"THAT WAS US!" Melody practically shouts. Her voice glitters with playful cheer, eyelashes fluttering the way they always do when a cute guy enters the scene. One would never guess she was a puddle of tears five minutes ago.

"Hi." She leans across the table, gingerly taking the boy's hand in hers. "I'm Melody Krieger. This is Bailey."

Both heads swivel in my direction. It feels as though everyone in the cafeteria has turned to gawk at me. All eyes on me. Melody's sparkling green eyes and the boy's—

Brown.

His eyes are soft, a deep chocolate brown. Unlike the boy in my dreams, whose eyes were crystalline waters infested with hungry sharks, these eyes have a warm, laid-back allure to them.

And his hair—it has a tousled, unkempt appearance, but purposely so, as if it took at least a half hour to perfect. No trace of the nightmare boy's slick, classic style. Also missing is the Autumncrow letterman jacket, but otherwise the boy is a dead ringer for the puppeteer—same angular face, same athletic silhouette. Even his smile is identical to the one that has haunted my dreams for the past three months.

No ... not identical. Like his eyes, this boy's smile is gentle. No trace of menace whatsoever. This is a perfectly affable teenage boy, altogether ordinary if not for his dashing good looks and the dark stubble lining his jaw.

He seems a bit older than the other guys at Autumncrow. It could be that he was held back a year at some point. He is well past the acne stage, that's for sure. And he has a self-assured swagger about him, as though he has grown into himself.

My panicked heart gradually eases back into a normal rhythm.

"Well, good God, Bailey," Melody pipes in.

I jolt from my thoughts. It's hard to say how long I've been sitting here with my jaw hanging open, but it's clear I've embarrassed Melody in front of this boy one time too many.

"I swear she can speak," Melody assures him.

He chuckles and pushes his shaggy hair off his forehead only for it to fall back into place, covering his thick, dark eyebrows. "It's cool. I'm Dennis. This is my first day here."

"Same." Melody breathes the word out in a dreamlike sigh. Her elbow is propped on the table, chin resting in her palm as she drinks him in with longing eyes.

She's falling in love, I realize. *Again.*

"Oh, you're new here too?" Dennis asks.

"Huh?" Melody snaps out of her trance. "No. Sorry. I meant it's my first day back to school." She shakes her head in embarrassment. "Brain fart."

The new boy flashes a lopsided grin and grabs the apple from his lunch tray. "It's all good. This is actually my first day in Autumncrow. I arrived in town last night. With my mom."

He polishes the apple with the hem of his brown bomber jacket, moving it in circles, around and around. Turning.

Cranking.

I feel a tug in my gut. Is it real or simply a trick of the mind? I can't be sure.

"Come. Follow me in . . ."

My heart is racing again.

"Wow, so you're total fresh meat!" Melody laughs. "Welcome to Autumncrow. What do you think so far?"

"It's . . . different," Dennis answers. "I can't believe everyone is decorating for Halloween already."

"Oh, that's normal around here. We're, like, the Halloween capital of the world. It's weird, I know." Melody laughs again. Loudly. Everything is loud.

"Yeah," Dennis says, smiling. "That's what I hear. The people are nice though. They're very"—his smile widens as he shifts his gaze to me—"interesting."

It's him. It has to be him. He's here, and Melody is falling for him already, and he's dangerous.

Or you've lost your mind. Get a grip, Bailey.

"Hey . . ." The boy named Dennis looks back at Melody.

He points a thumb toward me. "Is she okay?"

"I'm okay."

Did I just say that? I don't know if that was me. It sounded like me, but I'm not sure. *Everything is so loud.*

Melody, her brow crinkled with concern, waves a hand in front of my face. I pull back.

"He's right, Bailey. You don't look so hot." Melody follows this up by mouthing a secret message just for me: *"What's the matter with you?"*

"I'm okay," I say before pulling out my go-to excuse: "I'm just tired."

Melody shrugs and says to the boy, "She never sleeps. She has nightmares."

Dennis nods, staring at me long and hard. "I get nightmares too."

"Oh," I say.

I can hear it now—that slow, lovelorn refrain suspended like fog in the back of my mind.

"When I'm alone with only dreams of you that won't come true, what'll I do?"

"You two should *totally* compare notes," Melody says. "Hey! You guys might even share the same dreams. I think I read about that in one of my horoscope magazines."

"Could be." Dennis winks at me.

I feel like I might be sick.

Dennis may not be the dream boy's perfect doppelgänger, but they are still too much alike. *Too much.*

"So, Dennis . . ." Melody folds her fingers together on the tabletop, preparing to pump the boy for info like the aspiring reporter she is. "What brings you to town? Are

49

your parents Halloween junkies? Paranormal investigators? Psychics? I need the scoop."

Dennis shakes his head. "No, nothing like that. It's . . . just Mom and me." He frowns. "My dad used to live here, so we're in town just long enough to collect his assets and settle his debts."

"Assets?" Melody seems puzzled.

"Like, his belongings and stuff, I guess? I dunno. Mom is handling most of it." Dennis isn't smiling anymore. He stares down at his lunch, shifting uncomfortably in his seat. He returns the apple to his tray without taking a bite. At the same time, the tension in my gut slackens.

Dennis continues: "I just have to go to school here until we can go back home."

"Where's home?"

"Cincinnati."

"I like the zoo there," Melody says, nodding. "But what's up with your dad?"

"Dad?" Dennis perks upright, wincing as if Melody had uttered a crude slur.

"Yeah, you said something about . . . settling his debts? What's his deal?"

"He died," I interject.

Both Melody and Dennis turn to look at me. I open and close my mouth, trying to figure out what to say next. I hadn't intended to say anything at all, but that's what the boy was implying, wasn't it? That his dad had passed away?

"Yeah," Dennis says, sparing me the need to speak further. He looks down at his burger and apple again and pushes the tray away. "He died this summer."

"Oh . . . I'm so sorry. I didn't mean to press. I just—"

Melody averts her eyes, stares toward the ceiling. Now even she is at a loss for words, but you can't hold Mel down for long. She quickly recovers with: "So your dad lived here?"

"Yeah, his whole life," Dennis says. "And don't apologize. I actually didn't know my dad. We weren't close or anything. My parents met here in Autumncrow and split before I was born. I grew up in Florida, and then Mom and I moved to Cincinnati when I was around ten. I never got so much as a phone call or birthday card from my dad, so he may as well be a stranger to me."

"I wish I lived in Florida," Melody says. "Would I have known your dad?"

Dennis looks around the cafeteria, an awkward grin on his face. "Um . . . yeah, probably." He scratches his eyebrow. "Kallum Greendale."

Melody narrows her eyes in concentration. "Kallum . . . *Oh.* Your dad was the janitor here?"

If she's trying to hide the disgust on her face, she isn't doing a very good job.

"Uh-huh." Dennis vigorously rubs his palms on his jeans and stares off toward the windows lining the outer wall of the cafeteria, the ones overlooking the football field. A banner is draped over the windows, proclaiming "GO SCARECROWS" in bold burnt-orange letters against a black background.

"That's a shame," Melody says, shaking her head solemnly. "Mr. Greendale was a real . . . nice."

Dennis bursts into rich, husky laughter. "A real nice?" He cracks up again, the awkwardness draining from his face. He grips his gut as though it pains him to laugh this hard.

Melody blushes.

51

"I'm sorry," Dennis says, noticing Melody's embarrassment and fighting to regain composure. "It's just . . . I know my dad was a slimeball. You don't have to pretend you liked him."

"What? He wasn't a slimeball," Melody protests unconvincingly.

"If you say so, but I have it on good authority that he wasn't the most agreeable person," Dennis argues with a luminous grin. Spirits seemingly lifted, he pulls his lunch tray close and grabs his burger, taking a hearty bite. "I like you, Melody Krieger," he says through a mouthful of food. "You're cool."

Melody blushes again. "I like you too, Dennis Greendale."

The pair exchange soft, bashful smiles. If their attraction to each other wasn't already apparent, the wheels are definitely spinning now. Just like that, the boy's hooks are in.

You know this isn't right. Nothing about this is right. Everything is wrong here. Dangerous . . . he's dangerous!

The bell rings, announcing fifth period. Most students have cleared out already. A few stragglers are dumping their lunch trays and racing for their lockers, eager to avoid being tardy on the first day of school.

But not Tommy Burke.

He is standing alone against the windowed wall of the cafeteria, beside the double doors leading to the football field. His hands are stuffed deep into the pockets of his leather jacket as he glares at Melody and Dennis, jaw clenched. Trembling.

He locks eyes with me for a beat, then looks away, pushing through the doors and taking off into the thrumming rain. The doors swing shut behind him, announcing his departure with an echoey *bang!*

"You coming?"

I glance up. Melody and the boy are on their feet, staring down at me.

"I'm going to walk Dennis to his fifth-period study hall. He doesn't know where it's at," Melody explains. "You wanna walk with us?"

Dennis is smiling at me—a wide, friendly smile. Too friendly, I decide.

I look down. "No. I . . . I need to run to the restroom first."

"You have Mr. Hammer for fifth period, right?" Melody asks me. "He'll kill you if you're late."

I glance up at Dennis, staring him right in the eye. Though I want to look away, I hold my gaze. "Not if I kill him first," I say.

Dennis's smile falters, but only slightly.

"Jeez, psycho much?" Melody snickers. "Okay, let's go." She hooks one arm in Dennis's—the way she and I usually walk—and guides him to the great hall.

I jump from my seat and follow them out of the cafeteria, bolting the opposite direction down the hall in a sprint for the restroom—the same one Mel and I had visited just before the boy from my nightmares casually introduced himself as the newest member of our senior class.

Darting into one of the stalls, I throw myself onto the grimy floor in front of the toilet and vomit.

CHAPTER 6

A CHILLY BREEZE RUSTLES the tree branches above, shaking loose the remnants of the day's storm from the vibrant autumn leaves. I lift my backpack over my head and listen to the droplets pitter-patter against the fabric. My hair is shielded from the errant beads of water, but the bag does nothing to save me when a soggy fallen leaf blindsides me from the left, nailing me in the face with a wet smack.

I groan, stopping to peel the leaf from my cheek. I toss it to the ground with a flick of the wrist and continue my trek home. Another angry gust whips through my hair, stinging my eyes and making me wish once more that I had let Mom drive me to school. It has only gotten colder since the storm moved through.

At least the rain stopped, I tell myself, trying to look on the bright side but feeling just as gloomy as the cloudy after-noon sky. I wipe my wet nose with the sleeve of my sweater and trudge onward toward Main Street.

Downtown is just as sodden as anywhere else in the val-ley, but the sidewalks continue to hum with their usual electricity, powered by locals and out-of-towners alike, undeterred in their pursuit of coffee, souvenirs, and other autumnal treats.

I scurry past pedestrians, praying I don't encounter any-one I know. I'm not in the mood for conversation.

Bed. I want to go home to my warm, cozy bed. I want to draw the covers tightly over my head and shut out the day. Shut out Melody and the boy who says his name is Dennis Greendale. Shut out life.

I wipe a tear from my cheek and close my eyes for just a second. *God, I'm so tired.*

Nearly faltering under the dense weight of exhaustion, I fight the urge to lie down on the sidewalk and let the shop-pers trample over me as they run their errands. They're all so deep under Autumncrow's spell, I doubt they'd notice or care.

Once I get home, I'll let myself venture as close to the brink of sleep as possible without actually drifting off. Sleeping means dreaming, and that's the last thing I want. But I can set my clock radio and teeter on the edge of sleep for a while before the alarm sounds. Anything for a little re-lief.

Shutting my weary eyes momentarily, I think back to Nancy Thompson from *A Nightmare on Elm Street* and si-lently wish I could do what she did, chugging coffee to stay awake and out of Freddy's clawed grasp. Sadly, caffeine has never had much of an effect on me.

I'm still relishing that sweet feeling of surrender to the heaviness of my eyelids when, all of a sudden, someone bumps into me. I open my eyes and utter a soft gasp of surprise.

"Watch it!" huffs a man hauling an armload of videotapes on his way out of Undead Video.

I give the old grouch a scowl as he lumbers away. Guess I should keep my eyes peeled next time.

I stop in front of the video store to admire the new window display featuring life-size replicas of Jason Voorhees from the *Friday the 13th* films and—oh look, speak of the devil! It's Freddy Krueger himself about to go head-to-head with the machete-wielding maniac.

Taped inside the window to the left of the display is a movie poster for *Jason Goes to Hell*. "IN THEATERS NOW, COMING SOON TO VIDEO," a sign below the poster reads.

So much for the surprise ending, I think to myself.

It all makes me think of Melody—not that she's ever been far from my thoughts, my worry mounting with each passing second as I wonder if she's with Dennis right now when she was supposed to be walking home with me.

I try once more to squash those worries and focus on the display, on the memories of Melody's sleepovers at my house this past summer in the aftermath of her breakup with Tommy. We called it the "Sad Bastards Club," and it mainly involved us staying up late watching horror films, bingeing on fistfuls of popcorn and extra-large slices from Autumn-Dough Pizzeria.

Just last week, we sat through a back-to-back all-nighter

of the *Friday* films leading up to *Jason Goes to Hell*, which we then saw on opening night at the theater in town. Melody and I were blown away by the final shot, agreeing that we should do a Freddy marathon next.

That marathon has yet to happen, and considering the way Melody was mooning over Dennis today, it probably never will.

It's like Tommy Burke all over again, I realize.

Once Melody started dating Tommy, I was no longer a priority. We'd still hang out sometimes, but Tommy was always there, front and center, forever the deciding factor in everything we did. Soon I was making excuses whenever Melody invited me along, preferring to stay at home and read or watch old movies with my dad.

In hindsight, I'm kind of glad things worked out the way they did. It gave me a little more time with Dad before he went missing.

"Hey!"

I gasp and spin on my heels away from the window display. Melody is hanging out the passenger window of a faded brown station wagon. She's smiling, but it's the smile she puts on when she's trying to hide her anger or frustration.

"What's going on?" she asks. "I've been looking everywhere for you. You weren't at our spot."

Our after-school meeting spot used to be the choking oak in the schoolyard. One of us would wait there until the other showed up, and then we'd walk home together.

But Melody should have known it would be the last place I'd want to meet this school year.

This seems to dawn on her, because her face suddenly

reddens. "I'm sorry . . . I guess we should find a new meeting spot, huh?"

"It's okay," I say with a shrug. "I assumed you'd be hanging out with Dennis anyway."

I lean to the right, looking past Melody to get a better view of the person in the driver's seat.

Dennis smiles and waves at me.

I feel like I'm spinning again.

"Is that what this is about?" Melody huffs, the faux smile quickly fading from her face.

I tug on the straps of my backpack and shrug.

Melody takes a few very slow, very deliberate blinks and then bites her lip in contemplation. Finally, she releases a sigh and begrudgingly steps out of the car. "Sorry, Dennis," she says, peeking through the window. "Bailey and I are going to walk from here."

"Oh," Dennis mutters, disappointed. "Sure you don't want me to drive you gals home?"

"No, it's okay. I'll see you tonight for the all-exclusive Autumncrow tour." Melody winks. "And get ready, 'cause I've got some crazy stories about this place. Hope you're not afraid of ghosts."

"Let's just hope the ghosts aren't afraid of me . . ." Dennis says, affecting a sinister tone.

He and Melody burst into laughter, but I don't.

Dennis drums the steering wheel and nods. "Cool. Tonight then. Catch ya later."

He pulls away from the curb, makes a U-turn, and takes off back toward the school.

Melody looks at me and smiles, genuinely this time. "You feeling better? You were looking pretty rough earlier.

Then again, you always look like a zombie these days."

I know she's only teasing, but the words sting regardless. Probably because I know they're true.

"I'm feeling better," I lie. "Just eager to get home."

Melody nods. "Me too. I'm glad we made it through the first day."

Let's hope we can make it through the next . . .

"See the new display?" I motion over my shoulder at the video store.

"Oh yeah. Cool." Melody skips ahead. She would have been all over the display two weeks ago, but she seems completely bored with it now. "You coming or what?"

Sighing, I follow along.

I want to ask Melody about Dennis, press her for more information about the new boy, but I don't know how to pry without seeming suspicious. She'll know something's up, and I don't think she's ready to hear that the boy from my nightmares is attending our high school.

Melody would probably drag me to the counselor herself if I told her that.

"Hey, wanna hang with me and Dennis tonight?" Melody asks. "You know more about the weird stuff in this town than I do, so you'd be a better tour guide."

"Um . . . I . . ."

What do I say? Part of me feels inclined to tag along for Melody's safety, but the other part doesn't want to go anywhere near Dennis.

"You have work again or something?" Melody asks, awaiting my reply.

"No. I . . . have homework."

God, when did I get this bad at lying?

59

"Homework on the first day? None of my teachers assigned homework." Mel narrows her eyes. She definitely doesn't believe me.

Fortunately, I don't have to say anything further. A woman's voice calls out to us from down the way.

"Hey, girls! Care for an after-school snack?"

Ahead, a young woman is sitting on a bale of hay outside Madame Tinkett's Sweets, surrounded by ceramic jack-o'-lanterns. She is dressed in a witchy low-cut gown made of satin as purple as the night sky with a black lace shawl that crisscrosses her cleavage in a spiderweb pattern. Her jade necklace matches the color of her glistening eyes.

She's dressed like Autumn Crow, I realize. She's identical to the old portrait of Autumn on display in the high school's main office.

"I have caramel apple fudge today," Madame Tinkett says, extending a bat-shaped platter of generous fudge samples in our direction with her free hand. A wide-eyed baby girl dressed in a onesie as orange as the surrounding jack-o'-lanterns is cradled in the woman's other arm.

"Yes, please!" Melody covers the distance between us and the shopkeeper in three even strides. She plucks a block of fudge off the platter and plops it into her mouth.

The woman holds the samples out to me. Usually, I'd take the biggest piece, but today the fudge looks completely unappetizing. I swear I can still taste the vomit in my mouth from earlier this afternoon.

"No, thank you, Jodie," I say kindly. "Maybe tomorrow."

Jodie Tinkett—Madame Tinkett herself—shrugs and says, "Suit yourself."

Having grown up in Autumncrow with parents who worked on the main drag and then having worked here all summer myself, I'm on a first-name basis with all the local shopkeepers—and their kids.

"Hi, Christine," I say, wiggling a finger under the baby's chubby chin. She giggles and hides her face in her mother's shawl.

"She's shy now, but wait until she's our age," Melody says. "She'll be a little party animal."

I give Melody a playful slap on the shoulder.

"What?" she mouths.

That's Melody for you, always saying something inappropriate. I often remind her to "have a little couth," to which she invariably replies, "Speak English!"

Fortunately, Jodie Tinkett doesn't break out in hives at the thought of her baby girl growing into a wild teenager. "I guess I just need to enjoy my time with her while it lasts," she says, planting a kiss atop Christine's soft head.

"Thanks for the fudge, but we'd better get going," Melody says. "Bailey has a *ton* of homework to do."

I look downward, feeling my cheeks turn crimson. I know Melody notices, because she lets out a sharp *"ha!"* before walking ahead.

I wave goodbye to Jodie and follow along, rounding the corner onto Abraham Street and passing Eleanor McGuffin's house for the second time today. One of the scarecrows in her yard waves at me from its cross. I tell myself it was just the wind.

Mel is going on and on about her date with Dennis tonight, about how she's going to show him around before they grab dinner.

"Just milkshakes and stuff. At the diner," Melody says. "Is your mom working tonight?"

Before I can answer yes, a motorcycle pulls up to the curb next to us. Tommy Burke hops off the seat without even giving his bike a chance to fully brake.

My heart leaps into my throat.

"I need to talk to you," Tommy says, stepping in front of us. At first, I think he's angry, but something about his expression burns with panic.

"Good afternoon to you too, Tommy," Melody mutters. She steps around him, but he cuts her off.

"Listen," he says, his uncharacteristically disheveled blond hair hanging over his eyes. "Who's that guy you were hanging out with today?"

"Oh God." Melody rolls her eyes and attempts once again to push past Tommy.

He grabs her by the shoulders, wrapping his long fingers tightly around her biceps and squeezing.

"Ow!" Melody cries.

"Hey! What's the big deal?" I shout, stepping forward and attempting to pull Melody away from him.

Tommy ignores me and holds on tighter, eyes piercing into Melody's. "Who is he? Where'd he come from?"

"What do you care? Get your filthy hands off me." Melody struggles, fighting Tommy's stone-hard grip.

"Please, Melody," he begs. "Please, talk to me. I . . . I made a mistake, okay? I'm sorry."

"You're making a mistake now, you jackass," Melody shouts. "Now let go of me!"

"Please, Mel . . . Just tell me his name, okay? I don't trust him. Something isn't right."

Tommy is showing no signs of backing down, so I do the only thing I can think of: I stomp on his foot as hard as I can.

Unleashing a yelp of pain, Tommy finally releases Melody and reaches down for his foot. Mel stumbles away, almost falling onto the sidewalk but regaining her balance just in time.

I push Tommy off his feet, shoving him with all my strength into Eleanor McGuffin's yard. He blunders backward, arms flailing, trying to grab on to something but finding only air. He lands on his back, breath whooshing out of his lungs, the crown of his head thumping against the wooden stake of a scarecrow.

Tommy looks up at the scarecrow. The scarecrow looks down at him.

"Ow," he mutters.

I rush over to Melody. "Are you okay?"

"Yeah," she says. "Thanks for going into ninja mode."

"Of course. Now let's go," I say, looking over at Tommy. He's clearly disoriented, but he's already rising to his feet. "He's getting up. Run!"

The two of us hightail it, pausing just long enough for Melody to kick over Tommy's motorcycle. It hits the pavement with a crash.

"Suck on that!" Melody shouts over her shoulder as we sprint down the sidewalk as fast as we can. "Oh my God, I've been wanting to trash his stupid bike all summer."

By the time we reach my house, we are out of breath but totally in the clear. Keeling over on my living room floor, we spend the rest of the afternoon laughing and howling "Suck on that!"

CHAPTER 7

WITH MOM AT THE DINER and Rae fast asleep upstairs, I am resting in solitude on the living room couch, trying to keep my mind from wandering to Melody and whatever she and Dennis are up to on their date. Lulled into a trance by the pulsing drums of yet another downpour against the roof of the house, I stare blankly at the pages of a V.C. Andrews paperback. The stormy weather is perfect for a little late-night reading, but I can't make out the words. Every time I try to focus on the print, it quickly morphs into blurry black blobs.

If only I could stop running the events of the day over and over in my head—the repeated run-ins with Dennis the dream boy, the fight with Tommy . . . I've spent all evening mulling over what Tommy was trying to say about Dennis.

"I don't trust him. Something isn't right."
"Where did he come from?"

I've had the urge to call Tommy ever since Melody left early this evening, to ask him what he meant and what it is about Dennis that has him set on edge. He's got to know something I don't.

Or he's just a jealous ex-boyfriend, Bailey. Ever think of that?

I give up on the book and toss it aside, burying my face in my hands.

No. Calling Tommy Burke would just open up a whole new can of worms. I have enough to deal with. I'm not sure I need to go looking for extra trouble.

I sweep the idea away and raise my gaze to the antique grandfather clock across the living room.

It's already half past eleven.

The adrenaline rush from this afternoon's excitement must have given me a second wind. I almost forgot about how tired I was.

Good. Maybe I can make it through the night without dozing off.

The front door bursts open, bringing my pulse to an abrupt pause. I leap off the couch in a panic . . . and relax when Mom steps into the foyer, folding a dripping umbrella.

I flop back down onto the couch and breathe a relieved sigh. "What are you doing home so early?" I ask. "I thought you were working until one o'clock tonight."

Mom looks at me with tired eyes and pulls off her raincoat. "I was supposed to."

I stand again, slowly this time. "What's wrong?" Mom looks more than just tired. Her face is pallid, as white as the stray hairs that have begun to invade her otherwise deep red tresses.

"I wasn't feeling so great, so I had Cathy cover my shift." Mom opens the coat closet beside the front door and hangs up her jacket. "Besides, business is so slow at this hour."

"Think you're getting sick? How about some tea?"

"No, no." She waves my worries away. "I'm fine. I just need to get some sleep. All these hours at the diner ... I think this job is driving me crazy, Bailey. Now I'm seeing ghosts." Mom chuckles and shakes her head as she shambles to the staircase off the foyer.

"Ghosts? What do you mean?" A sinking feeling of dread takes hold in the pit of my stomach. "Is it something about—"

I almost say "Dad," but I cut myself short. My dad isn't a ghost. We're still holding out hope that he's alive out there somewhere, so that can't be who she means.

Blood.

So much blood.

"I'm sorry, Mrs. Hagen, but wherever your husband is, he's not likely to survive after losing that much—"

Blood.

I clench my jaw and blink away the gory memories in my head.

Mom stops at the foot of the staircase and turns toward me, her complexion becoming sallower with each tick of the grandfather clock. "I saw Melody at the diner. Is she ... dating someone new?"

I'm shaking now. Trembling. Vibrating. *God, why can't I stop shaking?* It's like the air-conditioning has suddenly clicked on and I'm standing in the path of its current.

"Yes," I say, a small quiver in my voice.

Mom nods. She doesn't ask me what the boy's name is or where he's from. Instead, she turns away from me and looks up the stairs. In a whisper so low I can scarcely hear it, she says, "That's not pos—" Without finishing her thought, Mom glances back at me and says, "Have a good night, my girl."

Ever so slowly, she begins to climb the stairs.

"Wait . . . Mom?" I rush to the darkened staircase and look up at her thin, reedy silhouette, framed by the soft amber halo of the night-light in the hall. She looks down at me, her face a mass of darkness. All I can see is a faint glimmer in her eyes, almost as if they are glowing.

I want to ask her more about what she saw at the diner, but I bite my tongue. Mom seems so rattled that I decide to let it go, at least for tonight. Instead, I say, "Did you see Dalton today?"

Dalton Hagen, the police deputy . . . and also my older brother.

"No. He didn't stop in," Mom says.

"Oh," I say, feeling just as disappointed as always.

I quietly plan to drop by the police station tomorrow after school and see if I can catch up with him.

"He's working on it, okay?" Mom adds. "He's doing his best."

"Sure," I say, though I know this isn't true. Dalton stopped trying weeks ago.

"Was your window open again last night?" Mom asks.

"My window?" I have to think about it for a moment, thrown off by her random question. "Yeah, just a crack."

"Keep it closed from now on. And locked. Okay?" Mom says nothing more, doesn't ask me how my first day of school went or if Rae got home safely. Instead, she climbs the creaky old stairs, hesitating at the top before turning left down the hall, away from her bedroom. I hear the low groan of an opening door—a door that, as far as I know, hasn't been touched all summer—followed by a *click* as it closes shut again.

Why did Mom go into the library?

She just misses him, I tell myself, but something doesn't feel right.

Nothing feels right.

Thinking of my open bedroom window and Mom's warning to keep it shut, I glance over my shoulder at the front door and wonder if Mom took her own advice and locked it when she came in. She was so distant, she may have forgotten. I walk over and turn the knob, letting in the smell of midnight rain and a distant growl of thunder.

I'm glad I thought to check the door. Chills worm down my spine at the thought of a murderous stranger so easily invading my family's home in the dark of night, dispatching us one by one with the silent slice of a blade.

Shh, don't think like that, I scold myself as I shut and bolt the door. *Stop being so grim. You're safe here.*

My blood runs cold when another voice creeps in, an inner voice that I don't recognize as my own. A sly, knowing voice without gender or form.

"You can lock your doors, but the devil is already inside, hiding beneath the floorboards . . . Can't you feel it?"

PART II
RAPTURE

CHAPTER 8

POPPING. SNAPPING. The furious sound of a body colliding with pavement. Bones breaking. Doll's bones. The cracking of a skull. My skull.

Pulling. Tugging. Closer and closer ... almost there now. A dark form lingering ahead.

Autumncrow High.

"Help us? Help us?"

The dream is the same as before except for one fresh addition: the van. A red van, its front end crushed into the trunk of the choking oak, toppled gravestones and a mangled section of fence lying in its wake. The windshield is a ghastly spiderweb of shattered glass covered in blood.

So much blood.

"What'll I do ... ?"

"Let me fix you . . ." The boy is standing over me. The dream boy. Dennis, but with those piercing blue eyes. The puppeteer.

Cranking. Turning.

"Follow me in . . ."

I wake up sobbing.

⁎

I stop in the middle of senior hall when, from a distance, I spot Melody at her locker. Her back against the locker door, she gazes dreamily up into Dennis Greendale's dark chocolate eyes.

He's standing close. The back of one index finger lightly traces Melody's forearm, tickling up and down, up and down, while he caresses her face with the other hand. He's smiling, and so is Melody—hers a soft, faraway smile as if deep in a trance.

And perhaps that's exactly what this is.

Melody closes her eyes as Dennis draws nearer, bringing his lips to hers in a tender, delicate kiss.

Unbelievable! Melody has known this guy's name for less than twenty-four hours and she's already making out with him in the halls.

The two linger there, unhurried, their lips moving slowly and in sync. Finally pulling himself away, Dennis whispers something in Melody's ear. She giggles and punches him impishly on the shoulder. With both hands raised in surrender, he playfully backs away from her.

"See ya later," he says with a wave and makes his way down the crowded hall.

I let out an exasperated sigh, more aggravated than ever, and scurry through the sea of students toward Melody. She remains in place, textbooks and Trapper Keeper cradled against her fuzzy pink sweater, watching Dennis as he walks away. Her eyes, I can't help but notice, drift downward to his backside.

"How were the milkshakes?" I ask, stepping up next to her.

Melody nearly jumps out of her skin. "Bailey! Hey there." Her face reddens. She knows I saw her locking lips with Dennis. "Um . . . milkshakes?"

"At the diner last night. You said you guys were going for milkshakes."

"Oh! Right. They were good." Mel tucks a strand of hair behind one ear and gazes past me to avoid eye contact.

"And the date?" I press.

"Also good." Try as she might to seem nonchalant, she's unable to contain a grin. "Actually, it was great." Mel casts a sheepish look down at her white flats. "Dennis is really sweet."

"Uh-huh." It's petty, but it's all I can muster.

Melody eventually meets my eyes, her grin now a frown. "Hey, I'm sorry I didn't walk to school with you this morning. Dennis gave me a lift."

I already knew this bit of info. Dennis's station wagon passed me on the way to school. As his car crept along through morning traffic, I caught Melody's voice drifting from the open windows. She was explaining the history of Abraham Street and Autumn Street, completely oblivious to me on the sidewalk. But perhaps that was for the better. Even if Melody had asked Dennis to stop the car and offered me a ride, I would have declined. I don't want to be in the same car with that boy. Ever.

Momentarily losing control of my thoughts, I'm helpless to stop the mental picture of Dennis's station wagon from twisting and contorting into a grisly vision of Dad's van. *Smoke wafting from the engine. Windshield splattered in blood.*

I close my eyes, fighting against the images in my head, begging them to go away.

"I'm guessing the dreams were pretty bad last night," Melody says. It's not a question.

I open my eyes and find her regarding me not just with worry but with fear. Mel seems terribly afraid for me.

"I'm okay," I tell her. "I just didn't get any sleep. I read for most of the night."

This is half true. After the nightmare, the last thing I wanted to do was go back to sleep. I never meant to fall asleep in the first place, but fatigue had its way with me. Upon waking, I retreated to the window seat in my room and attempted some light reading, putting aside V.C. Andrews for *Sweet Valley High* or maybe something else—I can't even remember. Of course, I couldn't focus. I must have sat there for hours, staring at the same page until dawn.

And to think I used to be such a big reader, I reflect mournfully. I remember back to the countless summer afternoons I spent reading on our porch swing when I was younger, ignoring the mosquitos come dusk just to squeeze in one more chapter. So much has changed these last few months.

Suddenly, Melody wraps her arms around me and pulls

me into a big embrace. Her chin digs into my shoulder, nailing a pressure point and causing a sharp pain, but I ignore it and hug her back, albeit hesitantly.

Melody sighs. "I love you. You know that?"

"I know," I say. "I . . . love you too."

And I do. Melody has been like a sister to me for as long as I can remember, but I'm not in the hugging mood at the moment. I'm so frustrated at Melody and terrified for her at the same time. And I don't know how to tell her.

Melody pulls away and checks my face for improvement, hoping one of her "famous Melody hugs" did the trick.

She frowns. "God, you . . . you . . ."

I raise my eyebrows.

"You . . . need a distraction," Melody finishes.

"Is that a kinder, gentler way of saying I 'look like a zombie'?" I ask, miming quotation marks.

Melody rolls her eyes. "It's my way of saying you need to go on a date."

Now it's my turn to roll my eyes.

"Seriously, Bailey, the date with Dennis last night made me feel a million times better. It was wonderful!"

Mel walks through the crowded hall toward our homeroom, and I follow along, hearing her voice but not really listening.

"At the end of the night, once the rain finally stopped, we went down to the lake and sat on the rocks to watch the stars. It was the most romantic time of my life. Tommy never did that kind of stuff with me. It was always just dinner and a movie, dinner and a movie, over and over. But this . . . this was on a whole other level! You really need to get a boyfriend. You should totally ask out that guy from Spooky's."

I stop walking. "Who? Brian?"

Melody pauses, looking back at me. "Yeah. Brian. Who else, dummy? He *so* likes you!"

"Melody," I say. "I'm sorry to ruin whatever fantasies are in your head about Brian and me, but he's, like, twenty-five."

"I mean, eh . . . that isn't *too* big an age gap."

"He's also gay."

Melody visibly deflates. "Oh . . ."

"His boyfriend stopped by Spooky's last weekend to say hi. They're cute together."

Melody nods slowly. "You're going to be single forever."

I shrug. "Give the dating thing a rest, will you? I'm not interested."

"Mm-hmm," Melody says, a sly smile spreading across her face. She points behind me. "Tell that to Bill Macklin."

I react instinctively, spinning on my heels and searching for Bill's face in the teeming hall.

"Made you look!"

I turn and give Melody the most intimidating glare I can muster. "Jerk."

She shrugs. "Just keeping ya on your toes."

Melody knows I had the biggest crush on Bill Macklin for years. Too bad I never worked up the guts to talk to him before he graduated last spring. Now he's starting at Autumncrow University. I rarely ever see him in town, but that's okay. Bill has been the furthest thing from my mind these last few months. Funny how fast you can get over a boy when he isn't around anymore . . . especially when you're also dealing with your dad's mysterious disappearance and your best friend's budding romance with the creepy boy from your nightmares.

Melody seizes my hand. "C'mon. Let's grab breakfast before homeroom. Ms. Peabody is serving biscuits and gravy in the cafeteria."

I resist her pull, tugging my hand away. "Just a sec. I . . . I think that's my brother over there by the stairs. I need to go talk to him."

That's him all right. Dalton stands out in the crowd, to say the least, thanks to his police uniform and enormous stature. He's always been a tall guy, much like our father. But while Dad was—*is*—on the thin side, Dalton has packed on a lot of muscle since joining the police force. In two years, he's transformed himself from an ordinary, lanky guy into a less hairy King Kong.

Leaving Melody behind without another word, I weave past my classmates as they scramble about the hall like ants at an outdoor potluck, only to be halted beneath a hanging "WELCOME BACK" banner by Monique Stevens, class president for the past three years (and no doubt hell-bent on securing a fourth and final term). She forces a clipboard into my hands.

"Good morning, Bailey," she says with the biggest, cheesiest smile imaginable. The spinach stuck in her teeth refuses to be ignored. *Only Monique would eat spinach before lunch,* I think. Otherwise, she is just as put together as always: black hair freshly straightened, yellow blouse pressed to perfection beneath a pair of overalls so blindingly white they may as well be Day-Glo.

"I hope you had a marvelous summer," Monique continues. "As I am sure you are aware, in 1959 Autumncrow High threw what would be its final prom, much to the disappointment of local teenagers ever since. You heard me correctly—these hallowed halls have gone thirty-four years without hosting a dance of any kind for the student body. How truly vile of the school board! How dare they take away something so important to the high school experience? The nerve!"

I look past Monique, making sure my brother is still hanging around. He is, thank God. I need to talk to him, and this will save me a trip to the police station. "Listen, I'm a little busy at the moment."

"This won't take much time, I assure you," Monique says, smiling even wider. "I am conducting a survey of the senior class of 1994 so that we can finally have a say in this matter. If the fates allow—and I'm referring to the goddamn school board—the blossoming youngsters of this fine establishment will be able to enjoy their very first school dance in a generation. Now, I know—"

"Monique," I say, cutting her pitch short, "I told you I'm busy. Really. So take your death wish and shove it, will you?" I fling the clipboard back at her.

"God, Bailey! When did you become such a snob?" Monique's jaw drops in astonishment. "This is not a death wish, okay? Why does everyone keep saying that? I just want my freaking high school prom!"

Monique stomps one foot and pushes past me, hustling the nearest student, a boy named Toby Mason. "Hey, Toby!" She just about throws the clipboard at him. "Here. Fill this out and sign your name. I'm done asking nicely."

Toby skims the fine print. "Hell no! We can't have another prom, Monique. You know that. It's banned. Do you want to be raptured too? Do you have a death wish?"

A screech of frustration rips through the hall.

I move on, flagging Dalton down with the wave of a hand. He sees me and closes his eyes, clearly in no mood to talk. But it's not like he can avoid me forever.

"Hey," I say, stepping in front of him.

"Hi." He scans the hall like an eagle hunting for prey. "I'm looking for someone. Do you know a Tommy Burke?"

"Tommy?" I feel equal parts disappointment and curiosity. "Why Tommy? You're not here about Dad?"

Dalton looks at me like I just slapped him in the face. "What? No, Bailey. I . . ." He releases a sigh as his face settles into a frown. "Listen, I'm still investigating Dad's disappearance, okay? But that's on my own time. When I'm on the clock, I have to set personal matters aside and do my duty. Today I'm looking for Tommy Burke."

I've heard this spiel about a dozen times already, the whole "I'm a police officer with a job to do" speech. But we all know the Autumncrow police department has done little to investigate Dad's disappearance. Hell, they do little to investigate *any* of the strange occurrences in this town. No sooner than something terrible happens—a kid vanishes, a man goes on a murderous rampage, a teenager's skinned corpse is found strung up in a tree—the department seems all but ready to forget all about it, moving on to smaller affairs like vandalism in the town square or smashed pumpkins at the nearest farm.

They even have Dalton parroting their bullshit, telling Mom and me in his proper police deputy manner that Dad had simply been in a car accident, that there was no way he could have survived that much blood loss.

"Then where is his body, Dalton?" I screamed the first time he tried to feed me that line. "If it was just a car accident, then where is his body?"

Despite having no explanation for this, the police were quick to close their investigation, leaving us in limbo. Thinking about it now makes me want to lash out at my brother, but I know it's out of his hands. Mom reminds me of this every chance she gets.

I bite back my anger and ask him, "Why are you looking for Tommy?"

"He broke into school early this morning. The secretary spotted him ransacking the file cabinets. Rather than confront him alone, she ran and phoned for help. Now he's nowhere to be found, but his bike is still in the parking lot. So that's where I come in."

Why would Tommy do such a thing? For a moment, I wonder what he was hunting for, but I already know the answer.

Dennis Greendale's student record. That has to be it. Leave it to Tommy to go digging up dirt on the new kid before he's even sure of his name. He's desperate and obsessed.

A sudden commotion breaks our conversation. Shouting. Cries of rage. Dalton springs into action, running down the hall toward the violent sounds. I follow him. Melody sees me on the move and hurries to catch up. "What's going on?" she asks.

I point to the growing crowd of students at the end of the hall. "It looks like a fight."

My brother is already pushing his way through the mob. A girl yells, "It's Deputy Hagen!"

"Step aside!" Dalton shouts. "Let me through."

The students scatter, spreading to either side of the hallway to make way for the intimidating officer. Left sitting alone in the middle of the floor is Tommy Burke, nursing a bloody nose that has already begun to swell.

"What the hell is going on here?" Dalton grabs Tommy by his bloody shirt and hoists him off the linoleum. "Well, I'll be damned. You're just the person I've been looking for."

Tommy winces. "You're pulling the skin, officer."

Dalton drops Tommy to his feet. "What's going on here, huh?"

Tommy shrugs, straightening his Misfits T-shirt. "Just messin' around."

"Likely story," Dalton mutters.

A girl on the sidelines chimes in. It's Agatha Something-or-Other, one of Melody's pals from the school paper. "He and that new kid were fighting."

Dalton looks around. "What new kid?"

"He ran off that way." Agatha points to the staircase at the east end of the hall.

Melody tenses beside me and clutches my arm. "Oh God, I hate this. I really, really hate this," she whispers. "I hope Dennis is okay."

I try to reply, but my mouth is wordless. All I can think is, *Tommy knows something. Tommy knows something.*

"Whatever," Dalton says, grabbing Tommy by his biceps. "Let's get you to the nurse. Then we'll call your parents. As for the rest of you"—he casts a granite stare at the swarm of onlooking teenagers and teachers—"as you were."

Good to see Dalton has expanded his police vocabulary.

Melody and I watch as Dalton escorts Tommy past us. The boy's left eye is beginning to bruise, and his bloody nose shows no signs of slowing. Melody glares at him, which he returns with a grave stare.

"We need to talk," he mutters.

"Zip it," Dalton says, rushing Tommy toward the nurse's office.

"Like hell," Melody says to me. "I never want to talk to that creep again. I need to go find Dennis. Will you cover for me in class? Tell Mr. Richards I'm sick or something?"

"I'm sure Dennis is okay," I argue, not wanting her to go looking for him. "Just come to class."

"No. I have to make sure he isn't hurt."

"Please, Melody," I beg.

The first warning bell rings, signaling the start of the school day. Everyone scurries for homeroom, but not Melody. Before the bell even stops, she has abandoned me, rushing down the staircase in search of Dennis. I want to go after her, but I hold myself back.

It's no use. No matter what I say, she'll insist on going to Dennis. That, or she'll ignore me or accuse me of being paranoid. Against my better judgment, I let Melody go, taking a deep breath and heading toward homeroom, all the while thinking about Tommy. Melody may have assumed he was talking to her, but the message was meant for me. Tommy's eyes were looking right into mine as he spoke the words.

"*We need to talk.*"

CHAPTER 9

I'M WALKING THROUGH the empty halls of Autumncrow High, the echoing squelch of my sneakers the only sound against the vaulted ceiling and stone walls. I don't usually walk unaccompanied here at school—terrible and often violent fates have been known to befall those who dare wander these grounds alone—but I was in the middle of class and had to pee. To be perfectly honest, it probably could have waited until lunch period, but I'd rather take my chances out here than endure another minute of mind-numbing lecture on the periodic table. For better or worse, the restroom nearest my third-period chemistry class is, well . . . not near at all.

At every turn, I carefully peer down the dimly lit corridor ahead, forever cautious of what might be waiting around a corner. I am greeted by lines of bright pumpkin-orange lockers, a trophy case packed to the brim with high school memorabilia, numerous hanging banners in support of the Autumncrow Scarecrows, and—

A man.

I utter a quiet gasp and stumble back into the stairwell, clutching the banister in one hand as I gape at the distant figure. He stands completely motionless in the center of the hallway, and for a moment I wonder if this is even a person at all. It could be a mannequin or some prop left behind by the theater department. But why would the drama club leave a dummy in the middle of the hallway?

I release my grip on the banister and take a step forward, not wanting to abandon my restroom mission just yet. "Hello?" I call out to him.

No response. No reaction. Just silence. Complete stillness.

It has to be a dummy, I tell myself. The figure is too far away to discern much detail, but I can see that it is tall and thin, gray-haired, and . . . wearing a tuxedo?

Yes, a tuxedo, complete with cummerbund and boutonniere. All gussied up for a dance that will never come again.

I take another step closer. And another. Chills whisper across my skin. The figure's face is an indistinct blur, but the longer I focus on the shadowy mass of it, the more my eyes seem to adjust as they would to a darkened room.

My eyes widen in shock. "Dad?"

A sudden dizziness throws my equilibrium out of control. The hallway begins to roll, tilting, turning . . . and now I'm spinning. The figure is gone, the hallway is gone, and

I'm on a carnival ride, whirling and twirling. Even after the ride is over, I can't stop spinning. I'm stumbling off the tea-cup, trying to catch my balance, but it's too late. I take a tumble, landing on the gravel path. Dad is kneeling over me. I start to cry as he examines my skinned knee.

"Shh, shh, shh. There, there," he whispers, smiling in relief. "You're okay. Just a scratch. Here, let me fix you."

Dad digs around in his pockets and manifests a Band-Aid. Unwrapping it, he patches me up as the neon colors of the Halloween carnival swirl around us like stars trapped in a kaleidoscope.

The memory ends as abruptly as it began. I find myself back in the school corridor, bracing myself against a locker. The figure is gone. Dad is gone.

Why do I feel like that was Dad? I couldn't discern his face, but something about his presence just *felt* like Dad. I could feel him the same way I always did when he'd arrive home from a long day at work. I never had to see or hear him come through the door; I just knew he was there.

And I know he's still here now.

"Daddy?" I repeat, a little louder this time. My heart is racing. My hands are trembling. Tears are threatening to spill down my cheeks. I step forward on quivering legs and ease myself toward the center of the hall, the very spot where the figure—*Dad*—was standing a moment ago. Another hall branches off at the middle of this one, and I realize he must have gone that way.

Finally regaining my strength, I push toward the other hall, walking faster and faster. I'm running now, rushing around the corner, hoping to see my father. Instead, I am met with yet another empty hallway, nearly identical to the one I just left behind.

"Daddy?" I shout. I'm bound to draw the attention of a teacher in one of the neighboring classrooms, but I don't care. I call for my father again, running faster down the hall, praying he'll hear me, that he'll rush to meet me and hug me and say, *"Shh, shh, shh. There, there. I'm here now. I'm here."*

I spot another bend ahead—one that I don't remember being there before—and round the corner. Another hallway. An endless hallway with endless orange lockers. Thousands of them. Stretching on and on and on . . .

The dizziness is coming back. I turn on my heels and look behind me, only to find more of the same: locker after locker, as far as I can see. A melody drifts down the hall, though I can't be sure which way it's coming from. The ballad is soft and tender: *"What'll I do with just a photograph to tell my troubles to?"*

"No . . ." I say under my breath, and before I know what I'm doing, I'm running again, running away this time, abandoning the search for my dad. All the while, the hallway continues to stretch and expand, growing longer before my eyes. I'm a kid again, running through the funhouse at the carnival, yelling over my shoulder at Dad, *"Bet you can't catch me!"*

I shake away the memory, trying as hard as I can to focus on what's ahead, when I hear another set of footsteps behind me, the sharp clicking of heels in stark contrast to the rubbery squeak of my sneakers.

Someone is following me.

I stop abruptly and turn, sobbing through jagged breaths as I am met with the shocking apparition of . . . a girl. A brunette no older than me. Her outfit looks like something from a production of *Bye Bye Birdie*: a white sweater with pink polka dots paired with a hot pink skirt that hits just below the knee. But something is terribly wrong. She is bathed from head to toe in blood as thick as chocolate syrup. It trickles and oozes from the gaping wound that separates her face into halves.

I cry out in shock as the girl—tears running down her bloodstained cheeks—opens her mouth and growls: "Run."

I cover my mouth in horror and fall back, collapsing onto floor, screaming at the top of my lungs, squeezing my eyes shut, too terrified to open them again, too afraid to see the girl—the girl with her face split right in two. I may just keep them shut forever.

"Bailey?"

I flinch at the sound of my name but quickly realize it's not the blood-soaked girl's raspy voice. It's not a female voice at all. Carefully opening my eyes one by one, I find myself on the cold dirt floor of the school's basement—a dank, musty labyrinth of twisting halls, rusted pipes, and steel shelving used for storage.

I've been down here once before, but it's been a couple of years, back when Melody and I were volunteering as stagehands for the school production of *Grease*. We were asked to pull some props out of storage, but we had no luck finding them among the endless rows of boxes. The drama instructor ended up letting us go a few days later, saying, "You gave it your all, girls, but I think I've got it from here."

How did I get down here? I stand up and brush the dirt from the seat of my jeans. I glance around, looking to see where the voice came from. Closer than expected, I spot the pale face of a boy with dark eyes staring at me through a barrier of corroded pipes dividing the hall in half.

"Hey," the boy says with a casual wave. He negotiates the meandering plumbing and rounds the boiler, finally coming into view. My breath hitches in my throat, and I step backward, colliding with the wet cinderblock wall behind me. I glance left, then right, trying to decide which way I should run. *Which way is out?*

"Hey, it's just me," Dennis says, taking another step in my direction.

I let out a short, shuddery whimper and cower against the wall.

Dennis freezes, his dark brows knit in confusion. "Whoa! Why are you so afraid of me, huh? What did I do?"

I'm breathing fast. My heart is beating hard against my rib cage. *Is this what a heart attack feels like?* "Please, stay back!" I say.

"Okay, okay!" Dennis tosses up his hands in surrender. "I'm not going to hurt you. I just heard you scream and got worried."

"What are you doing down here?" I ask though chattering teeth. My mind is a flurry of panicked questions. *What's going on? How the hell did I get down here? What happened to the girl?* "Where's my dad?" I ask aloud without even meaning to.

"Your ... dad?" Dennis is looking at me like I'm a lunatic. "Listen, I dunno about your dad. Why are *you* down here?"

"I asked you first!" I say.

"Well, I asked you second." Dennis crosses his arms and

narrows his eyes at me.

"I . . . uh . . ." I glance to my right again. I think that's the way to the stairs, if I remember correctly. I could make a run for it.

You won't get away in time. He'll catch you.

"I was headed for the restroom, but I got turned around," I finally say.

"Right. The restroom." Dennis nods and casts his eyes to the exposed beams in the ceiling, not believing me for a second, even though it's the truth.

"And what are *you* doing down here?" I repeat.

"I—" He pauses, his confusion and fluster more and more apparent. "I got lost," he mumbles and immediately cringes at his own explanation. "I just . . . I thought I heard something." He motions a hand behind him, toward the halls of the basement and whatever lingers there.

Dennis says nothing more, just shakes his head with a chuckle and peers back at me. There is an emptiness in his eyes, as though he might be more than just physically lost. It's like a part of him is somewhere else entirely.

He makes no effort to move. The two of us stand there for a moment, adrift in uncomfortable silence. Finally, Dennis says, "My dad died down here. Did you know that?"

I didn't. I had heard that Mr. Greendale died, of course, but I didn't know how or where. I shake my head.

"They found his body somewhere down here," Dennis says, eyes panning our gloomy surroundings. There is a trace of light from a string of bare bulbs rigged along the ceiling, but most of them are blown, keeping many areas shrouded in blackness. "Do you know how he died?"

I shake my head again.

"The cops said he died of a heart attack, but that was a lie. He took his own life."

I open and close my mouth, chills cascading down my back. A drop of water lands on my forehead, causing me to jump. I wipe it off and say, "If they said he had a heart attack, what makes you think—"

"I just know." Dennis cuts me off. His eyes are glistening in the amber light. "I mean . . ." He looks off down the hall, gazing through an open doorway into a dark room. I can't tell what's inside, but Dennis seems to see something. He sways slightly as his eyes burn into the darkness, as though perhaps he can see his father's body dangling from the ceiling.

"My dad died here too."

I don't mean to say it. I don't even think I believe it. The words just tumble out of my mouth.

Dennis turns toward me. "Really?"

I nod despite myself, hugging my shoulders to ward off the tremble in my bones. "That's what the police say, at least. I don't want it to be true. And it might not be; nobody really knows for sure. It happened in June, at the start of summer break. He didn't come home one evening, so Mom and I got worried and went out looking for him. We knew he'd left work, because the bookstore was all closed up and his van was gone. God, we probably drove around for three hours looking for him. We finally found his van here, in the schoolyard. He had crashed into the oak tree, knocked over a bunch of headstones. There was blood all over the windshield and the dashboard. All over the seats. Everywhere."

I'm crying now, and I can't stop. I can't stop talking either, much as I want to. *Why am I telling him this?*

"We don't know what would have brought him here, of all places, but there was his van. He'd barreled right through the iron fence."

"I'm so sorry," Dennis says.

"The weird thing is, his body was gone. All that blood, but no body. They thought he might have escaped the wreck and wandered off to find help. They organized search parties, looked everywhere. Nothing. It's like he just vanished."

The two of us stand in silence again, neither knowing how to continue. I've never shared this much about that horrible night with anyone besides Melody. I don't know why I told him. Perhaps it was that look in his eyes, that mournfulness I can't help but connect with. He's like a child down here, wandering around in the dark. Confused.

He's like me.

"Melody was looking for you earlier, after you and Tommy—" I pause, finally noticing his split lip. "She couldn't find you."

Dennis nods, gazes down at the floor.

"Where did you go?" I ask. "Why did you run?"

Dennis sniffles, and his eyes meet mine once more. Instead of answering my question, he asks me one of his own: "Did you love your dad?"

"I did," I answer, surprised. "I do."

Dennis nods and blinks back tears, a small quiver in his chin. "I hated mine."

With that, Dennis takes off down the passage, disappearing around a corner. The dull thud of his footsteps gradually fades away into nothing, leaving me alone in the cold, empty hall.

CHAPTER
10

"Go home."

I'm in the middle of prepping an order for Mr. and Mrs. Lovegrave—old family friends who've dropped by the café for some hot chocolate—when Brian hops over the counter and starts washing his hands in the sink. He isn't scheduled to work tonight, but here he is anyway, wearing his bright orange Spooky's apron, hair tucked neatly beneath a black bandana.

"I said go home," he tells me again. "When I get in tomorrow, I'll tell Sookie you left sick."

"Why? What's up?" I ask in confusion.

Brian draws close, drying his hands on a paper towel, and whispers, "What's up is that you look exhausted, Bailey." He gives me a worried glance, then pitches a thou-sand-watt smile at the Lovegraves. "Hey, y'all. Just one moment, okay? Sorry for the wait."

"I'm fine," I insist, keeping my voice low.

"Sure, sure." Brian rolls his eyes. "But really, go home. You need some sleep, hon. You look way tired."

The mere mention of sleep makes me want to pass out right here, right now, to doze for hours on the café floor. Brian must see the drowsy twitch in my eyes, because he gives me another look as if to say, "I rest my case."

"Fine." I give in and peel off my apron. "Why are you even here, though? I thought you and your friend were going to that concert tonight."

"No, that's next Thursday. I just wanted to check on you, kiddo. I had a hunch you might need me to fill in. Oh look! I was right." Brian grins and gets to work finishing those hot chocolates. "Order up!"

I won't be taking his suggestion of sleep when I get home—not after making the mistake of drifting off last night—but sitting on the couch and zoning out to some old reruns sure beats slogging through the rest of my shift. The café always stays open late, but this place is dead on weeknights, at least until mid-September when the Halloween crowd starts pouring into town. In the meantime, there isn't much to do besides wait for stray night owls and the occasional patron in need of an emergency grilled apple 'n' cheese sandwich.

Before leaving, I use the café's phone to make a quick call to my sister. On nights when Mom and I are working, Rae rides the school bus to her friend Heather's house a few doors down from ours and hangs tight until one of us can pick her up. Since I'm on Rae duty tonight, I let her know

I'll be there soon. Then I clock out, grab my denim jacket off the coatrack, and head into the already dark, misty evening, softened by the warm glow of wrought iron streetlamps and the neon colors of Spooky's buzzing sign. As soon as I step off the stoop, the crisp night air sinks its fangs into my skin. I hug myself against the cold, the thought of the coming winter months sending shivers up my spine.

I make my way toward the intersection of Main and Abraham. Up ahead, the last of the dinner crowd ambles out the revolving door of Drac's 24-Hour Bite. I can almost hear Mom's sigh of relief from all the way down the street.

The diner may still be open, but most of the other businesses on Main—minus Undead Video and Screamplay Cinema—are already bolted up for the night, so there is little cause for traffic. Besides those climbing into their cars to drive home and turn in for the night, I am the only person around.

Walking alone after nightfall in Autumncrow Valley comes highly discouraged, but here I am. Alone. Walking. A crescent moon hangs in the hazy sky above, watching and waiting for something terrible to happen.

Passing by the bookstore where Dad used to work, I take a moment to peer into the darkened shop window. It's oddly comforting to imagine he might be in there somewhere, lost among the maze of shelves, poring over books when he should be shelving them. I can almost hear Mr. Hanlon, the bookshop owner, scolding my dad now: *"Reading on the job again, Felix?"*

The flashing lights of the movie theater across the street reflect in the window glass, reminding me once again of that long-ago father–daughter date to Autumncrow's Halloween

Carnival, of sitting at the tippy top of the Ferris wheel while we waited to be let off the ride. I was transfixed by the glittering landscape of blinking lights branching out over the fairgrounds, a sight more beautiful to me than the Grand Canyon or anything else I'd seen in all my life. Up there on the Ferris wheel—so far up that even the sounds of the carnival barely reached our ears—Daddy and I were like royalty, admiring our kingdom from high above, happy together and safe.

To pass the time, Dad and I competed in a screaming match, each of us striving to make the longest echo over Autumncrow's valleys. "I'm going to make an echo so long, it goes all the way around the world and comes up behind us," I said.

Dad gave me that lopsided grin of his. "You can do it. Echoes don't just travel forward, you know? Once your voice leaves your lips, it scatters in every direction across time and space. No matter how far apart we are, you can be sure those echoes will reach me. They might even travel all the way back to when I was your age. I may not know what they mean, but I'll hear them."

I smile at the happy memory, though my heart feels sad. Pressing my forehead against the window glass, I close my eyes and whisper, "I miss you, Daddy," a familiar lump forming in my throat.

I hope what he said wasn't a bunch of nonsense. I don't know if he can hear me, but I like to pretend he can, wherever he is.

Could that have been him at school today? I still don't know what to make of it—some mixture of memory and sleep-deprived hallucination? A ghost?

With that, my thoughts turn to the girl in the old-fashioned dress. I blink away the gruesome image of her bloodied face split in half.

Who was she? I wonder as I round the corner onto Abraham Street. *Had she been a student at Autumncrow High?*

Have I completely lost my mind?

Out of nowhere, a car whips by on Main and blows through the intersection. From inside, a girl cries out, her words carrying through the stillness of the night, "Stop! What the hell are you doing!"

I whirl around just in time to see the car—a ramshackle station wagon—make a sharp right onto Black Lane, the same route I take every morning to school.

The girl's voice, I quickly realize, belonged to Melody. The car was Dennis's.

I reverse course without another thought and sprint after the car, turning onto Black Lane and running as fast as I can. The car soon disappears around a bend in the road, the hum of its motor fading beneath the thrum of cricket song and my own racing footsteps. Still, I don't slow. Sweat drips down my face despite the cold. My breath struggles to keep up with my frenzied heartbeat.

After a few minutes, the neighborhood homes become sparse, no longer clustered together like those near town. To my right, rambling mansions stand many acres from the road, and to my left is a massive cornfield, its stalks rustling and sighing in the chilly breeze. At last, I see the car up ahead, its taillights ablaze in the night.

Just as I thought. The station wagon is parked at the curb outside Autumncrow High. Dennis didn't bother parking in the lot behind school. Didn't even bother closing his door. The dome light illuminates the vehicle's interior, but I see no trace of Melody, at least not from this far away.

"Melody?" I shout. My voice echoes back to me from the cornfield across the street.

I cover the remaining distance between me and the car to steal a peek inside. For a moment, I'm terrified I'll find blood splashed across the dashboard, the windshield, the seats . . . but there is none. I draw a sigh of relief and cast my eyes to the towering black silhouette that is Autumncrow High, a dead shape against the moonlit lavender sky. It's too dark to see the choking oak, but I can sense its presence as though it were a living, breathing creature lying in wait for the chance to strike.

"Melody? Hello?" I call.

Nothing. No reply.

I hate the idea of going near the school at night, but I have to make sure Melody is okay. Dennis must have led her inside, unless they ran off into the cornfield together.

"Not here," the stalks seem to whisper in reply to my thoughts. *"Not in here. Alone. We are all alone."*

I shudder.

I don't know why on earth they'd come to school this late, unless perhaps for the same reason Dennis was in the basement earlier. I can't be sure, but he seemed to be looking for something . . . or someone.

I take a deep breath and walk toward the building, thinking twice before crossing into the schoolyard. From the dim recesses of my mind, the wreckage of Dad's van emerges, superimposed onto the scenery before me, raising the tiny hairs on my arms. I've been avoiding this route past the choking oak since returning to school, opting for the rear entrance instead, precisely in hopes of keeping these terrible memories from skirting about in my head.

But I've got to try the front doors, even if the odds of them being unlocked are slim.

I pass beneath the iron archway at the head of the property welcoming me to Autumncrow High. Goosebumps rise on my arms and legs as I walk along the path. I keep my eyes fastened on the doors ahead and do my best to ignore the oak's foreboding presence, but the school alone is enough to fill the pit of my stomach with sickening dread.

Peering up at the imposing schoolhouse—*it* peering down at *me*—I can't help but think of all the horrific atrocities that have transpired here in the shadows: the guttings and hangings, the dismemberments and maulings, the stabbings and . . .

How does anyone send their kids here and still sleep at night? How do we all just go on living in this town?

I'm not the first teenager in Autumncrow to ask these questions. The valley is a magical and bewitching place, to be sure, but that magic has a sinister side, and every kid in town knows it. We see everything. We remember everything. But eventually we grow up, and that's when the forgetting begins. Eyes become blind, ears are deafened, and soon all that's remembered are those happy times picking pumpkins at the pumpkin patch or catching the all-night horror movie marathon at the theater. We've all seen it happen, and I believe that's why no one ever leaves. The good memories hold so much gravity that even the most brutal of news reports are overshadowed and forgotten once the dead are scooped up and laid to rest, the unsightly mess tidied up before anyone else can see the carnage. The town moves on, the kids are sent back to school, and old patterns continue.

Sometimes even I forget. It's easy to get distracted here by the picturesque views and cozy small-town charm. But at moments like this, alone in the cold dark of night, I remember how vulnerable I am, how small and temporary.

Your time is coming, Bailey. Sooner than you think.

Or maybe you're already gone and just don't know it yet. Maybe that's why you can't imagine growing old, why you're so disconnected from those who were once so close. Because you're already dead. Because you're fading away.

Maybe you were never here. Maybe the world moved on before you ever had a chance, the ghost of a future that will never come to pass.

I let loose a whimper and swallow back tears, forcing these opaque thoughts into a closet deep inside my mind and slamming the door, locking it tight.

I step off the trampled path and climb the steps leading to the front doors of my school. I tug on the weathered iron handles, feeling their rough texture scrape against my palms.

Locked. Of course. They must have found another way in.

I turn and descend the steps, backtracking along the path through the schoolyard—the *graveyard*—when something moves near the base of the choking oak.

No, wait! Don't look at it!

But it's too late. I glance up instinctively, training my eyes on the tree and the ghostly figure standing beneath its gnarled branches. It rushes at me, a mass of shadow separating from shadow, and I scream, stumbling backward onto the grass, tripping over a petite headstone. I drop, landing so hard on my back that the air whooshes out of my lungs. *"Oof!"*

"Oh my God, Bailey! I'm *so* sorry. I wasn't trying to scare you, I *swear.*"

I open my eyes to see the figure looming above me, eclipsing the moon. "Melody?" I gasp, unable to see her darkened face.

"Yeah, it's me," she says, helping me to my feet. "Are you okay?"

"I..." I inhale a shaky breath, putting a hand against Melody's shoulder to steady myself. "I got the wind knocked out of me."

"Did you hit your head?"

"No. I think I'm okay."

"Good. That's good... So what exactly are you doing here, huh?" Melody asks, her voice betraying the slightest trace of hostility. "I thought a freaking ghost was out there in the cornfield wailing my name."

"I scared *you?"* I bellow. "You about gave me a heart attack running at me like that."

"I wasn't running," Mel protests, her irritation swelling. She pulls away. "Why are you even here? Were you following us?"

Still flustered, I take a seat on the nearest headstone, the one I tripped over a minute ago. Some might say it's disrespectful to perch on someone's grave like that, but hopefully they don't mind. "I was on my way home from work when you two NASCAR'd past me. I could hear you yelling. You sounded frantic. So, yeah, I followed you guys."

"Oh. Right." Melody crosses her arms to fight off the cold and gazes down at the ground. "Well . . . thanks. I was a little freaked."

"Why was he driving like that?"

"I don't know." Mel throws her hands up in the air. "Beats me. He's been weird all night. When I asked him what went down with Tommy earlier, he just acted all, like . . . aloof? Is that the word? He didn't want to talk, so I practically had to force it out of him. It sounds like Tommy jumped him in the hall for no apparent reason. Typical Tommy—all impulse, no self-control. If he only had a brain . . ."

It's a fitting sentiment for a former Autumncrow Scarecrow. In happier times, Melody even got an "IF I ONLY HAD A BRAIN" T-shirt airbrushed for him as a good-natured joke.

"Did you ask Dennis why he ran off?" I ask.

"Yeah, but he didn't want to talk about it. Like I said, he was being weird. We were supposed to go to the arcade tonight, but I suggested catching a movie instead since he was all distracted." Melody pauses and peers at me through the darkness. "Sorry I didn't invite you. You were working, so—"

"It's fine." I wave off her apology. "What happened next?"

"Well, back in the car after the movie, Dennis suddenly went all ballistic. He started asking me if I heard someone calling his name. There was no one calling for him, Bailey. It was like he was hearing voices in his head or something. Before I knew what was happening, he was speeding all the way here, even though I was begging him to pull over and let me out. He just ignored me like I was nothing."

Melody's voices hitches, and I hear her suppress a sob. "Hey, it's okay," I say, taking her hand and squeezing it. The events of the night must have really shaken her up. "Where is Dennis now?"

Melody sniffles. "In there," she says, angling a thumb back at the school building. "As soon as we got here, he stopped the car and just booked it, ran for one of the side windows and climbed through before I could catch up."

"You mean he broke a window?" I ask.

"No. It slid right open."

"Weird."

"I know. It's like he knew it would be unlocked. I was too scared to follow him inside, so I decided to wait for him out here. That's when I heard you wailing like a banshee."

"I was worried," I say, releasing her hand.

"Yeah, I know," she mutters. "Thanks for looking out for me. I . . . I don't know what he's doing. What if something happened to him in there?"

"He'll come back," I reassure her, though I have no way of knowing that. "Let's go wait by the car, okay? I'm getting the creeps over here."

"Maybe we should go hunt him down. It won't be so bad if we stick together."

"No way," I say, shaking my head. "I never want to go in there at night. Ever."

Melody swallows, a loud *gulp*. "No, you're right." She looks at the school and shudders. "Let's wait by the car."

We blunder toward Dennis's station wagon, eyes focused downward on the dark path so as not to trip, though it's too dark to see anyway. The small sliver of moon is of little help in that regard, but thankfully the car lights offer some visibility as we get closer.

We're only a few feet from the station wagon when Melody shrieks.

"What is it?" I ask her, freezing in place.

Melody points ahead, her outstretched finger trembling with fear. "Bailey," she whispers, "someone's in the car."

Terror tightens its grip around my heart. My breath stops as I glance toward the vehicle. Melody is right. Through the passenger window, I can see a man in the driver's seat. Whoever he is, he's staring straight ahead, ignoring us.

"Who is that?" I ask.

"I . . . I think—" Melody pauses and slouches, narrowing her eyes as she focuses on the man inside the car. "Dennis?" she calls.

The man slowly turns his head and leans over the passenger seat, peering at us through the glass. A smile appears on his face. A wide, white smile.

"Douchebag," Melody whispers. "It *is* him. What the hell is wrong with this guy? Freaking boys!" She marches toward the car, leaving me alone on the path.

Something's wrong.

Melody opens the passenger door and sticks her head inside the car. "Where did you go, Dennis? You left me standing out here in the cold! What's your damage, huh? Is this your idea of a joke?"

She's yelling. Loud. If there were any houses closer by, people would be stepping onto their lawns to assess the problem. But the nearest home is acres away, too far for anyone to hear. She can scream all she wants—no one but us is ever going to know.

Chills course my flesh. I take a reluctant step toward the car as Melody unleashes her rage on Dennis. He doesn't react, just stares at her from his place behind the steering wheel, grinning.

"Melody . . ." I whisper, but she ignores me.

"You've acted like a total weirdo all day, Dennis. A complete creepazoid," Melody barks. "What's going on? And why are you staring at me like that?"

Dennis continues to grin, remaining silent for a spell before finally speaking: "You finished?"

Melody scoffs. "You tell me. You've got a lot of explaining to do."

Dennis's grin widens, taking on almost uncanny proportions. He looks down and smooths his hands over his chest. "I found this," he says.

"Found what?" Melody asks.

"This jacket," Dennis replies. "Haven't you noticed it? I found it inside."

Jacket?

I step up behind Melody and peer over her shoulder. Dennis is wearing an Autumncrow High letterman jacket with the school's classic colors: black and burnt orange. But this jacket is far from new. The collar is ripped, and the sleeves are strewn with dark crimson stains.

"You stole somebody's jacket?" Melody asks.

"No. This is mine," Dennis says, beaming in glee. "I mean, it is now. Fits perfectly. Neat, right?"

"Yeah, sure. Real neat," Melody grumbles. "Look, Dennis—it's late, and I'm exhausted. Let's just forget this and go home, okay? It's still a school night."

"Sure thing, doll. Hop in!" Dennis pats the passenger seat.

Melody glances back at me, rolls her eyes, and gets into the car. I stand frozen for a moment, my teeth chattering, not from the cold but from anxiety.

"You coming?" Melody asks me.

I shake my head no.

Mel sighs. "Please get in. We'll give you a lift home."

I shake my head again. I can't speak. I can barely even move. From the car, Dennis stares past Melody, leering up at me with that horrible grin.

"Bailey!" Melody shouts. Her harsh tone rips me out of my dazed stupor. "For God's sake, it's not safe to walk home from here," she says. "Get in back, and we'll take you home. God, I'm *so* over this night." Melody huffs and sinks down into her seat, crossing her arms, a combination of angry parent and disgruntled kid.

Against my every instinct, I do as she says and climb into the back seat. Deep down, I want nothing more than to run home screaming, but my body is a prisoner to the icy fear crystalizing my blood. Somehow, acknowledging my dread in this moment feels more dangerous than pretending it isn't there.

The jacket . . . It's the same jacket, isn't it? The one from my dream.

Dennis starts the car, and it rumbles to life. He revs the engine, laughing. "I just love a late-night drive. Don't you?"

"Drive, Dennis." Melody rests her forehead against the side window, ignoring his question.

Dennis revs the engine a few more times, then flips on the radio. Whitney Houston blares from the speakers, belting her rendition of "I Will Always Love You." Dennis snarls in disgust and starts playing with the dial, sifting through station after station until a familiar old tune breaks through the crackle.

"What'll I do when I am wond'ring who is kissing you? What'll I do?"

I sit upright in my seat at the sound of the song, feeling as though I may cry.

"That's better," Dennis says, adjusting the rearview mirror so I can see him looking back at me. In the glow of the dashboard lights, his face takes on a ghoulish aura, but it's also something more than that. Gone is the deep chocolate brown of his eyes. All trace of their disarming warmth has vanished, awash in the bluest of icy oceans.

CHAPTER 11

"WHERE have you *been?*"

I've only just opened the door of the station wagon when Mom comes bursting out of the house. She races over the path in her white waitressing outfit, her hair—the same shade of red as mine—bundled in a tight bun. Rae is in tow, barely keeping up with Mom's relentless strides.

"Shit!" I whisper to Melody. "I told Rae I was coming to pick her up. I totally forgot."

"On the bright side, I hear those steel tables at the morgue are more comfortable than they look," Melody says dryly.

The dam that has kept my panic at bay through tonight's misadventures finally breaks. Anxiety courses through my body, flooding my every nerve. This evening is already one I hope never to repeat, but Mom's thoroughly displeased face says things are about to get a whole lot worse.

I step out of the car, hands held before me like a kitten trainer coming head-to-head with a tiger. "I'm so, *so* sorry."

Mom flings open the front gate and halts just inches from my face. "Apologize later," she snaps. "I had to leave work early because I got a hysterical phone call from Rae. She said you told her you were on your way and then never showed up."

"I wasn't hysterical," Rae protests, "just a little worried."

"Go inside," Mom barks at Rae without so much as looking at her. My sister rolls her eyes and marches back into the house.

"Do you know how worried I was?" Mom seethes at me through a furious scowl. "I thought something terrible had happened. I was about to search the entire neighborhood like we did for your . . . your fath—"

My mother freezes, looking past me in a state of shock. A tear breaks from one eye and falls down her cheek.

"Mom? What is it?" I turn, seeing Dennis on the other side of the station wagon, leaning against the hood of the car. The interior light pours from his open door and casts an eerie glow under his angular face. He looks like a kid at a sleepover with a flashlight held under his chin, ready to tell his friends a scary story.

The electric blue luster of Dennis's eyes only adds to the play of light and shadow. Though the rational part of my brain is eager to dismiss the change in color as a figment of my own restless imagination, my instincts tell me this is no hallucination.

"Hello, Mrs. Hagen," he says in a sticky-sweet tone. "It is Hagen, right? I'm afraid the mix-up is all my fault. Melody and I were out having a good ol' time when a flat tire spoiled our fun. Bailey here"—he motions at me—"was kind enough to stop and help us out. You have raised a lovely daughter, ma'am."

Dumbfounded, Mom merely stares back at Dennis, her eyes wide and unblinking. Melody rolls down her window and breaks the tense silence. "Hey there, Mrs. Hagen."

Mom starts, seemingly unaware of Mel's presence until now. "Oh! Hello, Melody."

"Hey," Melody repeats. "Listen, I'm so sorry. We didn't mean to take up Bailey's time. She was worried about me . . . I mean *us*. She was worried about us."

"Oh . . . yes," Mom says. "That's quite all right."

Something is amiss with Mom's demeanor. She seems disoriented. Scared, even, like she senses Dennis as a threat. This can't be on my account; I haven't told my mother a single thing about my dreams or the uncanny resemblance between the nightmare puppeteer and the boy standing before us.

I think back to last night when Mom came home from work, how spooked she seemed at having seen Melody out with Dennis. She knows something about this boy, something she isn't saying.

Mom finds my hand, grips it tightly, and pulls me toward the house. "Thank you for giving my daughter a ride," she calls without looking back. "You kids get home safe."

I give Melody a wave, but she doesn't see me. She's sitting in the passenger seat with her face buried in her hands, either from embarrassment or from fatigue—or both. It's Dennis who waves back, a slow, lingering gesture of farewell. He beams at me from across the hood of his car, his grin a ghastly jack-o'-lantern glowing in the night.

"Who is that boy?" Mom demands.

She slams the front door and crosses the foyer toward me in the blink of an eye, her face a twisted mask of emotions. *"Who?"* she demands again. "Where did he come from?"

Rae descends the dark stairwell and freezes on the bottom step. The alarm on her face mirrors exactly how I feel: a storm is coming.

"Mom, what's going on?" I ask, a baseball-sized lump in my throat.

Tell me what you know about him.

Mom ignores my question. "What's his name?" She comes even closer, her eyes probing mine for answers.

"Dennis," I answer, taking a step back. "Dennis Greendale."

"Greendale?" Mom grips her chest, staring at me like I've just slapped her across the face.

"He's new in town. He goes to school with us," I say. *"Please* tell me what's going on."

Mom grabs me by the shoulders, her fingertips sinking into my skin. I wince in pain. "Ow! Mom, you're hurting me!"

"Where did he come from?" she shouts, her frightened eyes spilling tears. She tenses her grip, gives me a hard shake that rattles my nerves completely. "What does he want?"

I'm crying now, and Rae has appeared at my side. She's trying to pry Mom's hands from me, begging her to let me go. But our mother is gone, totally lost in a spiral of terror and anger. I've never seen her like this before. Her face is as pale a corpse, her eyes feral and raging.

"WHAT WERE YOU DOING WITH HIM?" she

shrieks, clenching me tighter still.

Push her, I think. *You have to push her, or you won't get free.*

I don't want to do it. I've never laid a finger on my mother, and I don't believe she's ever laid a finger on me up until now. But I don't know how else to escape Mom's savage grip.

I give her a firm shove that sends her stumbling backward, hands flailing. She collides with the front door, grasping at the doorknob to keep from falling.

I rub my throbbing shoulders.

"Are you okay?" Rae asks me.

I don't answer. I watch as Mom rights herself and peers back at us across the foyer. The fear in her eyes remains, but the anger has dissolved into tears of remorse.

"I . . . I'm sorry, my girl," she says, putting a hand to her mouth in disbelief. "I'm so, so sorry. I don't know what came over me."

There's a moment's pause before I'm able to find my voice. "It's fine," I say, eager for the confrontation to be over, just wanting my mom to be her normal, sweet-natured self again. "I'm okay. Really. Forget it."

And I am okay. Shaken, yes, but I'll be fine. Rae, on the other hand, is trembling beside me, her teeth chattering. I take her hand in mine and give it a gentle squeeze.

Mom smooths back the flyaway hairs that have come undone from her bun and wipes the tears from her face. "I got so scared when I saw—" She freezes, and I can tell she's carefully considering her words. "I just got scared when I realized how easily I could lose you."

"Won't happen again," I say shortly.

Leave, I want to say. *Go back to work so I can attempt some damage control on your daughter.*

Rae is only eleven years old. What she just witnessed is bound to leave emotional scars.

As if reading my mind, Mom says, "I . . . guess I should get back to work."

I nod in response.

"Okay," Mom says, walking to the coat closet to retrieve her jacket. "I truly am sorry," she adds, slipping her arms into the sleeves. "To both of you. I shouldn't have gotten so angry."

"It's fine," I repeat.

Mom grabs her purse from a hook by the door. "We can talk more later. Just please, Bailey, promise me something."

I wait for her to continue.

"Stay away from that boy, okay?"

"Okay," I say.

I want to ask more, get to the bottom of whatever has her so frightened of Dennis Greendale. But after the way she just reacted, that doesn't seem wise. I'm not sure I'll ever be able to talk to her about him.

I'll just have to find out myself.

Without another word, Mom disappears out the door, leaving Rae and me in the foyer.

"Are you okay?" I turn to my sister, brushing the tears from her cheeks. Normally, she would push me away, tell me I'm going to mess up her makeup, but she doesn't this time. She hugs me instead, burying her face against my newly bruised shoulder and quietly sobbing.

"Hey, it's okay," I say, returning her embrace. "It was stupid of me to leave you hanging like that after I told you I was on my way. I'm sorry."

This is the first time Rae has hugged me in months. Since Dad disappeared, she hardly lets anyone touch her. She often makes the excuse that a hug will wrinkle her outfit, but she doesn't seem to care about that now.

"Mom never gets mad like that." Rae's sad voice is muffled against the fabric of my jacket. "She was like a monster."

"She was just scared," I say, combing my fingers through Rae's hair. "She was afraid . . . something might have happened to me."

Rae pulls away and looks into my eyes. "Like what happened to Daddy?"

I nod. "Yeah. Like what happened to Daddy."

New tears form in my little sister's eyes as her face contorts into a knot of bewildered agony. "I really miss him," she cries. "I miss him so much."

I'm too exhausted to hold my emotions back any longer. All summer long, I've done my best to put on a brave face for my family, to lock my grief away behind a door in my mind until Dad was found and brought back to us. But seeing Rae shed her recently toughened exterior like this, exposing just how delicate she really is, that door of mine begins to splinter and crack. Now I'm reminded of who I really am: a kid not much older than my sister, a kid who has lost her best friend and knows deep down that he's never coming home.

"I miss him too," I sob, wrapping my arms around my sister once more.

We cling to each other tightly, adrift in a sea of sorrow as the grandfather clock in the living room chimes midnight.

CHAPTER 12

FOR THE FIRST TIME since she was very small, Rae lets me tuck her in and wish her goodnight. Once her bedroom door is closed behind me, I cross the hall to Dad's library and test the doorknob. The door doesn't budge, confirming my suspicions: Mom is hiding something in there.

I stand on tiptoe and reach upward, running my hand along the top of the doorframe for the skeleton key that opens any door in the house. After a moment's search, I drop back onto my heels.

It isn't there.

I do an impromptu check of the other doorframes in the hall, trying my best to walk quietly so as not to alarm Rae. We've kept a skeleton key above one of these doors for as long as I can remember, but now it seems to have gone missing.

I glance down the shadowy hall at Mom's closed bedroom door. *It could be in there,* I decide, *stashed in her dresser or bedside table.* I haven't gone into Mom's room in months, and the thought of doing so now, for whatever reason, unnerves me.

It'll only be a second, I think. *Just run in, take a look around, and get out. If you don't find it, use a hairpin to pick the lock. It can't be that hard.*

I take a deep breath and push through the door, locating the light switch to my right. The soft glow of an antique lamp beside the bed illuminates a small portion of the bedroom, but the rest is left in shadow.

"Hello?" I whisper.

I don't know why I say it. It's not like anyone could be in here, watching from one of the dark corners. Right?

The darkness seems to stare back at me, asking if I'm willing to bet on that theory.

"Stop it," I mutter to myself. "Don't go creeping yourself out." The very idea that Mom wouldn't want me in the library has me jumping at shadows. But why else would she lock the door? There must be something in there that she doesn't want Rae or me to see.

Slowly, I creep across the room to the bedside table, the floorboards whining beneath my wool stockings.

Clink!

I freeze, half expecting to see someone—*him*—cranking that vile contraption of his, crystalline eyes gleaming in the lamplight. But all I see is an old chest of drawers, a floral-pattern reading chair, and thick burgundy drapes pulled taut across the bedroom window.

"Find the key and leave," I remind myself.

I sneak to the bedside table, on which sits the lamp, a phone, a large leather-bound book, and Mom's reading glasses. I open the drawer, doubtful Mom would make a hiding place of such an obvious spot. I shuffle through a pile of faded receipts and old to-do lists, finding nothing useful—no key.

I sigh and slide the drawer shut, hearing a second brief *clink* across the room. I toss another glance over my shoulder, knowing it's only the settling of the house I'm hearing. Even so, I have to check to be sure I'm really alone.

A small shape on the floor catches my eye.

I stand. I blink. I make sure the shadows aren't just playing tricks with my eyes. But no, this is real. In the center of the floor no more than five feet away, in a spot that was barren just a moment ago, is a clunky old skeleton key.

"Hello?" I say again, knowing now that I'm not alone. Someone else must be here, must be hiding . . . *but where?* Behind the drapes? If so, I'd see their feet poking from beneath. I'd see the fabric stirring with their every breath.

I overlooked it, I tell myself. *The key was right there when I came in, and I just didn't see it. Silly me!*

Yes. Silly you, say the shadows of the bedroom. *Silly you . . .*

I snatch the key from the carpet and tiptoe back to the hall as quickly as possible, closing Mom's door behind me. The dreadful feeling of being watched fades away instantly, which somehow worries me even more.

The night-light in the hall casts a soft glow over the family portraits covering the walls, morphing the smiling faces of Mom, Dad, Dalton, Rae, and myself into ghastly things, reminding me of those grinning scarecrows in Eleanor McGuffin's Halloween display. A shiver trickles down my spine as I walk past the portraits toward Dad's library, all the while feeling as though the eyes in each photo are trailing me, disapproving of my sneaking about.

Ready to leave the eeriness of the hallway behind, I unlock the library door and push it open for the first time in months. Greeting me is the musty scent of old books, a smell I didn't realize how much I'd missed until now. I turn on the light and feel my emotions swell yet again at the sight of Mom and Dad's vast assemblage of titles. Floor-to-ceiling shelves line every wall, packed to full capacity with every kind of volume imaginable. Fantasy and science fiction, cookbooks and tomes about gardening, detective stories and true crime paperbacks, Mom's collection of gothics and Greek mythology—it's all here. But taking up most of the shelf space, unsurprisingly, is row upon row of horror novels, Dad's personal favorite.

I smile, feeling a warmth in my heart that rivals the cold stone in my throat. Stepping forward, I run my fingers over the curved spines, remembering the many hours I've spent stretched out on the library floor, reading these harrowing tales or sometimes just staring at the covers while Dad sat at his desk with a cup of coffee and a book of his own.

All summer long, I've been afraid to step inside this room, worried I'd only miss Dad more. Instead, I feel closer to him now than I would have dreamed possible.

This weekend, I'm going to come in here and tidy the place up, whether Mom likes it or not. Dad would appreciate that. I'll dust the shelves, open the windows, let some fresh air in. I'll even organize the books stacked atop the old steamer trunk under the window. Dad must not have had a chance to do it himself.

I amble over to the trunk and sift through the pile of tattered tomes, already trying to determine where to shelve them. Their dusty covers bear no titles or authors' names, and the gold lettering on the spines is worn and illegible from many years of use. I open the top book of the stack to the first page and read the title: *Bindings and Banishings*.

I pause for a moment and lift the hefty volume closer to my face, reading the title again and again.

Do these words mean what I think they mean?

Propping the book's spine against the trunk, I leaf through its contents, finding text and illustrations the likes of which I've seen only in movies—treatises on magic and curses, on spells and . . .

Witchcraft.

My pulse rises. I set the first book aside and begin paging through the others, finding more of the same—dog-eared folios crowded with protection rituals and binding spells in an ornate script I can barely comprehend.

"What the hell is going on here?" I say to no one in particular.

Did these books belong to Dad, or are they Mom's? Is that why Mom came in here last night, to read through these?

To practice magic?

I can't help but chuckle at the thought. *Nonsense.* Mom isn't a witch, and Dad was no conjuror either. That's crazy. Dad worked at The Little Bookshoppe of Curiosities, a bookstore specializing in the occult and the macabre. He was a nerd for stuff like this. It's not any deeper than that.

Case closed. Mystery solved.

And yet . . .

Catching sight of something awry, I clear the lid of the steamer trunk and drop to my knees. There was a lock on the trunk that had remained clamped tight since I was a kid. I asked Dad about it once, but all he said was that the trunk was old and the key was lost ages ago. Now the lock is busted, mangled as though someone took the jaws of life to the thing. Was it these strange books that had been kept inside?

I lift upward on the heavy lid and prop it against the window frame. From above, the pale light of the crescent moon twinkles through the rippled panes of glass, filtering over the mostly empty trunk's remaining contents: a single Autumncrow High yearbook dated 1959 and a black-and-white photograph ripped right down the middle.

With trembling hands, I reach for the pieces of the photo and feel my heart stop when I bring the two halves together. Looking back at me is a teenage boy, seventeen at most, posing for a class portrait. He's sporting an Autumncrow High letterman jacket. His dark hair is slicked back except for a single ringlet that curves along his forehead. Even in black and white, the boy's eyes are piercing, as though made of snow. And his smile . . . that wide, sinister smile . . .

The caption below the photo reads "Kallum Greendale, Class of 1959."

Dennis's father.

I struggle to reconcile the image of this attractive young man with the Mr. Greendale I knew and loathed. In my mind, he had never been a teenager at all—just a perpetually middle-aged janitor whose spiteful demeanor made him seem even older. I see the absurdity of that now, but I still don't understand why (or *how*) his teenage incarnation has been stalking my nightmares.

I drop both halves of the photo into the trunk and lunge for the yearbook, flipping it open and scanning each page in quick succession.

Nineteen fifty-nine. If Mom and Dad were in school that fateful year, they certainly never mentioned it to me. I know they started dating as seniors at Autumncrow High, but I never bothered to do the math. Could their prom have been *that* prom, the last one the school would ever host? If it was, they must not have attended, despite what I've always assumed. The Rapture spared no one.

More questions jump to mind, but before I can articulate them, I land on a page proclaiming "Homecoming King and Queen, October 10, 1958."

It's like looking at a black-and-white photograph of myself. There's my mom, dressed in a beautiful sleeveless gown. Elegant white gloves adorn her hands and arms, ending just past the elbow. Her hair is the same length as mine, curled and fluffed to perfection. And the boy next to her . . .

"No." I shake my head, unable to believe my eyes. "It can't be." But it is. Close beside my mother in the photo—hands wrapped around her waist—is Kallum Greendale, his eyes glinting like stars in the camera's flash.

The following page only further cements my shock and dismay. In a series of snapshots from the homecoming dance, the two of them are carrying on like lovebirds, dancing together and embracing. Mom and Mr. Greendale weren't just homecoming royalty, I realize; they were a bona fide couple.

I suddenly feel like I'm falling into the yearbook, tumbling down, down into its yellowed pages. It's unmistakable. The boy with my mother in these photos is the boy from my nightmares, the same boy who drove me home earlier this evening.

How can that be?

The devil is already inside.

I gasp when I hear the whispered voice.

Swiftly turning to look behind me, I peer through the gaping doorway, seeing nothing but long shadows cast by the night-light in the hall. No one is there. Not a soul.

That voice . . . That was the same strange, inhuman rasp I heard last night as I was locking the front door. At the time, I convinced myself it was all in my head, my own internal voice getting me all worked up. Now I'm not so sure.

The feeling I experienced in the bedroom—that creeping sense of being watched—has returned, as though some unseen specter is spying on me from the ceiling. I do my best to ignore the uncomfortable sensation and turn my attention back to the yearbook, frantically examining its contents for any leads about what transpired that year at Autumncrow High.

What about Mom and Dad? I thought they were high school sweethearts.

In a collage of candid photos, dozens of students are making goofy faces or modeling against their lockers. Mister Hayman, Autumncrow High's mascot, an aptly named scarecrow with a burlap sack for a head, poses on the basketball court holding a handmade poster that reads "If I only had a brain." A group of cheerleaders are laughing together on the football field. There are various snapshots from formal school gatherings and events, but for the most part, these are photos of teenagers hanging loose and having fun. "November 1958," reads the heading.

One photo in particular catches my eye, that of a young couple bundled up in warm layers and snuggling beneath what I immediately recognize as the choking oak. She's resting her head on his chest, smiling the happiest of smiles as he lays a kiss atop her head.

Mom and Dad.

It seems my mother and Kallum must have parted ways sometime between their homecoming in October and the following month when this photo was taken, because she and my father were clearly an item here. Seeing them together in this shot, as happy and in love as two people can be, I feel the ghostly chill in the room diminish. The Mom and Dad from my memory are not much different from this fresh young couple in the photo. They never fell out of love.

I'm near the back of the yearbook now, fairly certain I've already seen all there is to see, despite my growing list of questions. But these last few pages prove me wrong.

"In Memory of the Class of 1959," the heading reads. "Those Lost Will Not Be Forgotten."

Row after endless row is lined with portraits of the students and staff who vanished from the prom of 1959. One of them, I notice, is circled in red ink. I lift the yearbook for a closer look and see a young girl, her short dark hair pinned back from her round smiling face. "Macy Welling," the caption reads. I recognize the girl immediately.

The last time I saw her, her face was split in two.

CHAPTER 13

I HAVE TO call Melody.

I slam the yearbook shut and make my way over to the mahogany office desk in the center of the room, home to Dad's old rotary dial.

Oh God, why didn't I call her sooner? I scold myself. I should have called right away to make sure she got home safely. What if Dennis—*Kallum?*—didn't take Melody home? He could have done something to her. Something awful.

Horrifying images of Melody's cold blue corpse intrude on my mind, her torso slashed and hanging open like an unzipped jacket, spilling forth a bloody mess of viscera. With my heart pounding in my throat, I dial Melody's house and listen to the monotonous ringing of the phone for what feels like an eternity.

Please pick up! Please, please answer.

There's a click on the other end of the line. "Hello?"

"Mrs. Krieger," I say, breathless. "Hi. This is Bailey."

"Bailey?" Melody's mother murmurs. Her voice is thick with sleep. "Do you have any idea how late it is?"

"Oh. I'm sorry," I say, finally realizing the time. The digital clock on Dad's desk reads a quarter to one. "I just wanted to make sure Melody got home safely."

"Well, I believe so. Her curfew is at midnight."

Believing isn't good enough! I want to shout. "Can you please check on her for me?"

"What's this all about?" she asks, sounding a little more awake. "Did something happen?"

"No," I say. *I hope not.* "I'd just like to know she made it home. And could I perhaps speak to her, too, if she's awake?"

"I dunno, Bailey. It's really late, and it's a school night. You should be in bed yourself."

"Right," I mutter. "Bed."

There's a moment's pause. "Let me check on her real quick, okay? If she's awake, I'll put her on. But don't go making a habit of these late-night phone calls." I hear Mrs. Krieger set the phone down.

I wait, tapping my fingertips on the desktop, my eyes fixed on the steamer trunk and the mysterious spell books stacked in a heap beside it.

"Please be okay," I whisper. "I don't know what I'd do without you."

There are sounds resembling the shuffling of feet and the creaking of floorboards. Then a very tired, very pissed-off voice comes on the line. "What is it?"

I release a shuddery breath. "Melody?"

"That's my name. Don't wear it out," Melody says grog-gily. "I was sleeping like a baby, so I'm warning you, Hagen—this better be good."

"I was just worried you might not have made it home," I say, trying to hold back tears.

"Why? I live right around the corner. You think I got in an accident in the thirty seconds it takes to drive over here? Werewolf attack perhaps?"

"No," I say. "It's just . . . Dennis was being really . . ."

"Weird," Melody finishes for me. "Yeah, I know. But he did just lose his dad, so let's give him a break. Grief does things to people."

I can't help but cringe at her tone-deaf defense. "Sure."

"He'll be fine tomorrow. Probably just needs to sleep it off. Kinda like how I want to be sleeping off this crazy night right about now."

"I'm sorry for calling so late. But listen . . ." I hesitate, unsure of what to say next. "Maybe you should slow things down with Dennis. I have a bad feeling about him."

Silence.

"You still there?" I ask.

"Yeah."

"Everything okay?"

"Uh-huh." Melody's voice is flat, but her delivery is as sharp as knives.

I can feel my face reddening. "We don't know anything about him."

"You don't," Melody says. "But I'm getting to know him. That usually comes first in the dating process."

There it is again, the "I have experience with this, and you don't" implication. While it may be true, that doesn't mean I'm totally clueless. If anything, Melody's boy-craziness often clouds her judgment. Sometimes it takes an outside perspective to see a situation clearly, to notice signs of danger that might otherwise be overlooked. And I've seen the signs.

"This can wait until morning," Mel grumbles. "Thanks for checking on me and everything, but I'd like to get back to bed."

"Wait," I say before she can hang up. "I need to talk to you, and I don't want to wait until tomorrow. I'm scared."

"I'm guessing your mom freaked out on you pretty bad."

"It's not just that." I think back to Mom's outburst, how she grabbed me by the shoulders and shook me until I thought my head would topple off. Then I picture her casting spells in the library, chanting from the books spread out before her. Maybe it's not so silly after all. If she has been practicing magic, I hope the protection spells I read about are the extent of it . . .

"Then what is it?" Melody asks. "Please spit it out. I don't want to stand here all night."

"I already told you," I say. "It's Dennis. I don't trust him."

"Have you been talking to Tommy?" Melody asks, clearly annoyed.

"What? No."

"Because you sound just like him."

"I haven't talked to him, Melody. That's crazy."

"No, what's crazy is how you act every time I start dating someone," Melody says.

"What do you mean?"

"What do you think?" she fires back. "When I started dating Tommy, you got all weird. I'd invite you on *my* dates—and that alone was uncomfortable for me, but I didn't want you to feel abandoned. Then, despite refusing to come along, you'd act like I was replacing you. After I tried to include you!"

I'm too shocked to say anything. I expected her to call me a nutcase when I told her how I felt about Dennis, but I never thought she'd throw all this in my face. It isn't exactly true what she's saying, but it still stings to hear her say it.

"Melody . . ." I finally speak. "That's not what this is about."

"Of course it is! You're acting the same way you did with Tommy."

"No, I'm not," I say, feeling myself getting annoyed. "I mean, yes, I did get upset when you were hanging out with Tommy all the time, but that was because it was always about him. Tommy never wanted to do the things you and I liked to do, and he was *always* there. You never made time for just the two of us."

"I did too!" Melody argues. "Remember I got us those concert tickets to see The Smashing Pumpkins?"

"Those tickets were originally for you and Tommy," I remind her.

"No, they weren't."

"Yes, they were. His name was on my ticket."

Melody doesn't respond.

"Hello?" I say.

There are a few more seconds of silence before Melody speaks again. Her voice is softer now, a little sad. "I did try to make time for us."

I sigh. "Again, that has nothing to do with Dennis. I understand that you and Tommy were serious, but you just met Dennis yesterday."

"I know. I just like him."

"I can see that," I say. "But Melody, he was acting so bizarre tonight, like a totally different person. And earlier today . . ."

"What about earlier? The fight with Tommy?"

"No, after the fight," I clarify. "In the basement."

"The basement?"

"Yes. I went down there today, and Dennis was wandering around. He seemed lost."

"Well, he doesn't know his way around yet. Was he looking for the restroom?" Melody asks.

"No, not that kind of lost. It was like he was in a daze. When I asked what he was doing down there, he couldn't give me a decent answer. He said he thought he heard something."

Melody stays silent for a beat. "Like his name being called?"

"I don't know. He didn't say. It was just weird. And with the way he was acting tonight, I'm worried that . . ."

How do I say this?

"What?" Melody demands.

"Remember the boy in my dreams?"

"Yeah, so?"

"Well . . ." I pause again. "Dennis looks just like him."

"Huh?"

"The boy from my nightmares and Dennis. They look almost exactly the same, and . . . I think they are the same."

Even more silence.

This isn't going well.

"Melody, I know it sounds insane, but it'll make more sense when I show you what I found in my dad's library. There are all these weird spell books, and I even found a yearbook from 1959—my parents were seniors the year of the Rapture! I had no idea. They were in the same class with Kallum Greendale. My mom even dated him for a while. It's so weird—one month she and Kallum were homecoming king and queen, and the next she was dating my dad."

I'm rambling now without so much as taking a breath, fearful that Melody will interrupt to inform me of my lunacy and promptly hang up the phone.

"And then there was the prom," I say, "and you know how that went down. And I'm pretty sure something terrible happened to this girl named Macy Welling. And then there's Dennis's eyes changing color tonight—surely you noticed it too—and the way Mom looked at him as if she were seeing . . . seeing . . ."

Kallum.

I trail off, finally gulping in a huge breath of air. My heart is racing like I've just run a marathon.

Melody remains silent.

"I know you think I'm crazy," I say, "but please at least come over and take a look at everything I found. Not now, but maybe tomorrow after school. I won't have to work, and my mom will be gone all night. We'll have plenty of time to read through it all. Okay?"

Nothing. No reply.

"Melody?"

There is finally a noise on Mel's end, whispers followed

by the clatter of someone fidgeting with the receiver. "Um ... hello?"

"Mrs. Krieger?"

"Bailey! You're still on the line," Melody's mother says.

"Where's Melody?" I ask, confused.

"She, um ... went back up to her room a minute ago," Mrs. Krieger says. "She must have forgotten to hang up the phone."

My heart sinks. I'm immediately brought back when Mel and I were fourteen years old. She had begged and begged to borrow my brand-new copy of *Disintegration* by The Cure. I reluctantly agreed, and then days later she returned the cassette to me all tangled up, saying her player had eaten it. When I got home, I carefully wound the tape back onto the reel, but it never sounded the same again. I was so mad, I called her up and yelled for five minutes straight. When I finally stopped to take a breath, I realized she wasn't even on the line anymore. She had set the phone down while I was shouting to go watch TV in her living room.

And now she has done it to me again. There's no telling how much she heard and how much was just me ranting to myself.

"Well," Mrs. Krieger says, "I'll let you go. I'd better get back to bed myself. Goodnight."

"Wait!" I say.

"What is it now?" she asks, flustered. "Is everything okay?"

"Yeah," I say. "I just have a question."

God, I hope this isn't a bust. The Krieger family must think I've lost my mind tonight!

"Go on," she says reluctantly.

"Well . . . you went to Autumncrow High, right?"

"Go Scarecrows!" she answers with a giggle. Her irritation and wariness wither away immediately. "I've lived in this town my whole life, so of course I did. Why do you ask?"

"I was just curious what year you graduated," I say, crossing my fingers that she'll know something about my parents and Kallum Greendale. She seems close in age, so it's worth a shot.

"That would be 1961," Mrs. Krieger says. "I just barely missed the Rapture. You've heard of that, right?"

The mere mention of the Rapture of 1959 sends spiders crawling down my spine. "Yes. That's why we don't have prom anymore."

The woman scoffs. "It's all a bit silly, if you ask me. I say you kids should be allowed to have your prom. The Rapture happened so long ago, and I'm sure there's a rational explanation for it. Besides, nothing like that is ever going to happen again."

How can you rationally explain hundreds of students and chaperones disappearing from a school prom without a trace? I want to ask, but I bite my tongue.

"Did you know my parents?" I ask instead.

"Oh, of course. They were very popular. Well, maybe not Felix, but your mother was a cheerleader and head of *all* the clubs. I was a sophomore at the time, so I always looked up to her. Everyone wanted to be like Cassandra Martin."

"I didn't know she was a cheerleader," I say glumly. In fact, now that I think of it, I know very little about the teenage years of either of my parents. I never thought to ask, and they never had much to say about it.

"Oh, don't let that get you down," Mrs. Krieger says. "I've grown close to your mom since you and Melody became friends, and she once told me the pressure of being the star student got to be too much for her. Her heart just wasn't in it. So that's probably why she doesn't like to discuss it. After Cassandra and your dad started dating, she withdrew from everything and stuck close to him. Felix was so kind to her. They were always trading books in the hall or sneaking kisses. Such cuties." She giggles. "It's a good thing they skipped prom that year."

"Yeah. Good thing," I say. For whatever reason, I always pictured my parents going to their prom, but now I'm glad they didn't. That would have been the end of their story. "Mrs. Krieger . . . do you know of Kallum Greendale?"

"Oh . . . yes. Gee, that's a name I haven't thought of in a while. Is he still the janitor at the school?"

"Well, he was," I say. "He passed away this summer."

"I didn't hear about that. Shame." Her tone lacks any hint of emotion. It seems Mrs. Krieger wasn't too fond of Kallum Greendale either.

"He dated my mother, right?"

"As a matter of fact, yes. But it didn't last long. Just a couple of years."

"*Years?*"

"Well, I guess that's a long time to date someone when you're a teenager." Mrs. Krieger laughs again. "They were an item all throughout high school until early in their senior year. That's when your mother and father became close."

I can't help but wonder if Dad came between Mom and Kallum in some way. Their parting seemed awfully sudden.

"Do you know what happened between her and Kallum?"

"Oh, I don't know, honey" Melody's mom replies. "It was so long ago, and I wasn't very close to them back then. I was young and ran with a different crowd. Kallum always struck me as the jealous type, to be honest, a little too possessive. I don't fault Cassandra for leaving him. But everything unraveled for him after that."

"Unraveled how?"

"I don't think he was ever quite right, to tell you the truth, but he absolutely went off the deep end. Started getting into trouble. Lots of feuding with the other boys. I don't think it was just the breakup, though; he sustained some kind of injury and couldn't finish the season. I guess he'd only ever seen himself as the all-American teen dream football hero, and when that fell apart . . . what was left?"

"I see," I say quietly.

"He ended up dropping out of school, which might have been a blessing in disguise, since it meant he missed the Rapture. But then he came back the very next year as our janitor. I guess the school took pity on him and wanted to give him another chance. Kind of ironic when you think about it—spending the rest of his life in high school like that."

The picture is coming into focus, but there are still so many missing pieces. How do my nightmares fit into this? For that matter, what about what happened to Dad? Is it all connected somehow? I shudder at the thought.

"Oh-oh, I hear my husband calling," Mrs. Krieger says abruptly. "I need to go. Good night, Bailey."

I'm about to ask her for just a few more minutes of her time, but a *click* ends the call. I have so many more questions, but I think I've gotten all there is to get from Mrs. Krieger.

I sigh and drop into Dad's office chair, hearing the pop and groan of its wooden joints. Though the clock on the desk reads just past one, I feel completely awake for the first time in weeks. There's no way I could even dream of sleeping with all these questions cluttering my mind, and for this I'm grateful. There will be no drifting off to sleep by accident tonight and no nightly visit from the puppeteer ... Kallum Greendale.

I need answers. I need to know who Kallum really is—or *what* he is—and how he's managed to ... what? Haunt my dreams from beyond the grave? Come back from the dead to pose as his son? Whatever the case may be, there has to be something he's after, something he hopes to accomplish. And what of blood-soaked Macy Welling? *Damn it!* I should have asked Melody's mom about her too.

Melody. If all this is really happening and I'm not just losing my mind, she could be in real danger.

Suddenly, I have an idea.

I pick up the receiver once more and dial a number I still know by heart. I've dialed it countless times before to reach Melody once she stopped spending her free time at home.

He'll be up, I think. *One o'clock is nothing to a teenage boy.*

Sure enough, someone answers the phone by the second ring and says, "Sup?"

"Hey, Tommy," I say. "It's Bailey. I'm ready to talk."

CHAPTER 14

I CAN'T BELIEVE I'm doing this. But here I am, riding on the back of a motorcycle in the middle of the night, arms wrapped around the waist of my best friend's ex-boyfriend.

Melody would hate me if she could see me right now, as would my mother. And Rae will totally lose it if she wakes up and realizes I've left her in the house all alone. But I'm not too terribly worried. My sister snoozes right through her alarm most mornings. With any luck, she'll be none the wiser and won't be able to rat me out to Mom for slipping away.

This is important, I tell myself. *You're looking for answers. You're trying to protect Melody.*

The slumbering town of Autumncrow Valley zips by in a flurry of unlit homes and darkened storefronts. I grit my teeth against the biting cold and cling tighter to Tommy's middle. How can he stand to drive this thing in the cooler months? I'm freezing my buns off.

I've only been on a motorcycle once before, a long time ago when we were staying at Uncle Pete's cabin for a weekend. He offered to give me and my brother a ride around his property, but I wimped out after a few seconds. I wish I could do the same now, but before I can tell Tommy I'm getting cold feet about this entire stupid idea, we're pulling into the parking lot behind the high school.

Without even waiting for Tommy to kill the ignition, I leap off the motorcycle and peer up at the school's formidable silhouette for the second time tonight. Just a few short hours ago, I was telling Melody I never wanted to set foot in this place after dark. Now I'm about to do just that.

I feel a twinge of regret for having called Tommy to begin with, for giving him the opportunity to propose this ridiculous mission. After I filled him in on the evening's events—conveniently leaving out any mention of living nightmares or spell books—he insisted we get back to school to investigate as soon as possible. As in *tonight*. I argued with him at first, but he was adamant it was the only way we'd be able to search the student records without getting caught.

"We need answers now, and nighttime's our best chance. I meant to find the new kid's record this morning," he said, "but I wasn't sure where to look or even who I was looking for, and I ran out of time. I had to jet when I heard Principal Tremblay coming down the hall. I thought I'd gotten away with it too, but I guess the secretary had already seen me."

It took a bit of convincing, but Tommy's influence finally reigned supreme. After all, what else was I going to do for the rest of the night? *Sleep?*

"You ready?" Tommy asks, climbing off the bike.

"No," I say.

"Yeah, me either. This place skeeves me out."

"Well, it was your idea."

"True. Let's go. I know a way in." Tommy takes the lead and makes a beeline for the side of the building, stopping just outside a classroom window. "This was open a hair when I got here this morning. I guess Ms. Fredrickson wanted to let the lab air out a bit."

He fits his fingertips into the slight crack between the bottom of the window and the sill. It pushes right open. "Voilà."

This must be the same window, I think. *The same one Dennis used earlier tonight.*

Hopping through, Tommy lands inside with a resounding wallop as his Nikes hit the linoleum. Then he turns and offers me a hand.

"I've got it," I say, waving him away.

Tommy throws his hands up in surrender and steps back, giving me space to hoist myself onto the windowsill and squeeze through the narrow gap. Except for the harsh fluorescent glow emanating from various reptile tanks and animal cages bordering the far side of the room, Ms. Fredrickson's biology lab is a mass of foreboding blackness, reminding me of the shadowed corners of Mom's bedroom.

Again, the unpleasant sensation of being observed by some unseen presence creeps up on me. Tommy must feel it too, because he's scanning the room with a hard stare, taking extra care to peer deeply into the shadows. Finally, he says, "To the office?"

I nod, and we slowly make our way across the room to the even darker school hall. The only trace of light is cast by the glowing red "EXIT" signs positioned at each end of the corridor.

"Glad you remembered to bring a flashlight," I say.

Tommy nods. "The office isn't far from here. Just at the top of the stairs off the entry hall."

"I'm well aware," I say, rolling my eyes. I can't keep the resentment from seeping into my tone. Tommy is responsible for breaking Melody's heart, after all. If it weren't for that, she never would have fallen for Dennis in the first place.

We walk toward the front of the school, staying as quiet as possible, not for fear of being caught—if the empty parking lot is any indication, we're the only ones here—but for the lingering tingle of dread that has followed us from the biology lab. I keep watch at all times, terrified Macy Welling will come running down the dark hall, the long gash in her face vomiting gore.

Tommy finally speaks. "You broke my mirror, you know?"

"Huh?"

"When you knocked over my motorcycle, you broke one of my mirrors. Now you've got seven years' bad luck."

"Oh. Sorry." I don't mean it, of course, and he knows it. Hardly seems worth clarifying it was Melody who kicked his bike over, not me. Instead, I change the subject: "So what happened after my brother picked you up?"

"Nothing much. They called my parents. I got suspended."

"Yikes."

"No big deal." He gives me a shrug. "At least it'll get me away from Kristi for a while. She's so clingy."

"Why are you even dating her?" I ask, a sudden flare of rage taking hold in my chest.

"I don't know," he mumbles. "I got lonely, I guess."

"You should have thought of that before you broke up with Melody," I snap.

"Listen, I know I made a mistake, okay?" Tommy argues. "Mel and I were just so serious, and I knew when the time came, she'd want me to go to some fancy college with her. But with my grades and my family's financial situation, I'll be lucky if I make it into Autumncrow U. So, yeah, I broke up with her. I thought it would make things easier."

"Is that the only reason?"

"I mean ... no." Tommy stops speaking for a moment, his pace slowing. "Melody started talking about getting married after college. I guess it freaked me out. We're only seventeen."

I bite my bottom lip. As much as I don't want to side with Tommy, I can see where he's coming from. He and Melody are so young. I'd flip out too if someone brought up marriage when homework is still my top priority.

Melody likes to dream big, though, and have life all mapped out. She plans to get out of Autumncrow and go to Ohio State to study journalism, and then she wants to move to a big city and work for a reputable newspaper. Tommy, on the other hand, would probably be happy to remain in Autumncrow his whole life. All the same, he had no right to let Melody down like that, and he certainly had no business accosting her the way he did in front of Mrs. McGuffin's house.

As if reading my mind, he says, "I'm not defending myself. I know I screwed up. I miss Melody, and it's killing me to see her with this guy. There's something not right about him."

With this I agree completely.

Rounding a corner, we pass the school library, the place I spent most of my free time as a freshman when I volunteered to help Mrs. Harvey organize the card catalog. That after-school activity fell to the wayside after the librarian's severed head was found shelved in the fiction section under the *H*s.

Unlike the rest of the doors in the school, the library's ornate wooden entrance is open wide, leaking the icky blackness within like paint from a punctured aluminum can.

"I hate that room," Tommy utters.

"Not surprised. No one ever mistook you for a reader," I say, but my attempt at humor falls flat.

"That's not what I mean. Something bad is in there. I can see it." He stops and penetrates the dark of the library with pointed eyes. "Do you see it there?" He points. "Between those rows of shelves? It's moving."

Chills skate across my back. "It's too dark. I don't see anything."

"I can see it," Tommy repeats. "It's big and furry, like a bear or something. But it has horns."

"Stop it," I say, grabbing Tommy's forearm and giving it a light tug. "Let's go."

"It's looking back at us. I think it's glad that we're here."

"Tommy, please!" I whisper frantically. "I want to go."

Now I see it too—a dark, hulking shape in the gloom, a shape whose presence I sensed in my hours of library volunteer work but never actually saw for myself.

Despite the evil being, Tommy's demeanor is calm. Cool. He breathes a laugh through his nose. "I always knew something bad was in there. You think that's what killed Mrs. Harvey?"

I don't answer. I leave Tommy behind and start speed-walking down the hall, wanting to put as much distance between me and the library as possible.

"Wait up!" Tommy calls, jogging to catch up.

I keep shuffling forward, not once slowing my step. I didn't know about Tommy's awareness of the supernatural—didn't know he was aware of much of *anything*—but I don't care about that right now. I'm just eager to get to the office and wrap up our harrowing little adventure as soon as possible. "We all see things here," I say dismissively.

"I see more than anyone else," he insists, sounding defensive. "Melody got all wigged out whenever I talked about the crap I've seen here, so I learned to stay quiet. But I see and hear a lot. That's how I know something's up with this Dennis guy, even if I can't put my finger on it."

"I know what you mean," I say. I may know a little more than Tommy does about our mystery boy, but I keep my mouth shut. Instead, I ask, "Since you see so much here, have you ever seen a girl with a messed-up face?"

Tommy freezes mid-step. I pause and peer back at him. His eyes are wide, pink lips slightly agape. Even in the darkness, I can see the blood has drained from his face.

"Polka-dot dress," I add. "Looks like someone out of an old teen beach movie."

Tommy nods. "Yeah, I've seen her." He pushes past me, rounding another corner and entering the grand hall. "Pretty much every day."

I promptly follow behind, but not before stealing one more glance over my shoulder at the library doors, a decision I instantly regret. There is no devilish monster peeping around the corner at me. Instead, the slight, fleeting form of a woman stumbles out of the library, an empty space where her head should be.

"No . . ." I whisper.

I launch myself forward, accidentally plowing into Tommy on my way to the stone staircase leading to the second story. I lead the way up, running as fast as I can, as though the stumbling headless librarian has any chance of catching up.

The office is the first room on the left. I stop running, bracing myself against the office door as I struggle to catch my breath. Tommy puts a hand on my shoulder. "You okay?"

I nod, though I'm most definitely not okay. I want so badly to go home.

Tommy takes a deep breath and turns the doorknob to the office. "Wow, I'm shocked they left this unlocked after what happened this morning. The adults in this town are so stupid and set in their ways. C'mon," he says, making a mad dash for the row of filing cabinets at the far end of the room, beneath the windows overlooking the schoolyard.

The branches of the choking oak scratch against the glass with each gust of wind, and I swear I can hear them whispering to me: *"Please let us in. We're so cold. Inside . . . Let us inside. We won't hurt. Never hurt."*

"This cabinet holds all the student records for our year," Tommy says, hitting a lamp on the nearest desk and filling the office with soft light. "I got through the first two drawers this morning before I had to bolt, but now I know what I'm looking for."

On the wall to my right is a large portrait of a woman in a deep purple gown. Though stoic, there is an ever-watchful glint in her emerald eyes. "Autumn Crow (Headmistress of Autumncrow Academy)," the copper plate below the painting says.

Unsettled by Mrs. Crow's knowing gaze, I cross the room to the cabinets and inspect the labels on each of them until I find the one marked "Class of 1959." I open the first drawer and begin sifting through the files.

"What are you doing?" Tommy asks.

"I'm looking for Dennis's dad's file."

"Didn't you say his dad was the janitor? What's it matter?"

"Keep looking," I say. "I'll help you in a minute."

When speaking to Tommy over the phone, I neglected to mention that my mom had dated Kallum, and I left out most of the details Mrs. Krieger had shared with me as well. None of it seemed necessary, and I doubted he'd care. Instead, I explained why Dennis had come to town in the first place, and I agreed with Tommy's suspicions—there is indeed something strange and off-kilter about the new boy. That's all Tommy needed to fuel his fire.

Tommy gets back to work, and I resume my search. Since the files are organized alphabetically, I unearth

Kallum's record first, followed by my father's and then my mother's. Reading through the yellowed pages, I find many of the same details Mrs. Krieger imparted to me earlier: my mother was a straight-A student and cheerleader (head cheerleader, in fact); my dad was a studious young man; and Kallum Greendale—a onetime star athlete—got into some trouble his senior year and ended up dropping out.

Among his juvenile transgressions were fights in the school halls, failing grades, playing hooky, theft from his peers, disrespect for authority—pretty much all the typical pitfalls of a turbulent adolescence.

But as Tommy said, the adults in this town are stupid and have always been out of touch with the younger generation. Given that these are just school records, they can hardly be expected to paint the full picture. There's sure to be tons of valuable information that the school overlooked. I'm not ready to give up yet, though. I still have one more record from 1959 I want to find—that of the mysterious Macy Welling.

I open the drawer closest to the floor and find the *W*s, thumbing through folder after folder until finally—

"Yes!" I say, grabbing Macy's folder and flipping it open. I am met with the same portrait I found circled in Mom's yearbook, but this one is blown up to eight by ten. Without a doubt, this is her—the same dead girl I met in the hall earlier today, the dead girl that Tommy has also reportedly seen.

"Find something?" he asks.

"Yeah," I say. "An answer sheet to the SATs."

"Whatever," he grumbles.

I set aside the photograph and find a smattering of notes

report cards, and a couple of newspaper clippings, all dated 1959.

"Prom Attendees Vanish from School," an article from the *Autumncrow Herald* reads. "AUTUMNCROW VALLEY, Ohio — Authorities were called to Autumncrow High School Saturday, March 14, amid troubling reports of loved ones not having returned home after the school's annual senior prom festivities. Upon inspection, the premises were found to be vacant, though there were signs of a dance having been held in the gymnasium earlier that evening and a great many vehicles left in the adjacent parking lot. The body of sixteen-year-old Macy Welling was discovered in the school basement with severe trauma to the head and face. Foul play is suspected. Among the missing are 213 students from Autumncrow High and neighboring schools, as well as 37 chaperones. Investigation ongoing."

I stare at the brief article in shock. All my life, I've heard about the prom of 1959, how everyone in attendance that night was whisked away into oblivion, never to be seen again. But a girl found dead in the basement? This is news to me. Not once in all the retellings of the Rapture has Macy Welling's name ever been mentioned.

Could her murder be something more than a tragic co-incidence? Is there some connection to what happened at the dance that same night?

In my head, I can picture the scene, the police showing up to find a gymnasium fully decked out for the big event. But where there should be students slowly swaying together on the dance floor, there is no one. Not a soul. Just a few spilled cups of punch and a record left spinning on the turntable, the loudspeakers oozing smooth doo-wop harmonies.

It's one of the few cases in Autumncrow's history that has had a lasting effect on the town, the one shared tragedy that nobody has fully forgotten. Everyone lost someone that night—a brother, a sister, a parent, a friend—and it took months longer than usual for the townspeople to recover. They eventually did, of course—Autumncrow never stays down for long—but the school's ensuing ban on the prom made it impossible to move on completely.

Many liken the happening to the mysterious disappearance of an entire settlement from the valley in the 1600s, two whole centuries before Autumncrow was founded. The eerie parallels with the lost colony of Roanoke Island are hard to ignore. It's all speculation, but my mind is reeling with so many questions at the moment that I'm willing to believe anything.

The next article is actually an obituary. I hold it up to the light and read: "On March 14, 1959, at the tender age of sixteen, Macy Berdine Welling passed away into the loving embrace of her Heavenly Creator. Macy was a lifelong resident of Autumncrow Valley, Ohio, a town she loved very much. Left to mourn are her mother and father . . ."

I check the back side of the clipping, praying for further information on the young girl's death. I feel a twinge of excitement when I see mention of her name but deflate when I realize the snippet of text relates to something completely different, the upcoming "long-awaited return of Gerald's Pumpkin Patch, thanks to young Macy *Freeman*."

A melancholic sensation fills my chest to think just how little Autumncrow has changed since 1959. Even in the aftermath of a mass disappearance and the brutal murder of a teenage girl, the town was still striving to maintain its wholesome autumnal aesthetics.

Finding nothing more of value, I slam the file shut in disgust and shove it back into the cabinet. "Any luck?" I ask Tommy.

"None. I've searched the *G*s twenty times but haven't found a single Greendale."

"Really?" I say, standing to my feet and walking to his side.

"Yeah. I don't get it. It's like Dennis doesn't even go to school here."

Chills cascade down my spine, not because of what Tommy said but because of what grabs my attention from outside the window. Past the school lawn, parked at the curb just as it was earlier tonight, is a dilapidated station wagon.

"That's his car," I say in a stunned whisper. I'm barely able to get the words out of my mouth.

"Huh?" Tommy leans forward and peers out the window.

A burst of panic shoots through my veins, bringing me out of my stupor. "He's here!" I shout, reaching for Tommy's hand. "We need to go."

I pull him toward the office door, but not before hitting my thigh on the secretary's desk, sending tchotchkes and a mountain of paperwork spilling to the floor. A heavy glass paperweight in the shape of a pumpkin hits the ground and rolls directly in my path. I step on it by mistake, and my foot twists in on itself as I hit the floor. The solid *pop* of my ankle is enough to make both of us shudder.

The pain is immediate. A shrill scream erupts from my mouth as I reach for my ankle. An even sharper pain shoots up my leg as soon as I make contact. Tears bubble to the surface of my eyes, pouring down my cheeks as I fight back a roar of excruciating agony.

"Shit! Are you okay?" Tommy asks. He stands over me, eyes wide with shock.

Before I can reply, a hulking black shape appears in the doorway. Tommy gasps in surprise as the figure—a man—springs into the office, brandishing a curved saw blade that glints in the amber lamplight like hellfire. Without hesitation or warning, the figure lunges at Tommy and whips the sharpened steel through the air in a single decisive arc.

The movement is so quick I hardly realize I'm seeing the teeth of the blade slice through Tommy's throat. But I do see it. And I hear the garbled moan that issues from his gaping esophagus as a black fountain of hot, sticky blood rains down on me.

CHAPTER 15

A HIGH-PITCHED SCREAM of terror fills the room and threatens to burst my eardrums before I finally recognize it as my own.

Tommy grasps at the oozing grin carved into his throat and rests his free hand on the nearest desk, leaning with an expression of intense concentration, as though focused on somehow bringing the loose folds of flesh back together. The desktop runs slick with Tommy's blood as he fights to remain standing.

It's no use. His knees buckle. He slams face-first into a corner of the desk. His nose cracks on impact. The collision sends his head snapping backward, his body spinning to face me as the life fades from his eyes and he falls, falls, falls in what seems like slow motion.

I can do nothing but watch helplessly as Tommy's yawning gullet bears down on me until I'm crushed beneath his weight. Inky jets of arterial spray spatter my face, spurting into my eyes, my nose, my mouth. I fight against the boy's dead bulk, finally pushing him off me and crawling away from his bleeding corpse.

The white-hot pain of my sprained ankle burns through my every nerve, but I'm too busy expelling Tommy's life-blood from my mouth to give it much notice. The coppery taste triggers my gag reflex, making me vomit until I have nothing left inside me. I take deep, heaving breaths and struggle to clear the blood from my stinging eyes, but no matter how hard I try, I can barely see my surroundings—can barely make out the contours of Tommy's killer looming over me.

This is another nightmare, I tell myself. *It's just different this time. That's all. Any moment now, I'll wake up and see my* Saved by the Bell *poster hanging on the wall at the end of my bed. Then I'll walk to school with Melody like this never happened. She'll complain about Tommy and won't even mention Dennis, because he isn't real. He never existed. This has all been one long nightmare.*

"Hello, Bailey," the man says, his voice slithering into my ears and scattering my thoughts.

I blink rapidly, straining to see through the blood clouding my eyes. "Wh-who are you?"

The man releases a soft chuckle. "I think you know who I am."

My heart is beating so fast I think it might explode. "D-Dennis?" I can scarcely bring myself to utter the name.

"Dennis isn't here anymore. Guess again."

Anymore?

A glimmer in the man's right hand catches my eye. It's the blade, the one he used to slash Tommy's throat, dripping with ropy strands of blood. Slowly, purposefully, he is dragging it along the hem of his jacket.

He's cleaning it before he kills me.

The grim thought brings even more tears to my eyes, finally dissipating the crimson fog from my sight. My surroundings are a bit sharper now, a little more defined. I focus on Tommy's killer and see the Autumncrow letterman jacket, those frosty blue eyes that weren't there earlier today, and that crazed smile.

If Melody were here, she would believe beyond a shadow of a doubt that this is the same young man she met in the cafeteria yesterday. But I know better than that.

Dennis isn't here anymore.

I begin to sob. "You're Mr. Greendale . . . Kallum." The voice that comes out of me is hushed and childlike in its smallness.

"I suppose that's as good a guess as any," he says. "And it's mostly the truth, though I haven't felt like a Kallum in a long, long time."

Kallum. The dream boy. The puppeteer. Everything I have feared for the past few months—the essence of my nightmares personified—is standing before me, gripping a curved blade that looks to be some kind of pruning saw.

How? How can wretched old Kallum Greendale, Autumncrow High's recently deceased janitor, be standing here in front of me in this fresh young skin, looking exactly like his youthful self from Mom's yearbook? And what happened to Dennis?

"What do you want?" I ask, unable to pull my stare off his glistening blade.

"Look at me! I already have what I want," Kallum rests an open hand on his chest, his teenage son's flesh somehow made his own. "Every wrong has been undone, and now I'm free to start over. This isn't about me. This is about *her*, and I must give her what she is owed."

"*Who?* Melody?"

"That pretty blonde? No. She means nothing to me." Kallum flicks his weapon through the air as though Melody were a nuisance to be warded off like a buzzing fly. "Let's just hope she doesn't get in my way."

"It's my mother, then, isn't it? You're here for her."

Kallum pauses. "Yes and no. It's complicated."

"Tell me!" I scream. "What do you want from us?"

"I already told you, bitch!" Kallum roars, shedding his cool exterior. In a fit of rage, he lifts the saw into the air and brings it down. At first, I think he's about to stab me to death, but instead he sinks the blade deep into Tommy's gut and leaves it there, darting toward me and seizing my throat with his deft fingers. He squeezes, pressing against my trachea and stealing my breath away.

"It isn't about what I want!" he hisses. His crazed eyes are a treacherous sea of bottomless blue.

I choke on his grip, feeling my eyes bulge from the immediate buildup of pressure in my brain. Worming my fingers under his, I struggle to pry them from my neck, but they hold on to me like they're forged from iron.

"Everything I do is for *her*!"

I ball my hands into fists and pitch them at his face. But

I'm beginning to weaken. My vision is a blur of shape and shadow.

You're dying . . . He's killing you . . .

My legs flail about in panic, aiming for my attacker but hitting nothing.

"You've heard her, haven't you?" he says, ignoring my futile punches to his face. "You've heard her voice in your head too!"

I change tactics and begin a blind search of the sticky floor, fumbling around for Tommy's body. If he's within reach, I should be able to grab the saw planted in his belly.

Hurry! You're dying!

"It's all for her!" Kallum squeezes even tighter and shakes me, jerks my face to the side and forces my gaze to the old portrait hanging across the room. "For Autumn! AUTUMN!"

The Autumn Crow in the painting no longer wears that placid expression—she is glaring down at me with stygian eyes, dark pools of unfathomable malevolence.

Still hunting for the saw, I stretch my fingers as far as I can, feeling nothing but the hot, syrupy blood pooling on the floor around me.

So far away . . . He's too far.

"You're tired, aren't you, Bailey?" Kallum taunts me. "She wants you to sleep. *Autumn* wants you to sleep!"

Find something else. Don't give up!

"SLEEP!"

In my search, my hand knocks against a hard object to my right. I don't know what it is, but it's cold and small enough for me to wrap my fingers around. I get a handhold on the item and swing without aim. There is a *crack*, followed by a bellow of pain. Kallum relinquishes his grip, and I gasp for air again as he falls backward, clutching his cranium.

I don't waste a second. Though I'm starving for breath and my ankle is pulsating in misery, I grab on to the secretary's nearby desk and use it as leverage to pull myself to my feet. Then I reach down for the pruning saw protruding from Tommy's stomach.

Except it's no longer there.

A new pain ripples through my injured leg. I unleash a bloodcurdling shriek and find the puppeteer kneeling on the ground, grinning madly as he saws through my Achilles tendon.

I scream in agony once more and kick my uninjured foot at his face. My sneaker nails him hard in the teeth, sending him tumbling backward yet again. With all my weight now on my injured ankle and severed heel, my knee gives out. I topple over, landing in a heap atop Tommy's bloody carcass.

His dead eyes stare up into mine.

They blink.

"Tommy?" I whisper.

He says nothing back, just continues to stare at me with the truest emptiness possible. But in my head, I can hear a voice that sounds a lot like his. *"Run."*

I roll off Tommy's body and frantically pat the ground for the saw, hoping this youthful incarnation of Kallum Greendale dropped it when I kicked him in the face. But then I see it still clenched in one of his hands as he covers his bloodied, moaning mouth with the other.

Now's my chance.

I retrieve the pumpkin paperweight I tripped over earlier, in case I need it again, and limp past Kallum, moving as quickly as possible toward the open office door.

But Kallum sees me. He grunts. He stands.

No, no, no, no, NO!

Just as I reach the hallway, Kallum snatches me by my hair and jerks me back into the office. He lets me go with a shove, and I am sent stumbling backward, tripping over Tommy's body and sliding across the desktop smeared with his blood. I glide over the edge, bringing the desk chair with me in the process.

The chair careens into the wall of filing cabinets, throwing me onto the floor behind the desk. Kallum crawls over the desktop like a spider, flashing a messy red smirk courtesy of his freshly busted lip.

I grip the paperweight once more and force it upward as he lunges over the desk's edge and drops onto me. The object hits just right, pushing past his perverse grin and into his mouth.

Kallum shoots to his feet and staggers backward, leaning against the filing cabinets as he pulls the glass pumpkin from his mouth. Jagged fragments of teeth spill from their bloody sockets onto the floor.

He isn't holding his saw. Where did it go?

I sit up to search the floor for Kallum's weapon, but I'm blindsided by a stabbing pain in my middle. I freeze, watching a crimson stain blossom across my denim jacket, branching away from the hilt of the pruning saw buried in my abdomen.

I stare at the wooden handle as it pulses in sync with my

racing heartbeat, wondering if I'm just seeing things. I try to explain it away as a hallucination brought on by the fire of my mangled heel. *You're just delirious with pain and panic, Bailey. That's all.*

I can't hear Kallum's frenzied cries anymore. Everything is fading away. All that exists is me and the blade. I reach for the hilt and lightly touch it with the tip of a finger. This gentle contact sends a screeching crescendo of anguish through my every limb.

A near-silent scream floats out of my mouth, accompanied by the taste of my own blood.

With red oozing down the front of his letterman jacket, the puppeteer fixes me with an angry scowl and stomps forward. I don't think, I just react. I pull the saw from my stomach. Kallum reaches, arms outstretched like Frankenstein's monster, as I stab the saw through the air.

His scream is deafening as the pointed tip of the blade slips through his hand with surprising ease. I pull back on the weapon, hoping to use it again, but the serrated edge catches on bone and sinew, leaving it jammed in his palm. I kick him away instead, using my newly borrowed time to climb to my feet. Blood pours from my gut, and the room begins to tilt.

The hall . . . Get to the hall. Run!

But the puppeteer has already tugged the saw out of his gushing hand and is bounding toward me with the blade held high above his head.

This is it. This is how it all ends.

Unless . . .

I turn around, doing my best to keep the world in focus, and climb atop the row of filing cabinets. I turn the handle latching one of the tall, narrow windows lining the wall and push it open. Frigid night air spills into the office and kisses my skin.

"*Yes! In! Let us in!*" the branches of the choking oak implore, poking through the opening. One of them jabs into my gaping stomach, bringing stars to my eyes. But I try with all my might to abandon the pain and any trepidation I have about making the leap into the gnarled boughs of the oak.

Do it! Jump and grab on.

Two strong arms seize me from behind, wrapping around my torso and trapping me in place.

No . . .

The pruning saw catches the light of the crescent moon shimmering through the tree branches and comes down, plunging once more into my stomach. I feel a popping sensation as something ruptures inside me.

I gasp.

"There, there. Sleep." Kallum's whisper is slurred and indistinct. Bloody drool dribbles from his bottom lip and rolls down my neck. "Everything happens for a reason, but it didn't need to happen this way, Bailey. You're too much like your father, see? He got in my way too—got in *Autumn's* way." Kallum pulls the blade out of me. My blood trickles off its point, pitter-pattering out the window and onto the choking oak's famished branches. "Come," he sneers. "Let me fix you."

With this final remark, Kallum shoves me through the open window.

I fall, crashing down like a meteor through the limbs of the choking oak. They crackle and snap and splinter under my weight, leaving me powerless to halt my descent. Completely powerless, like a puppet on strings, left to the whims of an unseen hand, trapped inside a dream.

But this is no dream.

Grainy images begin to roll past my mind's eye like scenes on a View-Master reel: Rae is practicing handstands with me in our front yard as the summer sun sets . . . Mom is helping me carve my first jack-o'-lantern while Dalton boasts his pumpkin is scarier than mine . . . Daddy is all gussied up in a tuxedo, dashing as ever, as he sways with me at my fifth-grade father–daughter dance . . . Melody and I are laughing together at the movie theater . . . Melody and I are practicing our stupid secret handshake . . . Melody and I are hugging each other in the school hall.

"I love you. You know that?" she says.

Closing my tear-filled eyes, I hold my breath and wait for impact.

PART III
MELODY

CHAPTER 16

"LOVE you too."

My eyes, crusted over with sleep, crack open at the sound of the voice. "Huh?" I breathe, unsure whether someone actually just spoke to me or I simply imagined it within a dream.

"I know. I . . . love you too." The voice is quieter now. Dimmer. A hushed and tiny whisper.

"Mom?" I call softly. That is Mom I hear, right? Come to wake me up for school?

"Love you . . ." The whisper trails off as if scrubbed from the air, erased from existence completely. All I can hear now is the mechanical whir of my electric fan across the room. A scrap of notebook paper, pinned to the wall nearby, rustles in the breeze. It's a simple drawing of a ghost under a sheet, the one Bailey gave to me in kindergarten on the first day we met. "It's me," she said. I've had it ever since.

Propping myself up in bed on sleep-stiffened elbows, I notice just how dark it is out my window.

"Hey . . ." I murmur groggily. "Where's the sun?" I crane my head to glance at the green digits of my clock radio: 3:14. Definitely not time for school.

At the far end of the room, my bedroom door remains shut. I hang tight a moment, listening for voices in the hall or the creaking of floorboards, any telltale signs that Mom and Dad are the culprits who disturbed my beauty sleep. Nothing.

Must've been dreaming after all.

"Melody?"

With a gasp, I pull myself into a tight ball and crowd against the wall beside my bed. The semigloss paint is cold to the touch, bringing goosebumps to my flesh. I tug the blankets up around my chin and stare with fright into the shadows of my bedroom. The whisper didn't come from outside my door as I originally thought. It came from *inside* the room.

"Who's there?" I ask, scanning my hazy surroundings. My writing desk, messy with materials for the school paper, stands against the wall near my bed. An overstuffed backpack rests on the floor beside my desk chair, among the many piles of clothes Mom keeps asking me to throw in the wash. The heartthrobs and starlets on the magazine cutouts adorning my walls look strangely sinister in the darkness.

Standing in front of my bedroom window, moonlight trickling in through the narrow cracks between closed blinds, is a slim silhouette. A girlish figure.

My eyes widen in shock. A balloon inflates in my throat. I can't speak, can't scream for my parents, as much as I want to. I'm held captive in the presence of this shadow girl.

She doesn't budge or say anything more, just stands as still as a statue molded against moonlight, spine curved at the most grotesque angle. Her torso leans sideways, as though no longer supported by her back, and her head hangs limp like dead weight. She is a broken human-sized puppet suspended on invisible strings, her features faint and indistinct.

"Wh-who are you?" I stammer, finally regaining my speech, though it feels like I'm talking through six feet of dirt.

The figure stirs, a shuddery jerking motion, as if I've surprised her by speaking. Her frail shoulders quiver. A soft, short moan leaves her mouth, followed by a choked and lifeless whisper. "I don't think I'm here anymore."

Something about her tone is familiar, but while my brain is slow to match the voice to a face, my lips seem already to know the answer: "Bailey?"

Another sob, slow and sorrowful.

The wall's glossy sheen grows even cooler against my skin.

"Bailey?" I call out again.

The figure shifts slightly. Her sinewy hair tumbles past her shoulders and dangles in the air, ending at her elbow.

"Bailey, is that y—?" I freeze when I notice the girl's right forearm is missing, severed at the elbow.

My blood freezes.

The stranger—it can't be Bailey, it just *can't*—begins to breathe quickly, savagely, like a terrified animal. Then, in a voice thick with frenzy and panic, she growls, "Run."

I gasp. Tears are spilling down my cheeks as I grip the bedsheets, hoping they'll protect me somehow.

"Run. *Run*," she cries in a desperate, wheezing staccato. "*Run run run run run—*"

"Stop!" I shout, raising my hands to my ears and pressing as hard as I can. "Please, stop!" But the girl's agonized voice is still there, echoing in my ears, scratching inside my skull.

"*Run run run run run—*"

"STOP IT!" I squeeze my eyes closed, wanting to shut this nightmare out completely, but even from behind my eyelids I can see the girl's figure as she staggers across the room toward me.

I shriek in terror, opening my eyes and leaping out of bed. "Mom! Dad!" Reaching my bedroom door, I grab hold of the knob and turn.

The door doesn't budge.

I pull and tug, but it's stuck. *Goddamn it*, the door is stuck!

"Help! Help me!" My screams, my racing pulse, the girl's frantic refrain, her labored footsteps—they all meld together in my ears and overwhelm me completely. I'm horrified to turn around, but I'm twirling on my heels anyway, looking behind me to see the girl's silhouette rapidly approaching.

"*Run run run—*"

"NO!" At the mercy of pure adrenaline and reflex, my hand shoots outward and flips the switch by my door, flooding the room with light.

As the darkness dissipates, the girl's wiry frame flickers and distorts into that of a broad-shouldered man with a bloodied face and mangled lips that part in a roaring scream of rage as he bounds across the room toward me, his bloody fingers outstretched.

Before I have a moment to dart away or even cry once more for my parents, those thick fingers are around my throat, thumbs digging into my trachea and cutting off air supply. I grip at the man's wrists, squeezing, trying to push him away, but his hands are so strong.

"Sleep!" the shadow man yells. His piercing blue eyes drill into mine. Bloody saliva leaps from his cracked lips and spatters my face.

He shakes me by my neck, knocking the back of my skull against the bedroom door. Bewildered and desperate for air, I strike the man's face again and again. One of my blows hits his already busted mouth as my curled fingers slip between his wet lips, long enough for him to bite down with a combination of empty gum sockets and shattered teeth.

Pain screams up my forearm as I pull my hand away, but all that leaves my mouth is a choked gasp.

"SLEEP!" the man bellows once more before flinging me like a rag doll across the room. I crash against my bifold closet doors. Wood breaks and splinters beneath my weight. Wire hangers and clothing rain down on me, burying me in soft fabric and cold metal.

I lay motionless under the rubble of my closet, dazed and exhausted, but relief courses through my being when I hear the alarmed voices of my parents in the hall, followed by the sound of my bedroom door bursting open.

"Melody! Oh my God, Melody!" My mother's hands

find mine as I'm pulled up and out of the mess. The harsh glare from the ceiling light fixture assaults my eyes. I have to squint as I scan the room for the bloodied man and the broken-bodied girl I had seen in the darkness.

Nothing. No trace of either of them. Instead, I find my mom kneeling beside me, her hands clasping my shoulders and assessing me for injuries. Dad hovers over the scene with a white-knuckle grip on a baseball bat and starts grilling me with questions. "What the hell happened? Did you fall? Melody, what's going on?"

"I . . . uh, I . . . I don't—" I can't get my mouth to work.

"Andrew, she's shaking like you wouldn't believe," Mom says to Dad.

"Is she hurt?"

"I don't know. I don't see anything. Melody, take a deep breath. I need you to calm down so you can tell me what happened."

"A man!" The words finally leave my throat, but they come out louder than expected, and shrill. "There was a girl in front of the window, and then she turned into this bloody man. His face was all swollen and messed up, and he started attacking me, and . . . and he threw me. He threw me like I was nothing!"

Mom wraps her arms around me and smooths my hair, saying, "Shh, shh, shh. It's okay. Just breathe," while Dad dashes to the window, pulling up the blinds and checking the locks.

"Looks secure to me." He kneels and peers under the bed, forgetting that there isn't an *under*, just drawers built into the bedframe for my winter clothing. His incredulous expression tells me exactly what's on his mind.

"It wasn't a dream!" I shout.

"Well, Mel, I don't see anyone here," he says with a disgruntled tone, knees cracking as he stands. He rests the barrel of the bat on his shoulder.

"You probably had a scary dream and tripped when you got out of bed . . ." Mom doesn't seem entirely convinced of her own explanation; it would take a lot more than a stumble in the dark to wreck the closet doors this way.

"He was here," I whimper. "He was choking me."

She immediately examines my neck for bruises. "Honey, I don't see anything. Let's get you up and make sure you aren't hurt."

"He bit my finger," I recall, raising my hand to see—

Nothing. No bite marks. No blood.

Maybe I *was* dreaming.

"Okay, I agree with your mother," Dad says. "Stand up. C'mon."

The two help me to my feet. I'm quivering like a leaf in the wind, but I don't feel any pain in my legs. My extra-large Looney Tunes T-shirt, however, is torn in the back, exposing a long cut that runs parallel with my spine. Mom assures me it isn't anything serious and leads me to the bathroom to clean me up.

That girl . . . Her voice sounded so much like Bailey's. I shiver just thinking about her broken form stumbling toward me, shifting into that monstrous man, his terrible face battered beyond recognition. There was something vaguely familiar about him too, and yet he was more savage and violent than anyone I've ever encountered. Where did that bogeyman come from and what did he want with me? I have no clue, but I can't shake the feeling that the answers are hiding right in front of me.

Other bumps and bruises soon form on my arms and shoulders from the fall, but after about a hundred glances in the mirror to check my throat for finger marks, I finally accept that the whole thing must have been a terrible nightmare, probably brought on by tonight's phone call with Bailey.

And I feel totally stupid about it.

All this time, I've been so dismissive of Bailey's dreams. I've tried to pawn her off on the school counselor so she'd stop making such a big deal over something that isn't even real. But now that I've gotten a taste of it myself—seen the way Mom and Dad shake their heads at me, grinning and clicking their tongues—I know exactly how Bailey feels. And she's been going through it nearly every night since her dad disappeared in that accident. I should learn to listen to her better. After everything she said on the phone tonight, I know she needs me.

The heavy weight of guilt settles in my gut. I can't believe I left Bailey on the line like that after she'd gone on and on about dream boys and the Rapture and spell books. It doesn't matter how upset or angry I was that she'd judge my relationship with Dennis. At the end of the day, she has a point. I met the boy only two days ago. Bailey was simply looking out for me, and if she genuinely believes I'm being haunted by the evil boy of her dreams, the last thing I should do is ignore her. She isn't well, and I'm the only one who can help her through it.

In the morning, I tell myself, *I'll hear Bailey out. I'll listen to her like she's always listened to me.*

I owe her that.

CHAPTER
17

THE HARSH GUSTS of the coming storm howl through the early autumn leaves as I stroll along Abraham Street in the direction of Bailey's house. A chill slices through my windbreaker and settles into my bones.

Another dreary day, I think begrudgingly. *Farewell, sunny summer days. Farwell.*

I'm hoping we can hitch a ride with Bailey's mom this time around. We just barely made it to school the other day, and if the gathering clouds are any indication, I doubt we'll be as lucky today.

I cover the distance to Bailey's Victorian stucco and stop at the gate. The house looms above, appearing much taller than it ever has before. Vaulted peaks scratch at charcoal skies, threatening to cut the dense clouds apart and free

169

the flood within.

Grotesque images—images I've struggled to push aside all morning—race through my mind like crime scene photos on microfiche: the twisted, broken-bodied figure in front of my bedroom window and the strange yet familiar man coming at me with bloody fingers outstretched, shouting, *"SLEEP!"*

Both were the product of one seriously messed-up dream, I know that now. The ghostlike girl wasn't actually Bailey, and the man—whomever he was supposed to represent—wasn't real.

What *was* real was the crazed, out-of-character grin on Dennis's face as he drove me home last night, the way he giggled like a madman when he saw the scarecrow display in Eleanor McGuffin's yard. The way he tugged me toward him before I could wish him goodnight, his hands forming a vice-like grip around my waist, kissing me hard—*too* hard—as though he'd never kissed anybody in his life.

Which isn't true. He had done just fine down by the lake a couple of nights ago, his soft lips tenderly meeting mine for a few mind-numbing seconds before pulling away and saying, "It's late. I should get you home," much to my disappointment. But as much as I wanted him to keep going, I took Dennis's gentlemanly restraint as a good sign.

The illusion of Dennis's decorum, however, was shattered last night. I had all but punched him in the jaw to get his greedy paws off me, hurrying away from his car and wishing I had stayed the night with Bailey instead of going anywhere else with Dennis Greendale. I'd have much rather endured Mrs. Hagen's motherly wrath.

Bailey was right—something was off about Dennis's behavior. What was it she had said about his eyes? That they had changed color or something? God, I can't even remember what color Dennis's eyes are. I'm always too busy staring at his giant biceps and cute butt.

As I step through the Hagen front gate, I chance a glimpse at Bailey's bedroom window, scared to death I'll see her glaring down at me with those tired eyes of hers, hating my very existence. But where Bailey usually sits every morning is an empty space. Even the window—normally open a crack to let in the fresh morning air—is shut, curtains pulled taut against what little daylight the clouds allow.

I suppose I should take this as a sign that Bailey wants nothing to do with me after last night. I should probably go on to school alone and give her some space for a while—however long she needs.

I guess that's what I'd normally do—what most people do—but there's this nagging sensation deep within me that says no, that isn't the way. Waiting instead of apologizing will only make things worse, prolong the suffering for us both. No, I should swallow my pride for once and tell her I'm sorry.

Unless it's too late.

I don't know where the thought comes from, or why I'd even think of it in the first place. Why would it be too late? Bailey will forgive me. She may be a little stubborn at first, but if she sees that I'm trying to make it up to her, she'll eventually come around. Then I can help her with whatever she's struggling with.

I do my best to swallow the sudden lump in my throat as I ascend the porch steps, rapping gently on the front door.

A moment later, Rae pokes her head outside. She's dressed for school in a simple pink T-shirt and faded Levi's. A pastel yellow button-down is tied around her waist. On her head is a denim baseball cap, positioned backward. She's trendy as usual, but I'm surprised to see she isn't wearing any makeup, at least not yet.

God, she looks as tired as Bailey.

Deep circles darken her weary eyes. All this time, Bailey and I assumed Rae was using makeup to be trendy. Now I understand she's been doing it to hide a lack of sleep.

Is she having bad dreams too?

The question sends spiders skittering down my spine.

"Hey, mind if I come in?" I ask.

"Bailey isn't here." Rae rubs her drowsy eyes. "She must've gone to school early."

Of course. Bailey went to school early just to avoid me.

I sigh. "And your mom's at the diner, isn't she? So you're home alone?"

"Uh-huh."

I stare at the bags beneath Rae's eyes. "Need any help getting ready for school?"

"No. I just need to do my makeup. The bus will be here any minute."

I nod. "Okay. Well . . . I'll see you later, I guess."

Rae nods back, a frown etched on her face.

I begin to back away from the porch, but I pause. "Is everything okay? You upset about what happened last night?"

Rae casts her eyes to the ground. A loose lock of hair swings into her face, and she brushes it aside, tucking it behind her ear. "I'm fine. Just haven't been sleeping good."

"Bad dreams?" I ask, using my best reporting skills to feign ignorance.

She nods again, her frown deepening.

"What about?"

"Nothing much. Just that . . ."

I wait for her to continue before offering encouragement. "You can tell me. I'm here."

Her chin trembles, and her eyebrows knit together, as if in anger that her emotions would betray her stoic expression. "It's nothing. I just keep dreaming that I'm . . . I'm all . . ."

Her eyes finally meet mine. I expect to see tears, but there aren't any. Her eyes are empty. Glassy. Like the eyes of a doll. There is no trace of the girl I've known her whole life. "I just keep dreaming that I'm all alone," she finishes.

My heart breaks. "Rae, you aren't alone. At all. You have me and Bailey and your mom. And I know you have lots of friends at school."

"That's not what I mean. There's just no one around in my dreams. It's always just me. Mom is gone. Bailey is gone. Everyone in town. All gone. Except . . ." She stares past me, as if fighting to recall some buried memory. "Except there are these dark, blurry . . . things. They're always moving so fast I can barely see them, but out of the corner of my eye, they look kind of like kids. There's something wrong with them, though. Their faces don't look right." She raises her fear-filled eyes to meet mine. "They aren't real kids."

An ear-splitting screech shatters the stillness. I turn to see an Autumncrow Elementary bus pull up to the curb outside the Hagen residence.

"Guess I'll have to do my makeup on the ride." Rae

grabs her backpack from the foyer before stepping outside.

"Sorry to take up your time," I say as she locks up. "If you want to talk later, you can always—"

"Thanks."

Then she's gone. I'm left standing alone on the porch, watching as Rae boards the bus. She doesn't so much as offer a wave out the window before she's carted away.

There it is again—that stone in the back of my throat, along with a weird sense of impending doom that I've been unable to shake all morning.

Why does this goodbye feel so final?

A bolt of lightning brightens the dark sky, followed by an ominous rumble a few seconds later.

Hurrying across the yard, I push through the gate, stopping to consider whether to return home for my raincoat and umbrella. No, it's too late. If I go back now, I'll definitely be late for school and my counseling session with Ms. Price, and by then the storm will have arrived. Mom and Dad are already at work, so I'd have no one to drive me.

Better keep moving, Melody.

I quicken my pace, adding a hop to my step in hopes it'll warm my body against the cold, but the chill is unbeatable. It seems to be coming from within.

"I don't think I'm here anymore."

"Shut up," I mutter to the echo of last night's nightmare. I wipe a sudden tear from my eye. Then I laugh, a forced chuckle. What's the matter with me today? Is this what it's like to walk to school alone, without Bailey to distract me from my thoughts?

Is it the same for Bailey when I'm not around?

Guilt pulls my heart into my gut. I pause again, stomping one foot on the sidewalk in frustration. I must look like a five-year-old throwing a tantrum. I don't know why I feel this way, but something is seriously wrong, and it's driving me insane.

I toss my backpack on the ground in front of an old oak bordering the sidewalk and plop down on it. If it starts raining, so be it. I just need to stop for a moment and collect myself. I can hardly breathe.

Leaning forward, I rest my forehead in my hands. The image of Bailey's closed bedroom window appears in my head.

I start sobbing.

"DAMN IT!" I slam my fists against my knees and lean back against the rough bark of the tree. The branches above toss about in a colorful frenzy. Beyond them the sky flashes its anger, illuminating several dark, winged shapes hovering in the sky. Vultures.

I squeeze my eyelids shut. Tears trickle down my cheeks.

Why am I like this? What the hell *is going on with me?*

I open my eyes to find Agatha Spalding, photographer for the school paper, gawking at me from across the street.

"I'm fine, Agatha," I project. "Just freaking out, is all."

Agatha, camera strapped around her neck like always, nods in understanding and shuffles on her way.

I wipe the tears from my face and murmur, "Just freaking out, and I don't know why."

Reaching between my knees, I seize my backpack and pull it in front of me, undoing the zipper and sifting through the contents until I find my Walkman. I don't listen to it very often these days, but I could use the distraction today.

I place the headphones over my ears and press play, not even caring what tape is inside. Some vaguely familiar song begins mid-chorus in a strange, garbled tone. I listen in confusion.

"What'll I do when I am wond'ring who is kissing you? What'll I do?"

Sounds like something Dad would listen to on the oldies station. Did he borrow my Walkman again without asking?

I shrug and stand up, throwing my backpack over my shoulder and continuing the trek toward school. I've definitely heard this song before—recently, even—but I can't quite place it. It's pretty though. Reminds me of Dennis and the lakeshore the other night.

I've got my fingers crossed that Dennis will be back to his normal, sweet-natured self today. With any luck, Bailey will be back to normal too, though I'm starting to think she may never be the same again.

A raindrop hits my cheek. Another lands on my nose.

I sigh. I'm going to be soaked by the time I reach school, and so is Agatha. She's walking ahead of me on the other side of the road, head drawn downward, reminding me a lot of Bailey.

"When I'm alone with only dreams of you that won't come true, what'll I do?" the voice in my headphones ponders.

Agatha suddenly stops and casts about a perplexed stare. She turns her nose up at the sky, sniffing the air. I pause too, smelling the air for myself. Something stinks. Bad. I walk onward, cringing more and more with every step.

Agatha gazes at me across the way, saying something I

can't hear over the music. I lift my headphones on one side. "Huh?"

"What *is* that smell?"

I shrug and use the opportunity to quote from one of my favorite bad horror films. "Garbage day!"

Agatha hurries on in disgust, and I can't blame her. It smells like someone left their dead cat in a trashcan for waste control to pick up.

I continue on, passing Eleanor McGuffin's house with her Halloween maze of scary scarecrows, reminding me of the ugly scene that transpired here just a couple of days ago.

"Eat shit, Tommy Burke," I say under my breath.

Bailey and I really showed him. Even though the vile stench permeating the air is at its worst, I can't help but smile at the thought of pushing Tommy's bike on its side, of hearing the satisfying crunch of his rearview mirror as it bit the dust.

Tommy had it coming.

The distorted noise of the tape worsens, hissing and warbling, slowing down and speeding up. I stop and stare at the player in my hands as it begins to skip, repeating the same lyric over and over.

"What'll I do?—What'll I do?—What'll I do?—What'll I do?—"

I open the lid of the Walkman in a hurry and gasp as smoke lifts into the air, mingling with the already putrid scent of my surroundings. I cough, fanning the smoke away from my face until it clears and reveals the cassette inside.

My mouth gapes in disbelief. The bottom half of the tape is melted. I've never heard of a Walkman getting hot enough to melt a cassette, but that isn't the thing that perplexes me most. When I opened the player, I expected to see some unfamiliar tape, something Dad left behind by mistake, but this one is mine. It's my old single of "Pictures of You" by the Cure.

Years earlier, I bought a copy for me and a copy for Bailey, and I used to listen to that song for days on end, rewinding and replaying it, over and over.

Another flash of lightening ripples through the sky, followed by the clash of thunder and an immediate downpour. I drop my ruined Walkman on the ground and start hightailing it toward school, but the rain is the last thing on my mind as my sneakers pump along the wet sidewalk. If my Cure tape was in the player, where had that mysterious old song come from?

Goosebumps form on my arms and legs—and I'm not at all certain the cold rain is to blame.

Something's wrong. Terribly wrong.

CHAPTER 18

BEFORE HEADING TO THE OFFICE to check in for my weekly counseling session, I squeeze into the crowded girls' restroom near the front entrance of the school. I'm greeted by a frenzied group of girls in the midst of battle. The cause for this down-and-dirty fight to the death? A single hair dryer.

I take a deep breath and dive in, pushing my way through the rain-drenched crowd to a cracked mirror and dabbing myself with paper towels to the best of my ability before accepting the depressing truth: my clothes are totally soaked and will take the rest of the morning to dry. I cringe just thinking about the discomfort of sitting through morning classes in sopping clothing.

As for my ruined hair, the ringing of the first-period

warning bell tells me there isn't time to bother with it. A chorus of groans erupts from the surrounding girls. "I guess it's a lucky scrunchie kind of day," someone declares.

I agree and fish a light pink scrunchie out of my bag, tying my wet hair back with a shrug. It'll have to do. My mind is too full of midnight visitors and phantom ballads to care either way.

Exiting the restroom, I gaze down the way at Bailey's locker. She isn't there. Not that I expected her to be. Bailey has a way of vanishing completely when she wants to avoid someone. Lucky for her, I have counseling during homeroom today; otherwise, she wouldn't make it past first period without having to face me. I'll have other opportunities, though.

Making my way to the offices at the top of the stairs, I'm assaulted by the harsh scent of cleaning chemicals. I grimace and cover my nose. What's with all the potent smells this morning?

Ms. Beamis, the secretary, is rummaging through the drawers of her desk. Her youthful face is pinched with worry as she glances up at me with a frown. "I left a stack of documents on my desk when I closed up yesterday, and now I can't find a darn thing. All my supplies are out of place too. Seems like somebody has been meddling in the office again. Principal Tremblay won't be happy."

"What about that smell?" I ask.

Ms. Beamis lifts her chin and smells the air. Each sniff is accompanied by the squeak of her stuffy sinuses. "Oh dear. My allergies. I can't smell a thing."

I nod. "Is Ms. Price in yet?"

"She's in her office. I'll sign you in."

I thank Ms. Beamis and leave the office, grateful to be free of that overwhelming industrial scent.

Ms. Price's office is across the hall. I rap on the frosted glass window of the counselor's office door.

"Come in," calls a woman's husky voice.

I push through the door and shut it behind me just as the bell sounds. Ms. Price, a thin, middle-aged woman with short strawberry blond hair, sits behind her desk, my file spread open before her.

She smiles. "Coffee?"

"No, thanks." I lower myself into the chair in front of her desk and drop my bag at my feet.

"Really?" She eyes me with concern.

"It isn't a good day for caffeine."

"Is it your anxiety?"

I don't know how to explain my current state of mind, so I simply shrug.

Ms. Price opens her composition book and jots down some notes. "First week of school. It's bound to bring about a lot of new struggles. And old ones." She sets her pen down and folds her fingers over her cluttered desk. "Want to start with what's bothering you most?"

I utter a humorless laugh. "Where to begin?"

"How about with the rain," Ms. Price suggests with a knowing smirk.

This gets a real chuckle from me. "The rain is very wet."

"I can see that. You know, my first day of freshman year, it was raining cats and dogs. The bus missed my stop, of course, so I had to walk. As soon as I stepped through the doors—*boom!* I slipped and fell right on my keister. Everyone laughed at me. It was terrible, but at least I got the most

181

embarrassing moment of my high school experience out of the way first thing."

"*That* was your most embarrassing moment?" I think back to the many times I've made a fool of myself since becoming a high school student.

"I mean, it's hard to embarrass yourself further when you decide to never show your face in public again."

"That'll solve it," I say. "Great message to instill on my impressionable young mind."

"Well, I think everyone could benefit from spending a little more time at home." Ms. Price sips her coffee from a mug promoting Autumncrow's upcoming Halloween Carnival. "Speaking of, how are things at home?"

"Good. Same old." *Except for the ghostly apparitions in my bedroom.*

"Have you been opening up to your parents about your anxieties?"

"Uh-huh." *I'm trying to, at least.*

"Are they listening?"

"Yep." As I say this, I can hear the echo of Mom's voice saying, *"You probably had a scary dream . . ."*

"Good, I'm glad to hear that. How's Bailey?"

Another lie is about to leave my mouth, but I pull back. This is what I really wanted to talk to Ms. Price about. Why do I feel the need to act so cool all the time?

"I guess I'm a little worried about Bailey."

Ms. Price raises an eyebrow. "Should I be worried too?"

"No, no. I mean . . . I don't think so. Bailey is tough. She's just been paranoid lately. She thinks her dreams are coming true."

"The ones about the creepy boy?"

"Yeah. She called me late last night and started rambling about dream boys and spell books and the Rapture of '59. She sounded manic."

"Okay." Ms. Price picks up her pen and pushes the tip into the sleeve of her baggy orange sweater, using it to scratch her right forearm. "How did you respond?"

My face reddens. "I listened. But I didn't know what to say. I tossed the phone to my mom and told her to make something up. She told Bailey I'd gone on to bed."

"And how are you feeling about that?"

"Guilty." I'm suddenly very aware of the wet clothes clinging to my skin, trapping me.

Ms. Price jots down some more notes before putting her pen to rest again and pulling up her sleeve. She has a dark red rash covering her forearm. Flakes of loose skin fall like snow onto the contents of my file as she digs at the rash with long, painted fingernails. "Have you seen Bailey today?"

"No . . . but I'll see her in third period."

"Do you have any idea what you'll say to her?"

I pull my eyes away from the rash, trying my best not to stare. "I'd like to apologize. And I want to hear her out and give her a chance to explain. I want to be there for her the way she's always there for me. I don't think I've been a good friend lately. I've been . . . distracted."

"Senior year can be all-consuming. It doesn't always give you time for things you used to have time for. Don't beat yourself up about it. The best thing you can do is focus on yourself. You do you, as they say, and don't worry about everyone else. That includes Bailey. Are you still thinking of

183

running for class president?"

I shake my head no. I'd been entertaining the idea, but I never brought it up to anyone besides Ms. Price, especially not to Bailey. I kept meaning to, but I was worried she'd think I wouldn't have time for her anymore.

"What changed your mind?" Ms. Price asks, seemingly disappointed. "You'd make a great class president. The students at this school like you and look up to you."

"I guess it doesn't matter to me as much as I thought it did," I say.

Ms. Price stares at me for a beat. Then I watch as she scribbles another note. Small drops of blood are beading up to the surface of her inflamed skin, making me feel sick.

"How are things outside of school? Anything new on the horizon?"

"Yes, actually. I've been on a couple of dates with someone new. His name is Dennis."

"Dennis?" Ms. Price sits up in her seat, her face alight with intrigue. She pulls her sleeve down over her rash. "Who's Dennis?"

"He's a new student I met on the first day back."

"A new student you met the first day back?" Ms. Price leans forward over the desktop, her eyes widening in excitement.

"Yeah. We've been seeing each other every night."

"You've been seeing each other every night?" The counselor's smile expands. Her fingers crawl back up into her sleeve, scratching feverishly at her skin.

I shift uncomfortably in my seat. The way Ms. Price is smiling at me—it's not her usual smile.

Ms. Price's toothy grin fades when she realizes I'm not

matching her enthusiasm. "Are you still upset about Tommy?"

Scratch, scratch, scratch.

"No, I don't care about Tommy."

"Are you upset with this new boy then?"

Scratch, scratch, scratch.

I'm growing tired of Ms. Price's questions. The rapid-fire way she's asking them is so unlike the counselor I've grown to like. "I guess so. He's very up and down. Sweet one day, erratic the next."

"Oh." Ms. Price pauses, as if deep in thought, and the scratching ceases. "And the boy's name again?"

"Dennis Greendale. You remember Mr. Greendale, the janitor?"

"That name rings a bell, but I can't put a face to it."

Of course not. Bailey has mentioned this before—as soon as anyone dies in this town, it's almost as if they vanish from memory. I thought she was crazy for pointing it out, but then I started noticing it too. I'm not as superstitious as Bailey, but I must admit it's very weird.

"He passed away this summer," I explain. "Dennis is in town with his mom for a while to wrap up loose ends before they go back to Cincy."

Ms. Price's eyes lose focus again, looking directly at me but not seeing me.

"Do you mind waiting here for a moment?" she asks. "I want to go check on something."

"Yeah, sure. Is everything okay?"

"Uh-huh. I'll be right back." Ms. Price stands and hurries out of the room, leaving the door open behind her. I watch as she enters the office across the hall and speaks to

Ms. Beamis in a tone too low for me to hear. Then she walks behind the front desk and out of sight.

Weird. Over the summer, I attended countless counseling sessions with Ms. Price. She never acted this bizarre or rushed off so hastily before.

What is going on today?

I keep my eyes glued to the office doorway, waiting for her to reappear. I feel a growing sense of nervousness in the pit of my stomach, further intensified by the deathly silence of the empty hallway. Chills clamber up my arms and legs.

School halls are so eerie when the comforting squeak of high-top sneakers on linoleum are absent, when the yammering voices of students are kept at bay behind closed classroom doors.

I wait in the silence, checking the wall clock every few seconds to see how much time has passed. Ms. Price has been gone five minutes.

Six minutes.

Eight.

Ten.

I sigh and glance at the office door again. *What's taking her so long?*

I reach for my bag and am about to stand when someone passes by Ms. Price's open door, a girl about my age in a polka-dot dress. She turns her head and glances in at me, briefly revealing her gruesome, mutilated face.

My blood turns cold. Every limb of my body becomes heavy. I stare at the doorway, now empty, and grip the armrests of my chair in terror. I try to open my mouth, try to scream for Ms. Price, but I can't make a sound.

I drop my bag and stand to my feet, darting into the

hallway and looking to the left, in the direction of the girl.

Nothing. There's nothing to see but a long, empty corridor, dead-ending at a wall of vast windows.

Ms. Price walks out of the main office and stops midstride. "Melody. What's wrong?"

My jaw moves up and down, but I still can't get a word out.

"You look like you've seen a ghost."

Ghost? Did I see a ghost?

"Here. Let's go back to my office." Ms. Price gently takes me by the arm and leads me to my chair. She pours coffee into a Styrofoam cup and hands it to me. Even in my shocked state, I notice she forgot the shot of cream and three pouches of sugar she knows I like.

I stare at the thick, murky liquid and feel like I might vomit, not because of my hatred for black coffee but because of what it resembles.

Blood. Hot, sticky blood.

That girl in the hall, whoever she was . . . Her face had been split in two, blood oozing from the wound like a dark river.

I set the cup down on Ms. Price's desk without taking a sip.

"Are you okay?" she asks.

"I think so. I just thought I saw . . . someone."

"Dennis?"

The question takes me by surprise. "No. Why?"

Ms. Price folds her fingers on the desktop again. I notice her shirtsleeve is now cherry-red with blood. "Melody, have you seen this Dennis Greendale today?"

"Not since last night when he dropped me off at home."

"Do you have any classes with this boy?"

"No. Why?" That sick feeling in my gut deepens.

"Have you been to his house? Met his mother?"

"No, I haven't. I've just been on a couple of dates with him. Why are you giving me the third degree? What's going on?"

Ms. Price sighs. "It's part of my job to familiarize myself with all the new students that come through this school. Names, records, and so forth. I need to know who to look out for, who might need my guidance. So far, we have twenty-two new students this school year. A small number compared to the larger schools I've worked for, but this means I can easily keep track."

Ms. Price looks deep into my eyes. "I double-checked our records, but I can't find any documentation of a Dennis Greendale."

"What does that mean?" I ask.

"It means we don't have a student by that name at our school. It means I'm going to need you to tell me everything you know about this boy."

CHAPTER 19

"AS YOU ALL KNOW, I have quite the busy year ahead of me. Running for class president for the fourth year in a row is hard enough, and between my volunteer work, directing this year's production of *The Legend of Sleepy Hollow*, maintaining my perfect grade point average, and acting as editor of the school newspaper, I'm going to have my work cut out for me."

Monique Stevens paces slowly back and forth at the front of the newsroom, only too happy to stand in for Ms. Gordon while she's using the copy machine in the teachers' lounge. Her hands are clasped tightly over her stomach, shoulders drawn back, chin held high in a sad attempt at appearing powerful and righteous, when in reality she looks like any other self-important goody-goody who feels most at ease when she's calling the shots.

"Therefore," she says, "my thinking is as follows: Melody, you've been the paper's head reporter for ... how long? Two years?"

I give a noncommittal nod from my editing station, in no mood to be bothered by anyone, especially not Monique. I'd give anything to be alone with my thoughts right now, maybe fake a cold and get sent home early, to lie down in bed and ponder the distressing information I received today.

He isn't a student. Dennis Greendale isn't a student. He's been lying to me this whole time, and I fell for it.

"And you were head editor last year, is that correct?" Monique prods.

I nod again, not really hearing her.

Who is he then? Where the hell did he come from?

"Good." Monique shoots me that million-watt smile of hers. "You have a lot of experience here. I may occasionally lean on you for your expertise. I'm sure you won't mind."

"Wait, what?" I rise from my slouched posture as it finally dawns on me what Monique is implying.

"You're such an asset to what I'm trying to create with this paper, Melody. It's an honor to have you on my team."

"On *your* team?" My fingernails bite into my palms.

I should have known it would go down this way. When I tried out for this year's assistant advisor position, I was thinking it would look nice on my college applications, but of course the role went to Monique, as all roles do. Now she's going to dump all her work on me and take all the recognition and praise for herself.

Before I can fight back, Monique moves on. "So, for the

feature story, I'm going to have you write about the value and significance of high school dances, in particular the senior prom. I—"

"No."

Monique freezes and gives me that icy glare of hers. "Come again?"

"No. I'm not writing about prom."

Most students go out of their way to avoid an argument with Monique Stevens, knowing it's a fruitless cause. Best to bury your head in the sand and wait for the storm to pass.

I, on the other hand, don't mind butting heads when it's called for. Monique may think she's the queen bee of Autumncrow High, but she's no better than anyone else. Someone ought to take her down a peg, and it might as well be me. Sure, she's Mayor Sherman's spoiled niece, but I have something she doesn't: respect.

Like Ms. Price said, people actually like me at this school. They may not stand up to Monique on their own, but they'll stand behind someone who isn't afraid to knuckle down. Someone who doesn't put herself on a pedestal.

I lean back in my chair and cross my arms, feeling some of my old fire returning. "I'm head reporter, so I get a say in our feature story. My idea is to write a piece honoring those students and staff who passed away this summer. That's what we've always done at the start of the school year."

The other three team members nod their support, all except for Monique.

"Well, I don't much like the way this school has 'always done' things. What a morbid idea anyway. Such a depressing kickoff to the school paper. I'm getting goosebumps just thinking about it."

Jerry Evans, sole writer of the comic strip and class clown, chimes in: "Did you know the scientific term for goosebumps is 'skin boners'?"

"Did you know you're gross and full of shit?" Monique snaps.

"It's not a morbid idea. It's thoughtful," I say. "We have to do something to remind people of those who've passed; otherwise, they'll be forgotten forever. I'll do a write-up on prom for next week's paper, but I can tell you right now it won't be well received. People are very superstitious about school dances here."

Monique huffs. "It's all a heavy load of bull. Everyone knows that stupid Rapture is a warped fairy tale. This town is always cooking up *National Enquirer*-worthy trash to attract more tourists, but if townies actually bought into a single word of it, they wouldn't continue living in this hellhole. The FBI would be banging at every door if those stories held a single ounce of truth."

"Listen, I'm not sure I believe it all myself. It's probably okay to hold a school dance. I just think the time and energy would be best spent elsewhere."

"I second that."

The entire news team turns to face the back of the room in surprise. Shy and solemn Agatha, with her knee-high stockings and plaid skirt, blanches and casts her wide eyes downward.

"It's riskier than ever to hold a school dance," she adds, cleaning her camera lens nervously. "Things are getting worse here."

"Guys! The weird girl knows how to speak," Jerry stage-whispers.

"How do you mean?" I ask her, ignoring Jerry.

Agatha shrugs. "Something just feels off this year. So many murders and missing persons. More than any other summer before."

"It's true," Jerry says.

"And it's barely stopped storming in days."

"Nasty weather," Jerry agrees.

"And did you notice the fluorescents in the halls seem dimmer than they used to?"

"Budget cuts."

"Even the air itself feels heavier in the school. Oppressive."

"Allergies be damned."

"And that portrait of Autumn Crow that's hanging in the secretary's office? She looks venomous now."

Jerry has no comment for this one.

"What the hell does that mean?" Monique demands.

Agatha clicks her camera lens back into place. "I saw it when I came in this morning. Autumn used to have a solemn expression on her face, but that's gone now. She's glaring instead. It's a little scary. I asked Ms. Beamis about it, but she couldn't see what I saw. Adults never do."

An eerie silence fills the room.

I didn't notice anything amiss with the painting this morning, but then again, I was too distracted by the cleaning fumes to notice. I make a mental note to swing by the office again before school lets out, just to satisfy my curiosity.

Agatha sets her camera aside and smooths her skirt over her knees. "You remember all those stories about Abraham and Autumn Crow?

"Yeah, Autumn lost her marbles," Jerry says. "She slaughtered all those kids and then ate her own baby."

As usual, I feel sick to my stomach just thinking about it. What Jerry said is true, or at least that's how the more sordid version of the tale goes.

In 1810, at the age of twenty-five, Abraham Crow came to this part of Ohio with his nineteen-year-old bride, and together they founded the town of Autumncrow Valley. Autumn, a true pioneer in her own right, was a fervent advocate for children and education. She believed all children should be taught to read and write, regardless of social stature or skin color. This made her something of a controversial figure, but the Crows were anything but conventional to begin with.

Abraham had a particular interest in All Hallows' Eve and the occult. Though legend states he wasn't a practicing witch, he collected what he believed were enchanted objects and tools for witchcraft, many of which are displayed in the old Crow mansion at the edge of town, now in use as a museum.

The town quickly blossomed into a thriving community, and Autumn threw herself into her lifelong dream of schooling the next generation, founding Autumncrow Academy . . . on the very ground where Autumncrow High stands today.

A decade later, after years of quietly longing to bear a child of her own, Autumn nearly died giving birth to her one and only daughter. She was gravely ill and never fully recovered, abandoning her post at the academy and locking herself away inside her mansion, seldom to be seen in public ever again.

Around this time, one by one, the town's children began to disappear. Hysteria spread throughout the community. At the height of this frenzy, Autumn Crow was seen walking through town late one night, dressed in a black gown, clutching her half-devoured baby in her arms, blood dripping from her teeth. She claimed the infant had been speaking to her, telling her to do awful things, persuading her to devour the flesh of the young.

Before she could be taken into custody, she disappeared into the woods. Meanwhile, the remains of the lost children were unearthed in the forest bordering the Crow mansion, their bones picked clean.

Abraham, distraught over the murder of his daughter and shocked at the extent of his wife's wickedness, went out in search of Autumn. He returned on Halloween night, her corpse in his arms, declaring she had committed suicide.

And that's essentially where the story ends, although many variations of the tale exist, as with any local legend. I don't know how much of what they say is true, but the mental image of a woman eating her own baby has haunted me since I was a kid. Bailey too.

Once, during a sleepover when we were ten, I devised a plan to scare Bailey by dousing one of my baby dolls in ketchup like it was a freaking meatloaf or something. I hid the doll in Bailey's sleeping bag and waited for her reaction. She flipped out when she found it, screaming like a madwoman about the dead baby in her sleeping bag.

"It's okay," I told her. "Look—it's just a toy." But she insisted it was a real baby moments before, that its face had been chewed away, revealing the skull beneath. That it had whispered the words: "It won't be long, little girl."

I was afraid I'd really messed her up with that prank, and maybe I did. I've reminded her of that night since, but she doesn't seem to recall. It's like she's locked the memory away.

Thinking about it now brings about a fresh feeling of regret.

Third-period chemistry, I remind myself. *I'll get to apologize to her about last night very soon.*

Monique leans against the chalkboard, oblivious to the chalk dust that'll cover her backside for the rest of the day. "We've all heard the stories, Agatha. But that's all they are: a bunch of bogus stories. My mom—Mayor Sherman's sister, for those unaware—belongs to the historical society. She says it's all claptrap. Autumn Crow didn't eat her baby. She loved children. Her daughter was stillborn. That's why Autumn locked herself away. She was devastated and fell into a deep depression. As for the other children, Autumn was *obviously* the victim of a witch hunt. The superstitious townsfolk needed a way to make sense of it all, so they turned their backs on Autumn, a misunderstood woman ahead of her time. It's as simple as that."

Agatha nods but keeps her gaze low, obviously intimidated by Monique's daggerlike stare. "I hope that's true. I just have a bad feeling. Like this school year is cursed or something."

"This whole town is cursed." There's no trace of humor in Jerry's voice this time around. His words are genuine.

"You guys remember why Abraham had Autumn laid to rest in Kilgore, right?" Agatha says.

We all nod. Apparently, Abraham feared his wife's

grave would be desecrated if she were buried in Autumncrow Cemetery, so she was interred in a crypt in the neighboring town of Kilgore.

"Well, my dad's a cop, and he heard on the scanner this morning that Autumn Crow's crypt was broken into overnight and her coffin disturbed."

"Weird," Jerry and I say at the same time.

"I don't know what it means," Agatha says, "but I have a terrible feeling that something especially bad is going to happen. Very soon."

"Oh dear God, you're all pathetic." Monique rolls her eyes and throws her bookbag over her shoulder. "I don't have time for this. I have places to be."

She motions to a typed document pinned to the bulletin board beside the classroom door.

"On those pages, you will find content suggestions for each section of the newspaper. Leave your notes in the margins, and we'll get down to business on Monday. Melody— write about whatever you want this week, but you better have one hell of a persuasive piece about prom before next Friday."

With her hand on the doorknob, Monique turns to me one last time, a sly grin on her pompous face.

"I know school dances may not be your top priority, considering how unceremoniously you got dumped not too long ago, but some of us would like to attend prom this year instead of, say, cowering at home to binge on ice cream and watch rom-coms like you and precious, innocent Bailey are probably planning to do. Best not let your biases get in the way of delivering cold, hard facts to this school, hon. Just a tip."

Monique has barely a second to blink—and I have no time to rethink what I'm about to do—before I've covered the distance between us and pitched my fist at her uppity, unsuspecting face.

That part about knuckling down? I guess it wasn't so figurative after all.

CHAPTER 20

I LIFT THE ICE PACK from my knuckles for the millionth time in the past two hours. My hand is swollen, sore, and a dozen shades of blue and purple, but at least it's not broken. Monique was asking for it, but I never ever want to do that again. I wouldn't have guessed that punching someone in the face would make *me* feel this lousy in so many different ways, but now I know.

Boy, do I know!

I shift uncomfortably in the hard, plastic chair outside Principal Tremblay's office, feeling an ache in my lower back. I glance at a nearby wall clock. It's lunchtime. So much for talking to Bailey in third period. I've missed nearly half a day of school and will miss many more half days to come.

I've been suspended. For two whole weeks.

What have I done?

As a kid, I thought suspension sounded more like a prize than punishment. What's so terrible about getting a couple of weeks off school? Now, as a high school senior with plans for college, I get the picture.

Principal Tremblay's office door bursts open, sparking my nerves. Mom rushes out, averting her eyes from me as she passes by. Too ashamed to look at me, I guess. The click-clack of her high heels bounces off the cinderblock walls.

I hurry to catch up. "I'm sorry, Mom. I'm so, so sorry."

"No, you're not," she says, keeping up a pace I didn't think was possible in heels. "If you think this is sorry, just you wait. You broke the nose of the girl whose uncle is the most important man in Autumncrow. You're lucky they have more money than they need, because otherwise they'd sue us for all we're worth. I'm hoping we can settle on a deal that doesn't result in pressed charges, but when it comes to your hopes for a scholarship or attending a fancy college, you can kiss it all goodbye. *Sorry?* Melody Krieger, you'd better believe you're going to be."

"Mom, please slow down," I say, barely keeping up. My voice is thick with emotion, but I'm doing everything I can to hold the tears at bay. "I messed up. I know. I want to make it right. I don't know what got into me. When she said the thing about rom-coms, I snapped. I hate rom-coms."

Mom stops in her tracks so suddenly I almost barge into her. She turns and gives me a venomous glare. "I swear to Christ, if you think now is a good time for humor . . ."

"I'm not trying to be funny." I want to add that I really

200

do hate rom-coms, but it's not wise to poke the bear. "Monique brought Tommy into it, okay? Then she insulted me and Bailey and took a huge crap all over my credibility as a reporter. She cut deep, and I reacted."

Mom closes her tired eyes and pinches the bridge of her nose, as though warding off a headache. "Please, watch your language."

"Mom—"

She holds up a finger, cutting me off. "Not another word, Mel. I need to get back to work. You're lucky it stopped raining. Go straight home and think about what you did. We'll discuss this with your father tonight."

With a turn, Mom treads down the hall. I don't follow this time. I stand still, watching her disappear down the steps and out the front doors of Autumncrow High.

"Think about what you did . . ." I feel like a five-year-old again.

"I'm sorry," I say, though I'm not sure who the apology is for. Mom? Myself?

Certainly not Monique.

I return to the chair of shame outside Mr. Tremblay's office, lifting my backpack off the floor and throwing it over my shoulder. As I make my way to the exit, a cold sadness washes over me. I pull my windbreaker tighter around my body, but the icy grip holds firm, refusing to fade.

"I know . . ."

I gasp and whirl around, looking for the source of that familiar whisper, but I'm all alone in the dingy hallway.

Completely alone.

"Bailey?" My hushed tone is much too loud in the eerie stillness of the hall.

There's no reply, and why would there be? I imagined the voice. Bailey isn't here. She's probably enjoying her lunch in the cafeteria, relieved that I'm nowhere to be found. Whatever I thought I just heard, it was nothing more than an echo of last night's strange dream. That's it. And it *was* just a dream. That's the only explanation that makes any sense. I need to get a grip.

But what about that girl with the mangled face you saw this morning, Melody? Were you dreaming then too?

Being suspended is nothing like I pictured it. I imagined a police officer pulling me from class, escorting me to the door, and tossing me out on my face.

I guess reality isn't quite so exciting.

Ambling my way home, I marvel at how different my usual route looks at this time of day when the lunch crowd has descended on the town, not to mention all the delicious smells.

Though my gut is churning with guilt and anxiety, another sensation is starting to take over.

Hunger.

No sooner than I have the thought, I hear something creak overhead.

I pause and lift my gaze to the snarling mouth full of monstrous teeth hanging above me. Two long, bloody fangs sink into the words, "Drac's 24-Hour Bite." The brightly painted sign sways gently in the breeze.

My stomach rumbles as Mom's words replay in my head: *"Go straight home and think about what you did."*

Fat chance. A girl's gotta eat.

"Give me an Adam and Eve on a raft," a waitress calls as I step through the revolving doors. She greets me and tells me to take a seat somewhere. *Somewhere* being the operative word. The place is pulsing with the blood of lunch rush with no empty booths for grabs.

I settle in at the bar, sandwiched between a beefy middle-aged man in a baseball jersey and an old woman sipping from a bottle of cola. The enticing scents of fried foods and freshly baked pies do their best to lift my spirits, but the sounds of the kitchen—the incessant clatter of the chopping board, the sizzling of meats on the grill, and the shouting from the waitresses—keep me on edge. I wish someone would cue up a song on the jukebox and drown out all this noise.

The woman beside me takes a long generous sip through a straw, draining her bottle of cola and slamming it on the counter. The sudden racket makes my heart skip.

"I love a nice cold pop," she tells me.

"Mm-hmm," I say, helping myself to an abandoned menu and skimming the lunch specials.

"It's the simple things in life, you know?"

"Mm-hmm."

"Hey, Mel, how's it shaking?" Cathy Brewster, a young waitress with short, spiky black hair leans across the bar top and gives me a perfect smile, teeth stark white against her black lipstick. Cathy has always reminded me of a goth version of Cyndi Lauper.

"I'm fine. Can I get a cheeseburger and fries?"

"Put a yellow blanket on a dead cow with a side of Joan of Arc!" Cathy hollers to the kitchen staff. "Drink?"

203

"Get the cherry cola," my neighbor urges.

I shrug. "A cherry cola, please."

"Another for me too," the woman orders. "With extra cherries. I have a craving."

"You got it," Cathy says. "Good pop, eh, Mrs. McGuffin?"

"Mm-hmm."

I look at the old woman's face for the first time and blush. "Sorry, Eleanor. I didn't realize that was you sitting there."

"It's okay, dear." My former babysitter gives me a forgiving smile. "You must have a lot on your mind these days."

I nod. *Today especially.*

"How's the Halloween maze coming along?"

Eleanor's kind smile falters and her rosy cheeks fade to a chalky white. "The maze is finished. I needed to get away from the scarecrows for a bit. They're too real. It's starting to rattle me."

"Oh . . ."

Eleanor turns her face away, checking out of the conversation.

Strange. I can't put my finger on it, but she's not herself today.

I glance around the small but bustling diner, soaking in the atmosphere. Drac's looks like any other small-town diner, with its neon lights and checkered floors. But upon closer inspection, it more than lives up to its name, displaying a wide array of vampire movie memorabilia and artwork.

Only in Autumncrow.

"Order up!" Cathy sets a small plastic basket containing

fries and a hearty burger down in front of me and hands Mrs. McGuffin her drink. "Say, Melody—summer's over. Shouldn't you be in school?"

"Uh, yeah. The mystery meat wasn't doing it for me, so I came here instead," I say. "Where's Cassandra?"

Bailey's mom is normally buzzing around the diner during busy spells, encouraging customers to order the house salad. Now she's nowhere in sight.

"We do let her go home and get some shut-eye occasionally," Cathy says with a lighthearted smirk. "Poor woman can't catch a break. No sooner than she was out the door this morning, the school was calling for her, asking why Bailey didn't show up for class. I don't suppose you'd know anything about that." She looks at me askance over her cat-eye glasses.

"Huh? No. I had no idea."

"Oh, I see. For a second there, I thought you girls might be playing hooky today. I stand corrected." Cathy winks. "I've got orders up. Gotta run!"

"Wait. Cathy!" She's gone before I can even get the words out.

Bailey didn't go to school ... But Rae told me this morning that Bailey left early.

Oh God—what if something happened to Bailey on the way to school? What if someone snatched her up ... or ran her down with their car?

Disturbing visions reel through my brain, images of Bailey's flattened cadaver abandoned in a ditch like roadkill.

Suddenly, I feel too sick to eat anything.

A withered hand rests on my forearm. "Don't you fret, cupcake. It'll all be okay."

Eleanor gives me a reassuring pat, but I'm too distracted by the large weeping sores starting to soak through her sleeves to feel any kind of comfort. "Everything happens for a reason. All for a purpose."

"Thanks," I say. "Hey, what happened to your arm? Are you hurt?"

Eleanor ignores my question, repeating herself as her smile widens, revealing large gray teeth and receding gums, barely visible behind thin lips.

"Eleanor . . . are you okay?"

She looks different, unlike the cheerful woman I've known my entire life. I try to pull away from her grip, but she tightens her hold.

"Ouch! What's going on? You're hurting me."

A giggle leaves the woman's throat as she grabs on to me with her other hand, pulling me toward her with surprising strength. The blood from her arm smears onto the sleeve of my windbreaker.

"Ouch! Jeez, Eleanor, what are you doing?" I'm raising my voice now, but it's drowned out in the lunchtime chatter.

"I'm not hurting you," Eleanor says, smiling. Always smiling.

That's not her smile.

"Yes, you are," I argue.

"Oh no, dear. I'd never hurt you." She takes one of my fingers and bends it back.

"AAH!" I cry out in pain and slap Eleanor's knuckles with my free hand, surprising us both. She finally releases me. I grip my throbbing finger, staring at Eleanor in shock.

Her smile remains, but her bloodshot eyes blaze with

rage.

The entire diner has gone silent. Everyone has turned to watch the confrontation.

"My, my," Eleanor says, grinning. "You are a bitch."

"What?" My voice doesn't sound a part of me anymore.

"I always knew you'd grow up to be a good-for-nothing snake in the grass."

"Eleanor—"

"Wanna see what you did to me?" she asks, cutting me off. She holds up her arm and rolls back the bloodstained sleeve, revealing dozens of oozing boils. "Look what you did."

I stand from my stool, repulsed. "I didn't do that."

"Yes, you did. You hurt my arm."

What is she talking about? Why is she still smiling like that?

"I did not!" I yell, more to everyone else in the diner than to Eleanor.

The fry cook, a hulking man holding a spatula in one hand and a meat cleaver in the other, approaches the bar. "What's going on, you two?"

Eleanor bats her eyelashes at the man and giggles. "The little bitch hurt me, is all. See? My arm is ruined. Useless. May I?"

With the swipe of her uninjured hand, Eleanor snatches the meat cleaver from the fry cook's hand, lifts it into the air, and brings it down on her bleeding arm, chopping it off at the elbow in one blow.

The severed arm hits the diner floor. Blood sprays from Eleanor's elbow, spattering my face, soaking my hair and outfit.

Screaming. Everyone around me is screaming.

Several people run for the exit in terror, others rush forward to aid Eleanor. A young woman pulls the jacket off her own back and attempts to stop the bleeding.

All the while, Eleanor laughs. Hysterically.

Suddenly, I'm outside, running—no, *flying*—down Main Street, zipping past storefronts, pushing people aside. I turn onto Abraham Street, the usual route I take with Bailey after school, and keep going, pounding the sidewalk.

I see flashing lights up ahead. A cop car is parked in the middle of the road. Several cop cars actually, all parked horizontally across Abraham Street.

"Help," I say, but it comes out too quietly for anyone to hear. "Help me."

I throw myself against one of the cruisers and peer inside. Empty.

"Help!" My voice is getting louder, more desperate. And my legs, they won't stop trembling.

I run past the first car to the next, getting tangled in caution tape along the way. The second car is empty too, as is the third. "Somebody! Somebody, help!"

"Miss?"

Clipboard in hand, a young police officer approaches me. Taking notice of the blood on my face and jacket, she asks, "Are you hurt? Where is the blood coming from?"

"I ... I was at the diner," I say, but my tongue feels numb, like it can't form words properly.

"Okay, what happened there?" the officer presses calmly as she searches me for, I assume, the source of the blood.

"It's not mine," I explain. "She hurt my finger, but she

didn't cut me."

"Who?" the officer demands. "Who hurt you?"

"It's not my blood. I . . ." A sob pushes out of my throat. "My friend isn't at school. Do you know where she is?"

The police officer pulls away and waves her arm in the air, signaling at somebody behind me. "Hey! Can I get some help over here?"

I turn and see two other officers standing in a yard several doors down. I recognize one of them immediately.

"Dalton!" I take off toward him before he can react to the policewoman's request.

"Stop!" she shouts. "Don't go over there! This is a crime scene!"

"Dalton!" I yell, ignoring the woman's demands. "Do you know where Bailey is?"

"Melody? Stop! Don't come any closer," Dalton exclaims, rushing toward me. "You can't be here. Go back."

"Bailey didn't show up for school," I say.

"Is that blood?" Dalton asks.

The policewoman appears at my side. "She says it isn't hers. She seems to be in shock."

"Mrs. McGuffin chopped her arm off with a meat cleaver."

The two are silent for a moment. Dalton shoots the policewoman a dubious look. She shrugs in bewilderment.

"Are you talking about Eleanor McGuffin?" he asks.

"Yeah," I say, peering over Dalton's shoulder at the other officer who is preoccupied with something in a yard about a hundred feet away.

I notice that smell again, the same rank smell from this morning. The smell of rotting meat.

209

Caw! Caw! A crow pitches itself out of a nearby tree and descends on the yard, landing on the shoulder of a scarecrow.

"Get out of here!" the other officer yells at the crow. "Go on! Git!"

"Isn't that Eleanor's yard?" I ask.

Dalton sidesteps to obscure my view but doesn't respond.

"I need you to come back to the cruiser with me," the policewoman says.

"What's going on? Why is everything so strange today?" I peep over Dalton's other shoulder, at the cop shooing the crow away with his hands.

"Stupid bird. Get outta here!"

The crow remains, ignoring the man's cries and pecking at the head of the scare—

My stomach drops when I realize that isn't a scarecrow.

"Bailey?" My voice is a terrified whisper.

"Come with me," the policewoman demands, tugging on my arm.

Tugging on me like Eleanor did.

"Let go of me!" I scream. "Don't touch me!" I push past Dalton and barrel toward Eleanor McGuffin's front yard. "Bailey?"

"No! Stop her!" Dalton roars.

The other officer twirls around in shock, but he's too late to react. I freeze before Eleanor's Halloween display as my heart dies in my chest.

I gasp. I gasp again. I can't stop gasping.

I can't breathe.

Not Bailey. Tommy.

Hands restrain me from behind, pulling me away, down the street toward the cop cars, away from the horrific scene.

But no matter how far I'm pulled, no matter how tightly I shut my eyes, I'll forever see that image in my head—the grisly image of Tommy's body strung up like a scarecrow in Eleanor's front yard, an officer tugging the burlap sack off his face, the top of his head sawed clean off, nothing inside but empty space.

And as his flannel jacket flaps open in the wind, I catch a glimpse of his tattered and blood-soaked T-shirt, one I had made especially for him, emblazoned with those terrible words: "IF I ONLY HAD A BRAIN."

CHAPTER 21

DALTON HANDS ME a small cup of coffee. I peer down into the muddy black liquid, murmuring, "Still no cream and sugar."

"What's that?" Dalton asks.

I don't reply. Instead, I chew on the rim of the Styrofoam cup.

"Your dad will be here soon." Dalton slaps a stack of paperwork on his desk and takes a seat. "Can I get you anything else while you wait?"

Through swollen, bleary eyes, I peer up at Dalton and see a ghastly vision of Tommy crop up behind him, the crown of his head missing, arms outstretched like Jesus on the cross, empty eyes aimed skyward in anticipation of an oncoming storm.

I feel the storm coming too. It's twisting inside my heart, my gut, my soul. I'm rolling with it, tumbling, grasping for anything I can find, but there's nothing to hold on to. Nothing for miles and miles.

"Melody?" Dalton says. "Are you with me?"

"Um . . . I—I don't know."

Tommy's eyes roll down in his sockets and fix on me. "Run," he whispers.

I return my stare to my coffee cup and realize that a chunk of Styrofoam is missing from the rim. Did I accidentally swallow it?

My stomach growls, and the wall clock *tick-tick-ticks*.

"Run . . ."

I ignore Tommy's voice the best I can, telling myself not to look, to focus on the coffee. The thick, black coffee that looks like blood.

A bubbling brook of blood . . .

I squeeze my eyes shut as a stray tear falls down my cheek. "Did you call my dad?"

Dalton is silent for a moment. "Yes. As I said, he'll be here soon."

"Okay."

Dalton clears his throat. "I know you've had a real shock today, but I was hoping you might be able to tell me what happened at the diner in a little more detail."

"I already told you." I scrunch my eyes closed even tighter. "Why not question all the other people who were there? They saw it happen too."

"We're working on it. They saw how it ended, but you're the one who had a front-row seat for the complete exchange. Did Eleanor say anything to you about Tommy

Burke?"

"Please don't say his name." A tremor rakes through my body, my arms and legs shivering in unison. I wipe the tears from my cheeks with my sleeve. "Aren't I supposed to have a lawyer present for all this?"

"I'm not interrogating you, Melody. I'm just trying to fill out an eyewitness report."

"Shouldn't my parents at least be present?"

"We can wait for your dad if that'd make you more comfortable."

I ponder this for a moment. "No. On second thought, I don't want my parents involved in this. It'll scare them."

"It doesn't scare me," Dalton says.

I chance a glance in Dalton's direction. My soul sighs in relief when I see Tommy is no longer standing behind him.

"Eleanor didn't say a word about him," I say. "But she did say the scarecrow display was beginning to look too real. Something like that."

Dalton nods. Scribbles a note.

"Is Eleanor okay?" I ask.

"Yes. An officer spoke to her at the hospital. She'll have to learn to rely on her left hand from now on, but she'll recover. She remembers waking this morning to a foul smell, but she claims to have no recollection of anything else that transpired today."

"You don't think she could have possibly . . . I mean, she's not a suspect . . . is she?"

"We have no suspects at this point. Her outburst at the diner notwithstanding, I wouldn't think Eleanor is capable of something like this. But we don't have the full picture of what happened yet, either. All evidence at the scene suggests that the murder took place elsewhere, and I'm told the victim's motorcycle turned up in Mr. Gilroy's cornfield this morning. There are still a lot of missing pieces to this puzzle."

"The victim," I mumble.

"I'm trying to respect your wishes."

I set the coffee cup on the edge of Dalton's desk. "I guess it doesn't matter how you say it."

"It never does." Dalton frowns at me across his cluttered desk. I realize for the first time that his eyes are the same as Bailey's—an emerald city fallen into ruin.

"Did Tommy have any enemies?"

Again, I cringe at the sound of his name. "I don't know. He and I haven't spoken in months."

It's mostly true. A version of the truth I can live with in this moment, at least. I can't bear to recount to Dalton how ugly things got yesterday afternoon, not now that he's dead and gone.

"He got into a scuffle with someone at school yesterday," Dalton says. "Do you know anything about that?"

An icy finger traces my spine. "Dennis," I whisper.

"Who?"

"Dennis Greendale," I say. "Or at least I think that's his name. He's the new kid in town. We went out for milkshakes. Tom—" I choke on the name and take a deep breath. "My *ex* got jealous."

"So Tommy was fighting with this Dennis kid yesterday?"

"Yes."

"Okay, but you're not sure of his name?" Dalton leans forward, gripping his pen.

I pause.

Should I give Dennis away before he's had a chance to explain himself to me? My first instinct after finding out he wasn't a student at Autumncrow was to track him down and confront him, demand that he share whatever he's been hiding in hopes the answer would be less ominous than the conspiracy theories in my head. Perhaps the truth isn't so bad. Maybe it's all a big misunderstanding. Ms. Price could have been mistaken.

Or perhaps he murdered Tommy and strung up his body like a Halloween decoration.

I recall Bailey's warnings about him that I just shrugged off until now and Dennis's odd behavior last night . . . his maniacal laughter as we drove by Eleanor's scarecrow display.

"Melody?" Dalton brings me back to the cold, dark present.

"It turns out he's only posing as a student, so who knows if that's his real name or not?" I finally say. "He isn't enrolled. I don't know what his deal is. I mentioned him to the school counselor, and she said they have no record of him."

"Have you seen this boy since then?" Dalton probes.

I shake my head no.

Just then, the phone on Dalton's desk lights up. He grabs the receiver and presses a series of buttons while motioning at me to excuse himself and mouthing, *"One moment."*

I lean back in my seat and take a sip of coffee, cringing at its bitterness.

"Deputy Hagan speaking." Dalton turns ever so slightly

away from me and lowers his voice. "Hey, Mom . . . Listen, now isn't the best time . . . Okay . . . Yes . . . Are you sure?" As the barely audible voice on the other end of the line becomes more frantic and hurried, Dalton struggles to maintain an even tone. "Please calm down. This is what teenagers do. She's acting out . . . Look, I've got a lot to handle today. I'm sure she's fine. I'll send out an alert, okay? . . . No, Mom . . . That doesn't make any sense. I thought you said she skipped school today. Why would you go looking for her there? . . . Please don't . . . Okay, please just be careful. She'll turn up. I gotta go, Mom."

Dalton hangs up and scribbles a few lines on his notepad.

"Was that about Bailey?"

Dalton stops writing. "It was. And if you know where she is, I need you to come clean with me right now."

I swallow the lump in my throat. "She didn't tell me a thing . . . but then again, we didn't leave things on the best terms the last time we spoke."

"Oh, I see. So that's what this is about."

"I don't know. I don't think so. It's not like Bailey to just disappear."

Dalton lays down his pen. "I'm sure she's fine. She'll turn up. I just hope she does before Mom loses her mind."

"Something isn't right, Dalton. Everything feels wrong. I mean, not just what happened to . . ." My lip trembles. I can't say his name. "I'm scared. I feel like something terrible is coming."

"Take it easy, Mel. You're starting to sound like Bailey," Dalton says.

There's a knock at Dalton's open office door as Dad

walks in and immediately throws his arms around me, holding me, kissing my face.

"My baby girl," he says. "Are you okay?" Dad kneels before me as though I'm an altar of some kind and grips my hands. "I've been worried sick. Please tell me you're okay."

"She's still in shock," Dalton informs my dad. "Make sure she gets plenty of rest. In the meantime, we'll be investigating the matter and will keep you apprised of any new developments."

Bailey has joked about her brother's police lingo before, but I didn't realize just how excessive it's become. He doesn't seem like a real person.

Nobody seems real anymore.

"Can we go?" I ask.

"Of course."

Dad guides me to the door as though I'm at risk of falling at any second.

We pass a bizarre cast of characters on our way to the exit, but I can't take my eyes off a particular young boy, maybe twelve years old, lying on his stomach across a bench, his face anguished from his relentless dry heaving, a constant retching that echoes off the grand marbled walls of the police station.

I clutch tightly to my dad. If he's as disturbed by the boy as I am, he doesn't show it. *What's going on with everyone today?*

Dad steps forward and opens the door for me. The cool dusk air stings my cheeks.

"Where'd the day go?" I ask, gazing across Autumncrow's lamplit town square, only a faint swath of golden sunlight clinging to the horizon.

"It's getting dark so early these days," Dad says. "Let's get you home and have ourselves a warm bowl of soup."

The soup wasn't such a good idea after all. At the dinner table, staring down into the murky rust-colored broth filling the bowl, I felt like I was taking a peek inside Tommy's hollow skull. That was the last straw for me. I had to excuse myself from my parent's constant coddling and worried glances, or I was going to lose it.

"Okay, you can leave the table," Mom said, finally letting up. "But at least take the soup with you in case your appetite returns. Please."

I grabbed a Pop-Tart from the pantry instead and rushed off to my room.

But now that I'm here alone in bed with the smashed closet door reminding me of last night's bizarre occurrence, I wish I'd stayed in the kitchen. I felt much better hearing Mom say again and again that everything would be okay, even though I knew deep down it wasn't true.

Earlier, when she got home from work, Mom practically smothered me with affection, apologizing profusely for being so hard on me earlier. "My poor baby," she kept saying. "What a terrible day you've had."

The worst day of my life, I thought to myself. *It can't get any worse than this.*

Crumbs drop from my chin and sprinkle over my bedspread as I nibble on my Pop-Tart, ruminating on the last twenty-four hours and all the insanity that has transpired. No matter how many twisting avenues my thoughts take, the destination is always Bailey.

Apparently, her mother dialed mine this afternoon to ask if we knew where Bailey was. Mom proceeded to tell her about Bailey's uncharacteristic late-night phone call and all the questions Bailey asked about her parents' senior year. This only seemed to upset Cassandra more.

Jesus, Bailey . . . where did you go?

The idea that Bailey is missing and could be in danger makes me feel completely helpless and closed in. I have to do something. I have to help find her. What did Cassandra tell Dalton on the phone earlier? That she wanted to look for Bailey at school? It makes sense, I guess, given how the school seems to be a hub of constant chaos lately.

Maybe Cassandra is there now. Or maybe she's already back home with Bailey.

I reach for my phone and dial Bailey's house, praying as I twist the phone cord between my fingers that someone will answer and tell me she's safe and sound.

No such luck. After a few rings, the answering machine picks up. I curse under my breath and start to bring the phone down onto the cradle, but I stop short, blindsided by the bittersweet memory of so many slap-happy late-night calls I shared with Tommy when we were together.

I've never talked to Dennis on the phone, I realize, feeling gullible and very stupid. *I don't even have his number or his address. No way of reaching him.*

What if Bailey was right to be so worried about Dennis? What if he's responsible for what happened to Tommy? Dalton said Tommy's motorcycle was found in Mr. Grimley's cornfield, and that's right across the street from school, right where all of last's nights weirdness with Dennis played out.

If he's really that dangerous, then what might he try to do with Bailey?

That's it. I have to go to school and catch up with Cassandra, I tell myself. *I have to know if Bailey is okay. It's not like I can just lie here in bed and do nothing as my entire world comes apart at the seams.*

My parents would never agree to take me back to school after all that's happened today, nor would they even agree to drive by Bailey's house to see if she's returned home. But I've snuck out of the house many times before without anyone noticing. I can do it again.

As I stand from my bed, I wipe the nervous sweat of my palms on my trembling knees and steel myself before climbing out my bedroom window to face whatever fresh hell awaits me. There's no time to waste.

CHAPTER 22

I STAND AT THE FRONT STOOP of the Hagen residence. There is no car in the driveway, no lights on inside. Though I know there will be no answer, I rap on the door and wait, just to make sure, listening to the singsong of crickets give pulse to the night.

Nothing.

"Bailey, where are you?" I ask aloud.

I draw back and stand by the yard's elm, peering up at Bailey's closed bedroom window. I pick a pebble off the ground and heave, hitting the glass with a quiet *clink*. The window remains dark and shut off from the world. Shut off from me.

Ambling my way through the yard, I push through the gate and start toward town, taking the long way around to avoid Eleanor McGuffin's yard.

I'll never walk past that house again. Those strolls down Abraham Street are a thing of the past now. *A thing of the past* . . . just like Tommy Burke.

"He'll live on," I hear Ms. Price say from the not-so-distant future. *"He'll live forever in your heart and in the memories you made."*

That's what she said when Grammy died.

I try to think of the happy memories I made with Tommy when we were together, but all I uncover is the sight of his mangled corpse branded into my mind, a secret scar just for me.

I pass little Heather Gibson's house and spy the family sitting down to dinner through the open dining-room window. Rae is with them. It seems she spends more time with the Gibson family these days than she does her own. For tonight, I'm just happy she's not alone.

I remember how forlorn Rae appeared this morning, and how scared. I tried so hard to reassure her, but I realize now she has many reasons to be sad, and even more reasons to be afraid.

What if what Bailey says about Autumncrow is true? She's said many times that we are raised for slaughter here, brought up to smile through the worst until we've grown inured to the town's atrocities, willfully and blissfully ignorant until, at last, our own time comes: a flash of teeth in the darkness, a splash of red.

It's moments like this, alone in the cold dark of night, that remind me of how vulnerable I am, how small and temporary.

Mrs. Hagen's car is parked on the curb in front of Autumncrow High, nearly the exact place Dennis parked last night. The sight makes me shiver. If Bailey were here, she'd say this is an omen of some kind, that these little synchronicities are more than mere coincidence. I would have laughed her off before, but now, without her at my side, guiding me through this scary and unpredictable day, I'm picking up on these threads myself; like a blind person learning to rely on their other senses.

Stop it, I tell myself. *You're thinking about Bailey as if you've lost her. She's okay. It doesn't help to catastrophize. Bailey's okay. Bailey's okay. Bailey's okay.*

"Bailey's okay," I say aloud.

A breeze rustles the cornstalks across the street, and, for a moment, it's as though they're whispering to me: *"Liar. You're fooling yourself."*

I wipe sticky tears from my cheeks and trudge toward the front entrance, my heels clicking along the path through the graveyard. Each step is a descent deeper into hell with the school building sprawling before me like a dark beast, but I keep going. I tell myself that if Bailey and her mom are in there now, then so is the principal and possibly other staff members too. There's nothing to worry about. I'm not alone here.

"No, not alone," the field seems to say. *"Not alone at all."*

I take a deep, shuddering breath and pull on the handles of the front doors.

Locked. I guess I'll try the side entrance then . . .

I descend the steps and round the school to the side lot, the fallen leaves of the oak crunching under my feet like breaking bones.

BANG!

I stop and whirl around, clutching my chest.

A gunshot? No, something much bigger.

Cautiously, with my back pressed against the rough brick of the building, I ease my way to the corner and peer into the schoolyard, seeing nothing but the old oak tree, its skeletal arms dancing with the nightly gusts, casting faint shadows across Mrs. Hagen's vehicle and the cracked tombstones below. And then I notice the school's front doors, fully open to the night. Fallen leaves ride along on the breeze, clicking their way through the entrance like kids late to class.

No, not a gunshot. The doors must have blown open somehow and slammed against the brick.

But they were locked before . . .

Feeling no less anxious, I gaze through the entrance. The corridor stretches forever and ever, disappearing into the inky bowels of Autumncrow High.

"Mrs. Hagen? Bailey?"

My words, though whispered, somehow echo to the farthest reaches of the hall. There is no reply, just low-frequency rumblings that my mind interprets as either a generator kicking on . . . or a threatening growl.

I'm not breathing. I need to remember to breathe.

The entire outside world, in fact, seems to have held its breath. The winds have died down, and the cornstalks are no longer whispering among themselves. No more cricket song. No bats screeching overhead. Complete silence.

Breathe . . . Deep breaths . . . Breathe . . .

I don't take my own advice. I walk with hollow lungs into the darkness of Autumncrow High, leaving the doors open to let in as much moonglow as possible. As I pass the front staircase, I gaze upward to the balcony and see that the office lights are off. Whatever the reason for Mrs. Hagen's visit, it wasn't to check in at the office.

I walk on, passing the cafeteria, moving through the moonlit hall with its stained glass windows and marble columns, my strides becoming shorter and shorter as I grow more reluctant to go any farther. I soon find myself outside the library, its doors hanging wide open. But inside it is as dark as can be.

I sigh in frustration, finally finding my voice and calling out, "Mrs. Hagen?"

The silence is shattered. My voice ricochets off the walls and ceiling, filling me with regret.

Why did I do that? Why, why, why? I shouldn't be here. I've walked into a dangerous place, and I know it. Run. For God's sake, RUN!

A burst of adrenaline rushes through my veins as I realize what I'm doing—I'm standing in the halls of Autumncrow High after dark. Tommy's dead. My best friend is missing. My boyfriend is not who he says he is. I've even started seeing ghosts. And I've decided to come *here*?

I twirl around—fully prepared to flee for the exit—and let loose a horrified shriek when I see the same bloody girl from this morning just inches away from me, her face separated down the middle.

Both halves of the girl's face twist into a mass of sorrow

226

and rage. Her chin quivers as tears flood onto her crimson cheeks, her lips parting into a moan of agony. Her hands spring forward. One clasps the back of my head, causing a ripple of pain down my neck as her fingers worm around my hair. The other hand covers my eyes, blocking my vision entirely.

Before I can pull away, she pushes me down, down to the floor, then *through* the floor as if the linoleum were liquid, pushing me into a black abyss, submerging me fully before letting go.

I tumble deep, deep, deep into nothingness.

Thrashing.

Screaming.

CHAPTER 23

"I ANOINT THEE," says the little girl wearing the makeshift crown of daisies, "with the magical waters from the well of Crow mansion and welcome thee into this magical circle."

The second girl giggles from her crouched position on the forest floor, her long tresses of red hair shimmering in the golden daylight.

"Bailey? Is that you?"

Neither of the girls reacts to my voice. The redhead—the spitting image of Bailey at ten years old—continues to chuckle to herself as the hem of her baby-blue dress collects dirt.

No, this can't be Bailey. The Bailey I knew back then never would have worn something so prim. The dress, with its short, puffy sleeves, is something a schoolgirl would have worn decades ago.

The girl with the flower crown—also familiar to me, though I can't place her—huffs in annoyance. She's a scrappy little thing in dirtied overalls, which makes the pretty crown atop her head seem a bit out of place.

"Stop laughing!" she says. "You'll ruin the whole ceremony."

"You said 'magical' twice. You're only supposed to say it once." More giggling.

"I don't see how that really matters."

"You're right. Sorry." Bailey's lookalike smothers a grin and repositions herself. "I'm ready to be anointed now."

The other gets down to business, tracing her friend's forehead with foggy water taken from a Mason jar. "Dost thou pledge thyself to the coven of Autumn Crow?" she asks.

"I do."

"And dost thou pledge thine firstborn daughter to the coven as well?"

The kneeling girl is about to speak but pauses. "What if my firstborn is a boy?"

The anointer shrugs. "Then you better hope your next one is a girl. No boys allowed."

"Well, okay then. I do."

I check my surroundings and see that I'm in a small forest clearing. It's midday. The sun is at its highest peak in the autumn sky, filtering through the colorful leaves and showering the girls in radiant light. A blackbird sounds off in the distance, drawing my vision to a dilapidated and overgrown structure peeking through the trees.

The Crow mansion.

I've been here before on a few class trips, but that was after the house was restored in the mid-80s and turned into a museum. Before that, it stood abandoned, a ramshackle structure serving as little more than a hot spot for paranormal investigators and rambunctious teens looking for a place to haunt.

Which is exactly how it appears now.

If these girls don't notice me standing here in plain sight or hear my voice, and the house looks as it did a decade or more ago, then . . .

Am I really here? Am I dreaming?

"Is it done yet?" the red-haired girl asks.

The other girl glowers. "You are the most impatient witch there ever was, Cassandra Martin. And that's coming from me."

Cassandra Martin? Mrs. Hagen's maiden name is Martin.

My confusion gives way to terror.

What's going on here? Is this some kind of glimpse into the past? The thought sends shivers down my back.

"My knees are sore," Cassandra grumbles. "Mama's gonna ask about the bruises. I'll tell her it's all your fault."

"No snitching about the ceremony! It's secret. You tell her and I'll hex thee."

"Good luck trying to hex another witch, Macy." Cassandra smirks as she rises to her feet and rubs mud from her knees. "Especially now that I've been anointed. I have protection."

"Says who?"

"Says Autumn Crow. One day we'll actually conjure her, and she can tell you herself."

The scrappy girl, Macy, crosses her arms. "We need a third to close the circle before we can do that. Everyone knows a coven needs at least three witches."

"Oh, fine. When we get a third, that's when Autumn will tell you. She'll say I'm the most powerful witch of all."

"Bullshit."

Cassandra gasps. "Macy Welling! You watch your mouth, or I'll tell your mother."

"You better not!" Macy leaps at Cassandra and pushes her to the ground. The two begin rolling around in the dead leaves, wrestling and giggling.

The perfect fall afternoon.

In the blink of an eye, the scene changes. It's nighttime in a sleepy neighborhood. Moonbeams cascade through the thinning tree branches overhanging the street. The air is clean and crisp.

Two teenage girls are walking my way, communicating with exaggerated hand gestures. As they draw nearer, I recognize them as the girls from the forest, but they've grown into teenagers. I take one look at Cassandra and am overcome with a sadness I can't place. It's like seeing Bailey as she was only months ago, before her dad's disappearance turned her life upside down.

And the other girl . . .

It's her. The girl with the gnarly, bloodied face.

You put me here, I want to shout. *Why are you doing this to me?*

What are you trying to show me?

"So . . ." Macy pipes in after a brief gap in their conversation. "I see you're still wearing Kallum's varsity jacket."

The carefree smile melts from Cassandra's face. She doesn't respond, just pulls the jacket tighter around her body.

"Have you changed your mind then? About breaking up with Kallum?" Macy's tone is frosted at the edges.

"No," Cassandra says. "Finding the right opportunity has been a challenge, but I'm going to do it. Soon."

"Every moment spent with Kallum is a good opportunity, if you ask me. When are you going to bite the bullet and end it already? It's not like he's some kind of incredible catch. He treats you terribly, Cass."

"Yes, yes, I know." Cassandra rubs at her eyes, seeming exhausted all of a sudden.

"I don't mean to stress you out," Macy says. "I just care about you, okay? I want to see you free of him. We should burn that silly jacket so you don't have to wear Kallum on your shoulders anymore."

"I could never burn it," Cassandra says. "Kallum wouldn't be able to live without this thing. It's who he is. I just want to move on and get back to the person I used to be before Kallum Greendale took over my life. I'll give him his jacket back when the time is right."

"And when is that going to be?" Macy presses. "It's our senior year, for crying out loud. I hate to see you wasting it on that bozo. And for what? So you can pretend to be the perfect cheerleader with the perfect jock boyfriend? It's swell that you're Miss Popularity these days, but I'd really like to have the old Cassandra back."

Cassandra wipes a tear from her cheek. "Jeez, you can be really aggressive sometimes."

"It's tough love." Macy lays a hand on Cassandra's

shoulder. "I love you, Cass. You know that? You're my best friend."

Cassandra nods. "I know. Don't worry about me. I just need time. The worst thing you can do to someone like Kallum is injure his pride, and we've got homecoming next week. I'll let him have his night of glory. The crowd can cheer for him, and we'll pose for all the pictures. And once that's over, I'll find my opportunity. But I have to let him down easy. I haven't been putting this off because I don't want to break up with him. I've been putting it off be- cause..."

"Because you're scared," Macy finishes for her.

Cassandra nods. "I have to be very careful."

"I understand. But I do hope you go through with it sooner rather than later. I don't want this to spoil our Halloween."

"Well, that's just the thing," Cassandra points out. "Halloween falls on a Friday this year, the same night as the big game, and then we've got the Halloween bash. I'll be cheering at the game, and everybody on the team is going to be at the party... including Kallum. I imagine he'll still be licking his wounds after the breakup."

"You're right," Macy says with disappointment. "He'll probably ruin the whole evening for you."

"For both of us." Cassandra frowns. "Listen, I know you've been looking forward to the Halloween dance. You've been working on your Autumn Crow costume for months. Maybe you should go without me. That way at least one of us gets to enjoy herself."

"No way, I'm not going anywhere without you. Besides, I've been meaning to tell you, I have an even better idea for after the game. Why settle for dressing up like Autumn Crow when we can talk to the woman herself?"

Cassandra pauses. "What do you mean?"

Macy gives her a mischievous grin. "I mean, why not have ourselves an authentic Halloween experience at the Crow mansion? It will be spooky fun."

"You want to break in to the mansion?"

"It wouldn't be breaking in. It's easy to get into that place. Besides, we've explored it before. Remember our witching days back when we were kids? No one tried to stop us then."

"That's true." Cassandra ponders this for a moment. "I do miss those times, before life got so complicated. It was all fun and games back then."

"What makes you think it was all fun and games?" Macy grins mysteriously.

"Because it was. We were pretending to be witches. It was just kids' stuff."

Macy doesn't comment.

"It was just kids' stuff, right?"

"Well, we *were* kids."

Cassandra freezes again. "What's that supposed to mean?"

"I'm just saying, I think we made fabulous witches. With a little more practice, I bet we could have conjured Autumn Crow for real."

"You can't be serious," Cassandra says.

"Oh, I'm serious. I was thinking it might be fun to try it again one of these days."

"Try to contact Autumn Crow from beyond the grave?" Cassandra's voice creates an echo through the night.

"Shh! Do you want to wake everyone on the block?"

"If they'll come out here and knock some sense into you, then yes."

Macy crosses her arms and gives Cassandra a pointed glare. "What's with all the fuss? I thought you didn't believe in the supernatural."

"I don't know what I believe anymore. I've seen enough strange things in this town to make me question everything."

"Well, I'm just talking about a séance. You don't need to worry about Autumn rising from the dead to terrorize the town and eat all the babies," Macy teases.

"No, of course not. No one's coming back from the dead."

"If you really feel that way, then what's the harm in trying?"

"Where's this all coming from, Macy?"

"You know Felix Hagen from school? The one who works at the bookstore?"

"Yeah. He's a bit of a square, don't you think?"

"He's a sweetheart, and I'm pretty sure he has the hots for you—wink, wink, nudge, nudge. Anyways, I dropped by the shop last month and scoped out their occult section. He's very interested in this kind of thing."

"I see. So this has been brewing for a while."

"I've wanted to do this for ages! Oh, the questions I'd have for Autumn Crow! Like, did she really kill herself as Abraham claimed? Was she really a witch? And there are so many things I'd love to tell her too. I imagine she'd be shocked to hear the crazy things people say about her. I don't really buy into those bogus stories. At the end of the day, I bet she was a great gal, don't you think?"

"I don't know." Cassandra's eyes shift about uncomfortably, as if in fear that a sinister presence is watching from the shadows, stalking them.

Macy notices and rolls her eyes. "Don't be so skittish. Didn't you used to boast that Autumn Crow was going to proclaim you the most powerful witch of them all?"

"How many times do I have to tell you? I thought we were pretending."

"Well, I'm not pretending."

"Macy..." Cassandra looks at her friend like she doesn't know her anymore. It's a look Bailey has given me many times this past year. "It sounded like a fun idea at first, but I really don't know..."

"Come on! If you're in, that gives us a few weeks to make preparations. I'll tell Felix to study up on those spell books and help us figure out everything we'll need. This is going to be a Halloween to remember."

"I don't think so, Macy. I've had just about enough of this for tonight. I don't want anything to do with witchcraft. I'm spooked enough as it is with all the scary dreams I've been having lately."

"Oh please, Cass! For old time's sake." Macy puckers out her bottom lip pitifully.

Cassandra reluctantly gives in, realizing it's a lost cause. "Fine. Count me in, for old time's sake. I suppose I shouldn't be so paranoid. What's the worst that could happen?"

A shrill scream fills my brain as a new scene shatters the one before. I recognize Autumncrow High's dingy basement with its cursive signature of twisting and turning pipes, gurgling like the gut of a large animal digesting its prey. Another scream rips through the darkness of the basement as a shining ax blade plunges downward and lodges deep into Macy's horrified face.

I scream in shock and close my eyes.

No! Make it stop! I don't want to see anything else. Make it stop!

But it doesn't stop. The ground beneath me rumbles as some kind of energy surges outward and away, leaving an eerie stillness in its wake. For a moment, all is quiet. Then, suddenly, the rumbling comes roaring back with a vengeance. From above, the sounds of hell descend upon me. Crimson sounds. Sounds that flicker and throb and shatter. Mournful screams. Panicked voices crying, *"Help us! Help us!"* And then—

Laughter.

I open my eyes one at a time as relief floods my body. No more screams of terror and pain. I am somewhere else, somewhere that looks like a set from a Vincent Price movie: a dilapidated old bedroom with moth-eaten furnishings, broken windows, and rotting floorboards, made even spookier by the moonlight filtering through the open balcony doors. A circle of candles illuminates a trio of teens sitting in the middle of the room, hunkered over a large leather-bound book. Macy is there, and her face is very much in one piece. It's like time sprang forward, just for a moment, and then stepped back.

"These spells are a laugh," Macy says through tears of amusement. "What good does any of this do me? I want a spell to turn Kallum Greendale into the swine that he is. What use is a spell to 'fertilize the land'?"

"This book is really old," Cassandra says, wearing a black and burnt-orange cheerleading outfit. "We don't have to worry about these things now, but people back then used to harvest their own crops. If there was a drought or blight—"

"Then the townspeople were in deep trouble," an attractive boy with dark hair finishes. He gives Cassandra a lopsided grin, making her cheeks redden.

The boy before me may be much younger than the Felix Hagen I remember, but I'd know that grin anywhere. This is Bailey's dad.

"Well, that's no fun," Macy says. "Are you sure the resurrection spell is in here?" She begins furiously leafing through the book's brittle pages.

"Careful! I didn't get permission to take this from the store." Felix grabs the tome and pulls it toward him. "If this thing gets damaged, my boss will have a bird. He found it buried in a box of textbooks donated by the high school a few years ago. It's handwritten, completely one-of-a-kind, so be gentle. Also, for the fifth time, there is no resurrection spell. It's a summoning ritual. A simple séance."

He turns to a page toward the back of the book and points. "Here."

Macy lifts the book onto her lap and begins reading while Cassandra stands and stretches her legs. "Oops. I'm a klutz," she mutters, motioning at the floor. "My skirt messed up the circle."

"It's okay." Felix reaches inside a bag of salt and sprinkles a line of it at Cassandra's heels, connecting one broken end of the salt circle to the other. "All better. Just be careful not to break the circle during the spell, or we're toast."

"Let me guess," Macy says, "If that happens, Autumn Crow will come into the circle and possess us or something?"

"I don't know about that. I saw a spell in the book about binding a spirit to a living person, but it's complicated. For one thing, it requires something precious that belonged to the spirit in life. And that's assuming, of course, that any of this is actually true."

Cassandra and Macy stare at Felix in surprise.

"You mean, you don't really believe any of this?" Cassandra asks.

"I don't know. I've never actually tried it before, just read about it."

Macy sighs. "I hope we didn't skip the Halloween dance for nothing."

"I'd rather be here than at the dance," Cassandra admits. "After homecoming, I think I'm done with dances forever."

Macy reaches up and holds Cassandra's hand, giving it a reassuring squeeze. "You were right to break it off. You're too good for that knucklehead."

"You didn't see how upset he got. He said he'd make me regret it. I was so worried about spoiling homecoming for him, but now he thinks I waited until after the dance just to humiliate him. I wasn't trying to be cruel—I just couldn't do it anymore. What was I thinking? I should have found a better time."

Felix takes Cassandra's other hand. "No, you needed to get away from him. If he tries anything, we'll protect you."

She smiles down at Felix and leans forward, giving him a peck on the forehead. "I'm lucky to have you guys."

"This is sweet and all," Macy says, "but can we get down to business?" She pats the ground beside her, inviting Cassandra to sit.

Cassandra hesitates. "I still don't know about this."

"Is it the dreams again?" Felix asks.

Cassandra nods. "I've had them since I was a kid, but lately it's been every night. I'm looking down into an open grave with a closed casket inside. I don't know whose grave it is, but I'm filled with the deepest sadness imaginable, like I've lost everything in the world. Then I look around and realize I really have lost everything. I'm surrounded by hundreds of graves, and I know I'm the reason for it all."

"That's freaky, all right, but I can assure you it has nothing to do with this," Macy says. "It's only a dream, and this"—she motions at the circle—"is just a little All Hallows' fun. You said it yourself: kids' stuff."

"I guess so. Maybe I'm being silly." She shrugs and sits on the dirty floor with her friends.

"We don't have to do this," Felix tells her.

"No, it's okay. I shouldn't let my inner scaredy-cat get the best of me. Let's do it."

"Okay then, if you say so." Felix tells both girls to move to opposite ends of the circle so the distance between them is even, being careful to stay inside the ring, where it's safe. "Autumn spent a lot of time here in her final days, so I expect we'll get an answer before long."

I glance around the room as it dawns on me that I'm back at the Crow mansion, inside the house this time, possibly in the bedroom of Autumn Crow herself.

The teens begin the ritual, sitting cross-legged and closing their eyes as Felix speaks, inviting Autumn Crow to join them.

I want to shout at the teens to stop, warn them that something horrible is going to happen if they move forward with the séance. Like Cassandra, I feel it deep within my chest, a foreboding sense of dread. But I'm unable to speak.

"Autumn, if you're here, we ask that you come to us. Join us tonight on this All Hallows' Eve," Felix projects in a loud, clear tone.

Macy breaks out into a sudden round of giggles and Felix shoots her a daggerlike stare.

"Shh! You'll ruin the whole ceremony."

Now it's Cassandra's turn to laugh. "I seem to recall Macy saying the same thing to me once."

"Quiet, both of you," Felix whispers. "Listen!"

The girls grow silent, each glancing about the room with widened eyes, listening to the hum of crickets drifting through the open balcony doors and the croak of a frog off in the wilderness.

"What're we listening for?" Macy asks.

"Didn't you hear it? Footsteps. On the stairs," Felix says.

The girls stare at the closed bedroom door, listening for movement on the other side.

"I don't hear anything," Cassandra says.

"I don't anymore, but I definitely heard something."

"It was Autumn!" Macy exclaims. "She's responding to us. Keep going!"

Felix nods and closes his eyes. "Autumn? Are you here with us? Give us some kind of sign."

A gust of wind whistles through the balcony door, causing each candle to flicker out in tiny puffs of smoke.

Cassandra gasps and draws her knees to her chest. "Is she here?"

"I don't know," Felix replies. "It was probably just the—"

BANG! The bedroom door bursts open, causing the teens to jolt and cry out in surprise. A dark, bulky figure darts into the room and wastes no time, barreling straight for Felix and lifting him by the collar to his feet. The boy grabs a hold of his attacker's clenched fists and attempts to pry himself away.

"Felix!" Cassandra cries, leaping to her feet.

"No! Stay in the circle!" Felix demands.

"It's him!" Cassandra's voice is tight and panicked. "It's Kallum! He must have followed us here after the game."

The shape faces Cassandra, and though it's too dark to make out his features, I can see the whites of his eyes gleaming in the moonlight. "I warned you about these freaks," he growls. "I warned you!"

"Damn it," Macy says, tugging on Cassandra's skirt. "Look! He trampled on the salt. He broke the circle!"

Kallum Greendale, twisting Felix's collar tight around his throat, hauls the smaller boy out of the circle and toward the balcony overlooking the overgrown remains of the mansion's front garden. "I'll show you. I'll teach you for stealing my girl and poisoning her mind with all that witch nonsense!"

"Let go of me, you creep!" Felix's voice comes out a choked rasp as he strangles on his own collar, punching and scratching at Kallum's hands, fighting for freedom.

242

"Shut up!" Kallum throws his fist downward, colliding with Felix's nose with an audible pop. The boy's body instantly slackens, making it easy for Kallum to throw his unconscious body against the balcony's wooden railing.

"Oh my God, he's going to throw him over the edge!" Macy charges at Kallum and begins punching him with tiny fists, but he isn't the least bit bothered. He sneers at Macy and backhands her across the face, sending her flailing backward onto Autumn Crow's old mattress, raising a cloud of dust.

Cassandra stands in the center of the ruined circle, her hands hovering inches in front of her gaping mouth. Kallum glares at her from the balcony, moonlight gleaming in his icy eyes.

My stomach drops as everything Bailey told me about her nightmare boy and everything I know about Dennis— my dream boy—collide. When Dennis showed up at school, he was all warmth and kindness, but that quickly changed the night he put on what I now realize is his dad's dirty old varsity jacket. He became cold, manic, unhinged— a dead ringer for the boy glaring at Cassandra now, his face equal parts glee and rage, letterman jacket stained crimson from the blood gushing out of Felix's nostrils.

Though I don't understand how it's possible, this boy and the Dennis who dropped me off last night are not just father and son. They are one and the same.

"Stay," he orders, regarding Cassandra the way he would a pet, with dominion and a pointed finger. "You stay." He turns back to the task at hand, lifting Felix over the rail.

"No," Cassandra whispers as anger bubbles to the surface, burning away her fear. "NO!"

Rushing forward, she swipes the hefty spell book off the floor and lunges at Kallum. "I hate you! Do you hear me? I *HATE* YOU!" she screams, smashing the tome against the back of his head.

Kallum lets out a yelp of surprise as he releases Felix and twirls to face Cassandra.

"Cassie!" Now he is the animal, his expression steeped in hurt and betrayal.

"I HATE YOU!" Cassandra swings the book again, sideswiping Kallum across his stunned face.

Falling. Kallum is falling. He's flipping over the railing and plunging down, down, down into the unkempt garden. Cassandra drops the book and plugs her ears, blocking out the sickening crack Kallum's cranium makes as it connects with the ground below, instantly breaking his neck.

CHAPTER 24

KALLUM'S EMPTY EYES stare up at the puffy tufts of clouds kissing the moon as his lifeblood saturates the thirsty earth.

"He's dead," Felix says, abruptly pulling his fingers away from the pulse point on Kallum's bruised neck as though the dead boy might spring to life and bite off his fingers.

Cassandra, surrounded by tall weeds and wildflowers, gapes at Kallum's corpse with glazed eyes. "No. This isn't real. No, no, no. Not real. I'm only dreaming."

Macy pushes through the dense foliage of the garden and throws her arms around her friend, saying, "It's okay, Cass. It's all going to be okay."

Felix scrunches his eyes in pain and holds on to his head. "I think he broke my nose."

If Macy hears his complaint, she doesn't acknowledge

it. "What are we going to do? He's dead because of us. It doesn't even matter that it was in self-defense—we aren't supposed to be here. We're trespassing."

"It's just a dream," Cassandra reassures Macy. "It doesn't matter. None of this is real."

Macy and Felix share a worried look.

"We gotta get her to a doctor," Felix says. "And we have to go to the police and let them know what happened. We have no other—"

Kallum's cold, dead corpse sits up with a sharp inhale.

Felix cries out in alarm, falling from his crouched position and sprawling onto his back in the underbrush of the forgotten garden. Macy's scream of terror echoes through the darkness, scaring dozens of nesting birds from the surrounding trees. She grabs on to Cassandra, whose skin has paled several shades, matching the whites of her wide, unblinking eyes.

Kallum breathes like a drowned man taking his first gasps of air. He stares at the ground—*past* the ground—with bulging, inflamed eyes, grabbing fistfuls of grass and yanking upward, and repeatedly grinding his heels into the dirt as if to push himself away from something but getting nowhere.

"What'll I do?" he asks himself frantically. "What'll I do?"

Felix leaps to his feet and scampers backward, joining the girls and stepping in front of them, creating a protective shield in case Kallum attacks again. "He was dead a minute ago," he whispers over his shoulder. "I swear to God he was dead. He had no pulse. Zilch."

Kallum pays no mind to the trio. He rocks back and

forth, holding his dirty hands to his chest as tears drip onto his cheeks. "What'll I do? When I'm alone with only dreams of you that won't come true, what'll I do?"

"Kallum?"

Cassandra's voice pulls Kallum out of his trance. He looks up, finally taking notice of the teens, but there is no trace of malice in his eyes as before the fall. He's an innocent child after a traumatic event; severely rattled and incoherent. Small.

"What'll I do?" he cries with outstretched hands. "What'll I do?"

Cassandra pushes past Felix, effortlessly evading his and Macy's attempts to hold her back, and slowly walks toward Kallum, crouching low and laying a hand on his knee. She may have pushed through her shocked stupor, but her hands are still trembling.

"You—" Her voice catches in her throat. She swallows and tries again. "Kallum? Are you in pain? You took a hard fall."

Kallum, his face tilted skyward, closes his eyes and breathes deeply. A visible wave of peace washes over him, calming his shaking limbs. He seems to grow before my eyes, no longer tiny and helpless.

Cassandra, detecting the shift, pulls her hand away from Kallum's knee and shrinks back several paces. Macy reaches out and pulls Cassandra close to her and Felix.

"I know what happened. I remember what you did," Kallum says in an icy tone. "But now she's undone it."

The words hang in the air like oppressive humidity.

"Who?" Macy asks. "Who's undone what?"

Kallum opens his eyes and stares at them with a wide

grin. "She said it wasn't too late, that I could keep my life in exchange for a promise."

"Who?" Macy repeats. *"Who?"*

Bracing his hands on his knees, the boy climbs to his feet. Though he cringes in pain, he manages to stand. He stretches his arms, pops his neck, smooths his greasy hair away from his face, and gives the trio another knowing leer.

"She'll be seeing you soon enough," he says as he turns and limps through the garden and into the woods. "And I can tell you one thing," Kallum calls back to them. "You're all going to die."

Pain. Red-hot, fiery pain.

It yanks me out of the haze and lands me on my back outside the school library, staring at the vaulted ceiling overhead. The stark realization that this isn't another echo from the past hits me like a ton of bricks. This is the real here and now, and the pain shooting up my right leg is real too.

Though my head is as heavy as granite, I lift it from the floor and gaze downward at my feet. At first, I can barely make out the dark mass hunched over my lower half, but as my eyes adjust to the gloom, I'm able to discern finer details. Thick black fur covers the bulging muscles of the naked body crouched over me, its large pointed ears flanked by a set of ribbed horns, long and narrow. The hands—more human than not—clench around my right leg, digging long fingernails into my bleeding flesh. And the sounds, the horrible sounds of slurping and chomping, scuttle into my ears like black beetles looking for a home to infest.

I gasp, both from pain and terror, and the thing—the fearsome beast—responds. Its head snaps around, eyeing me like a predator with its milky white eyes that glow like headlights through morning fog. A bloody chunk of flesh—*my* flesh—falls from its open mouth chock-full of crooked fangs and lands with a wet slap against the gaping wound on my shin.

The beast draws in a wheezing breath and unleashes a bellowing roar, covering my face with gooey gobbets of spittle.

The only thing louder than the beast's angry cry is my scream.

I swing my available leg and kick the creature in the jaw, sending it careening onto its side. I'm free, if only for a second. Standing on trembling legs, I bite back the pain and limp down the hall as quickly as possible, dragging my wounded leg behind me. Where I'm headed is anyone's guess. I have no idea whether I'm running to the exit or deeper into the school. Everything around me is dark and hazy, blurred at the edges.

Just keep running. Don't stop, I plead with myself. *Don't let whatever that thing is catch you.*

That thing . . . Oh my God! It was eating me alive!

A panicked sob escapes my throat.

I try my hardest to tune out my own racing heartbeat, to listen for the sound of heavy breathing behind me, or the scrape of claws on the tiled floor, but all I hear is the clicking of my own heels.

No . . . not my heels. There's another set of footsteps behind me, clacking like typewriter keys. I glance over my shoulder as I sprint, seeing not a hideous beast but the slim form of a woman clumsily chasing after me, her blood-soaked sundress billowing around her knees, outstretched hands reaching, reaching for me, scratching at the air with overgrown fingernails. And where her head should be . . .

Oh God, it's gone! Her head is gone!

I fix my eyes onward, looking for a way out of this horrible nightmare, but the hall is stretching before me, getting longer, narrower, shrinking, expanding, swallowing me, pulling me deeper into the school's hungry maw.

I think I'm screaming, but that may be the shadowy figures hiding in the darkness, the little withered things that watch as I run past, woefully crying out, reaching with desperate hands like those of the headless woman chasing after me.

Watery bile burns my throat, and I swallow it back.

Let me out! Let me out!

The hallway continues to change. Lockers melt into pools of orange, stairways stretch into oblivion, and soon enough the hall is gone altogether, replaced by the grimy, twisted underground world that is Autumncrow High's basement. I don't stop to wonder how I got down here, how I could be upstairs one second and in the basement the next. I just keep running in fear that the headless woman or the horned beast may still be following behind, reaching for me with gnarled hands.

I shriek when something latches onto my shoulder and pushes me forward. I crumple to the earthen floor and watch as my worst fears materialize. Gone is the headless woman, but the beast is back, looming over me, its bare chest heaving with each furious breath, pale eyes gleaming with a voracious hunger.

The creature pounces, going directly for my throat. I grab its neck, knotting my fingers in its coarse fur and pushing with all my strength. The monster snaps at me, dribbling bloody saliva onto my face as I struggle to maintain my hold, to force its terrible teeth away from me.

Suddenly, the beast changes form, just as the hallway did a moment ago, shifting before my eyes into the headless woman and back again, over and over like a damaged filmstrip. For a split second, I even see Bailey's father in the creature's place, biting at me with gore-encrusted teeth and then flickering away.

"HELP!" I scream. "Somebody help me!"

My arms are weakening. Those strong jaws and bloody teeth are drawing nearer. Just when I think I can't hold on any longer, when I feel too tired to fight anymore, a sleek object whistles past me and sinks into the beast's shoulder, narrowly missing my own hands. I recoil as a doglike yelp of pain pierces the air. The evil thing falls backward, pulling at the ax lodged between its shoulder and neck, yanking it free. The safety ax clanks to the ground at the feet of the monster's attacker.

"Mrs. Hagen!" I sigh in relief.

Sweat dots the woman's upper lip and mats her tangled red locks. Dirt clings to her knuckles. She doesn't speak, just snatches the ax off the ground and holds it before her, silently daring the beast to attack. It glowers at her with those demonic eyes and emits a low growl as it slowly backs away on all fours, retreating to the shadows.

Its shoulder isn't bleeding, I realize before it disappears from view.

"What is that thing?"

Cassandra faces me, her expression grave. "We called it the watchdog when I went to school here, but I don't know what it is. Sometimes it's there, sometimes not. It can mimic any number of things, but always dead things. Dead friends. Dead teachers. It makes it hard to know who to trust."

"What do you mean?"

"That's probably what it wants," Cassandra continues, staring into the shadows of the basement, ignoring my question. She doesn't even seem surprised to see me here. It's like she was expecting me. "That's what the evil in this town wants. To confuse us, leave us unsettled and unhinged. Make us feel dizzy. Helpless. Isolated. It can't do that if we trust each other, so it tears us apart, makes sure we end up in the wilderness alone where there's no one to save us from being devoured." A tear rolls down Cassandra's cheek and fades into the collar of her shirt. "How am I supposed to protect my family if I can't even keep us together?"

The emptiness in her eyes suggests she's a million miles away. This isn't the Mrs. Hagen I'm used to seeing. For as long as I've known her, she's reminded me of a sitcom mom—infinitely strong and independent, putting her family first at all times. Nothing ever seemed to faze Mrs. Hagen. Even after her husband disappeared, she never let her chin fall—faithfully clocking in at the diner for shift after shift, ignoring the obvious strain she was putting on her body. I realize now that there was much more going on behind that exterior. This whole time, Cassandra has been harboring dark, painful secrets. I got a peek at those secrets earlier tonight, but there's more to learn. A lot more.

"Mrs. Hagen ... What are you doing here? Where's

Bailey? Tell me what's going on. Why—?" I groan at the sudden throb of my bloodied leg. The adrenaline had been keeping the pain at bay, but now it's flashing angry signals through my body, telling me I need urgent help.

"Shh . . ." Mrs. Hagen holds a finger to her lips and inspects my wound. "It's okay. I have all the same questions. I came here looking for Bailey. She's got to be here somewhere. I think *he's* here too."

"Who?"

"Kallum. Kallum Greendale."

The name sends chills skittering through my body as I recall the vision of the past that Macy gave me, how young Kallum Greendale wasted no time attempting to take Felix's life. He's always been a menace, and now . . .

"Dennis is Kallum somehow, isn't he?" I ask, feeling the impossible pieces come together in my mind. "Kallum probably never had a son to begin with."

"No, he had a son," Cassandra murmurs as she removes her jacket and ties it tight around my leg, creating a tourniquet to stop the bleeding. "Long after becoming the school custodian, he convinced a teacher to marry him. I don't know all the details, but it didn't last long. She left town to raise their baby on her own. So yes, Dennis is Kallum Greendale's son, but . . . I'm sorry, Melody. I'm afraid Dennis may be dead."

"Huh?"

Dennis. Dead. Dead Dennis. I roll the words over in my head, but they don't bite—they don't even sting. I think of Tommy's body too, his brains scooped out like jam from a jar, but I feel nothing. I can barely sense the pain in my leg anymore as Cassandra bandages me up. I've become numb inside and out. Completely numb.

Shock. That's what Bailey's brother said. I'm in shock.

"If I'm wrong and Dennis isn't dead," Cassandra goes on, looking me directly in the eyes for the first time, "then he's buried somewhere deep within his own body. Please believe me when I tell you that's not Dennis anymore. It may look like him, may sound like him, but don't be fooled. Kallum is a dangerous man. There's something evil inside him, an evil he's been feeding for years. He may even have sacrificed himself to it in some kind of last-ditch deal with the Devil."

"Sacrificed himself?"

"When he took his own life. Felix feared something sinister was afoot earlier this summer, and now I know he was right. I'm not sure how Kallum drew Dennis to Autumncrow, but that must have been his plan all along. That may even be why he wanted to father a child in the first place . . . so he could . . ."

Cassandra's face turns pale. It looks like she's about to be sick.

"So he could what?" I ask.

She swallows. "So he could take his son's body for his own and walk free again. Kallum gets what he wants, and so does Autumn Crow. He'll stop at nothing to keep his promise to her. We foiled him once before, but now his second chance is here . . . and that means so is Autumn's."

CHAPTER 25

"AUTUMN CROW? What—?"

Cassandra gives the tourniquet one last tightening pull and tugs me to my feet before I can say another word. I put too much weight on my leg and gasp in pain, almost falling over. Mrs. Hagen guides one of my arms around her shoulders and holds me steady as she leads me onward. All the while, my mind closes in on me.

The night of the séance, after Kallum's brush with death, he said he made a promise to someone—a woman. Could he have been talking about Autumn Crow herself? Is that what Cassandra was getting at?

Dread scratches its cold, dead fingers down my back as I realize even the most heinous tales about Autumn Crow may only be scratching the surface. If she's responsible for what's gone on tonight and everything that happened to Cassandra and her friends in 1959, what does that mean for us now?

"I want to go home," I say, breathless. "I want out of here."

"Deep breaths, Mel. I'll get you out of here soon. You need a doctor for that leg, but first I have to find my daughter."

"You think Kallum has her, don't you? You think he did something to her."

Cassandra doesn't speak, just keeps her gaze locked ahead as she effortlessly holds me upright.

"Answer me," I plead as tears burn my eyes. "Please tell me Bailey's okay. I need her. I need Bailey. I don't know what I'd do without—"

I freeze dead in my tracks, forcing Cassandra to stop with me. My mouth gapes, my hands tremble, tears stream down my cheeks as it dawns on me—*Oh God, no.*

Bailey is dead.

I fall away from Cassandra and tumble backward, backing against one of the slimy basement walls and grabbing my chest as pain stabs me in the heart.

"Melody. What is it? What's wrong?"

"That really was her in my bedroom last night." The tears welling in my eyes feel cold as frost. "It wasn't a dream. Oh my God, she's been trying to tell me to run, and I didn't listen."

I can barely speak. The knot in my throat is like a fist around my neck. It's choking me—like that bloody-faced man in my room last night, it's choking me.

The bloody-faced man . . .

"Kallum. That was him, wasn't it?" I utter in equal parts terror and grief. "Those eyes ... Those blue eyes. He was there in my room, like some kind of angry ghost."

I close my bleary eyes and grip my head as the world spins around me. "I don't understand. Nothing makes sense! I want Bailey. *Bailey!*" I'm shouting into the shadows now, calling out to her.

"Shh ... Please, you have to stop! He'll hear you," Cassandra whispers urgently. She's crying now, sobbing like I am. She knows it too—Bailey is gone.

A mournful wail leaves my throat. "I felt it. All day long, I felt she was gone, but I didn't know ... I didn't know."

"Please don't talk like this." Cassandra reaches out and pulls me to her chest, cradling me the way a mother would a small child. "Bailey isn't gone. She's here; I know she is. Kallum is using her to get to me. I'm the one he wants?"

"Using her to get to you how?" I ask through the sadness and anger. "Does this have to do with what happened to you at the Crow mansion?"

Cassandra lifts her red-rimmed eyes. "How do you know about that?"

"Macy. She showed me. She took me back somehow."

"Macy?" The name leaves Mrs. Hagen's lips in a melancholic whisper. "Where did you see Macy?"

"Upstairs. She showed me what happened that night. She probably would've shown me more, but that thing came along and brought me out of it." I point down the hall where we'd last seen the creature. "What happened to Macy?"

Cassandra stares past me, unblinking, like she's reliving a terrible memory. "He murdered her."

"Kallum?"

She nods. "We never should have conducted that sé-ance. When Kallum died that night, Autumn Crow was with us. She brought him back in exchange for a promise. Macy died trying to keep him from making good on it."

"What do you mean?"

"Kallum always had an angry side," Cassandra says, "but after that night, his anger consumed him. Autumn may have restored his life after the fall from the balcony, but there was something she didn't fix: his legs. His whole world had revolved around being an all-star athlete, and then that limp of his kept him from finishing out the sea-son. The Scarecrows went on to the playoffs without him. He grew resentful of everyone—his teammates, his class-mates . . . us most of all."

After what happened to Tommy, the mere mention of the Scarecrows causes bile to rise in my throat. I swallow it back and keep listening.

"But that wasn't all. He soon learned that whatever magic had preserved his life that Halloween night was rooted in the depths of this town, but that magic wasn't able to reach beyond Autumncrow's borders. If he ever tried to leave the valley, he'd die. He confronted me by the choking oak one afternoon to tell me so himself. He was so angry, I thought he was going to kill me. His college football dreams went up in smoke, and he ultimately dropped out of school. The three of us didn't see much of him after that. At least not until prom came around."

I remember what Bailey said on the phone about her parents being seniors in 1959, the year of . . .

"The Rapture," I say.

"Yes. Macy caught on that Kallum had chosen prom night to deliver on his promise to Autumn, the perfect opportunity to exact revenge on the entire school. We warned students, told teachers. No one listened."

"What was he planning to do?"

"We didn't know for sure, but the last thing he said that night at the Crow mansion stayed with me: 'She'll be seeing you soon enough.' If he intended to raise Autumn Crow from the grave, we had to stop him. Felix pored over every spell book he could get his hands on and determined our best bet would be a circle of protection around Autumn's crypt, to bind it against any other forces. So, on the day of the prom, the three of us went to Kilgore and cast the circle. Felix and I intended to stay at the crypt all night until we were certain we were in the clear, but Macy wasn't satisfied. She . . ." Cassandra pauses, looks down in shame. "She went to the prom to keep an eye on things . . . in case Kallum showed up. I shouldn't have let her go alone. The next thing we knew, she was dead. My best friend . . ." She closes her eyes and breathes deeply.

"And you think Kallum did it?"

"I know he did. He was counting on her confronting him so he could feed her to the town. Her death—the death of an innocent—was the last thing he needed to make it all happen."

The ground suddenly rumbles beneath our feet, vibrating the walls, shaking loose bits of stone from the ceiling. The quaking ceases, but I have a feeling there's more to come.

"Was that an earthquake?" *Have we ever had an earthquake here before?*

"We should keep moving," Cassandra says instead of answering my question.

As she leads me along the dark corridor, I try to ignore the sounds of scurrying little feet in the darkness—creatures likely stirred from their hiding places by the tremors.

"So then ... did you not stop him after all? I'm confused."

"No, we kept him from resurrecting Autumn that night ... but at a higher cost than we ever could have imagined."

"Are you talking about the Rapture?"

Cassandra hesitates. For a moment I worry she's going to steer the conversation in yet another direction—but then she pauses in her tracks and gazes at me with the saddest eyes.

"What I'm about to tell you is something I hoped to take to my grave, but it's no longer the time for secrets, no matter how ashamed I am to speak them." She breathes deeply. "There is an evil entrenched in the soil of this town, and when it feeds, it spreads. Autumn was laid to rest in Kilgore to keep her safely out of its grasp, but Kallum used Macy's death to give the evil a wider reach ... all the way to Autumn's crypt. Felix and I saw it happen, saw it race through the ground like a shockwave, headed right for us ... and then we watched in horror as our protective circle sent it bounding right back to the source. The details of what happened next are murky ... because no one who witnessed it was ever seen or heard from again."

Chills race down my spine as I step back in shock. "You're saying the circle around Autumn's grave caused the Rapture?"

There it is again, that guilt on Cassandra's face. "We

had no way of knowing what would happen. We were dumb kids dabbling in things we didn't understand. But it was our fault."

I open my mouth to speak, to console Cassandra and tell her she's being unfair with herself, but I can't form the words. Though they were only trying save the town, Cassandra and her friends ushered in the most catastrophic event in Autumncrow's dark history.

Cassandra continues, her eyes bloodshot with tears. "It was our fault the Rapture ever happened and our fault Autumn poisoned Kallum's mind in the first place. If we hadn't held that séance, I'd still have my best friend. And my husband."

"Is Mr. Hagen . . . ?" I don't want to speak the word. All this time, Bailey was convinced her dad was still alive somewhere. I wanted to believe it too, but I think we all knew deep down that it wasn't so.

"He's dead," Cassandra whimpers. "I don't know that for sure, but I can feel it. This summer, when we caught wind of Kallum's death, I thought we were finally free. All this time, we'd been trapped in Autumncrow too, keeping watch over things in case Kallum ever tried something again. I was ready to pack up the kids and get out of here . . . but Felix worried it wasn't really over yet. He needed to make sure. So he went to the school that night . . . and never came home."

"What do you think happened to him?"

Mrs. Hagen peers into the darkness behind us. At times, it feels like the beast is still back there, hiding in the shadows, trailing us.

"I try not to imagine it," she says.

A sickness worms in my gut when I picture Felix Hagen's crashed van, the broken windshield spattered in blood.

A scene plays in my mind's eye like a movie. A dark shape zips across Felix's path, causing him to swerve and crash into the choking oak. The watchdog bursts through one of the windows and bites into his throat, tearing him limb from limb and devouring him, leaving nothing but a bloody crash and a sliver of hope for his impossible return.

"This town is hungry, Melody. The more it eats, the more it craves," Cassandra says. "Kallum kept it fed for decades, and now Autumn is more powerful than ever. Except . . ." She halts.

"Except what?"

"Except she may be after something more." Mrs. Hagen squints through the darkness. "Do you see that?"

I follow her outstretched finger and see a light streaming into the hall from a room up ahead, a light that flickers like fire.

"The boiler room," I say.

Cassandra swallows. The light dances in her eyes like fiery coals. "Be very quiet and hold on to this." She slides the wooden handle of the ax into my palm. "Don't be afraid to use it. Understood?"

I nod, and together we approach the boiler room, terror pulsing in my veins. What's waiting in that room for us? Bailey, bound and gagged, waiting for us to rescue her? Dennis?

No, not Dennis, I remind myself. If everything Cassandra said is true, then Dennis is gone, his body taken over by Kallum. How could he do such a thing to his own child? Just thinking about it makes me as nauseous as the idea of Autumn Crow gnawing at her own baby.

When we reach the doorway, Cassandra places a hand on my shoulder and peeks inside. She's trembling.

"What do you see? Is it Bailey?"

"No. But it looks like someone's been living here."

Cassandra steps into the room, and I reluctantly follow, using the ax as a crutch. Illuminating our surroundings is an old coal-burning furnace, flames raging inside, making the air feel dry and oven-like. A dirty old mattress lies in a corner, surrounded by food scraps, crushed pop cans, and empty bags of chips. I recognize the half-eaten remnants of a cafeteria pizza topped with sparse cheese and cubed pepperoni meat.

Dennis has been crashing here. That's how he knew exactly which classroom window would be unlocked when he brought me here last night. He knew because he left it unlocked himself. Is his mother even here with him as he claimed? Probably not if he was never enrolled in school.

Everything he's told me has been a lie.

Cassandra stands at the other end of the room, studying a workbench bookended by metal cabinets and cluttered with a busted boombox and various maintenance tools: garden sheers, a scythe, hammers, screwdrivers, and some kind of long saw with a rusty-looking blade. She runs her finger over its surface, and a forlorn expression spreads across her face.

"What is it?" I ask.

"This looks like blood."

She's right; it does. A dark part of me wonders what it would take to cut through a person's skull. Would a saw like

263

this suffice, or would one need something more powerful?

Don't think like that, I scold myself, but it's impossible not to. After what I've seen today, I don't think my mind will ever be the same again.

"Are you sure he's here?" I ask. "I didn't see Dennis's car outside."

"Could be parked in the woods behind the school," Cassandra suggests. "He's here. I can feel him."

We jump in surprise when the boombox on the work-bench bursts to life. Cassandra joins me on my side of the room, and we watch as the tuner turns all on its own, scanning through static until settling on a melody I instantly recognize as the song my Walkman was playing earlier this morning.

"What'll I do when I am wond'ring who is kissing you? What'll I do?"

"What's happen—?" The word dies on my tongue when I hear footsteps in the hall. Heavy footsteps accompanied by deep grunts, heavy breathing, and something else... Sliding? Dragging?

"It's him," Cassandra whispers. She puts her hands on either side on my face and looks deep into my eyes. "I want you to hide in one of those cabinets over there. Don't come out until I tell you to. If anything should happen to me, stay put until you know for sure it's safe. And if he finds you, kill him." She grips her fingers over mine, forcing me to grip the ax more tightly. "Do you hear me? Kill him."

Tears are already streaming down my cheeks. "I'm scared," I say.

"Me too." Cassandra's chin quivers. "But I've known for a long time this day would come. It's time to face him and protect what I have left."

Mrs. Hagen places a kiss on my forehead and whispers, "I don't have much time, so I can only say this once: I knew you'd be here tonight, Melody. I wasn't there for Macy when I should have been, something I've regretted to this day and will never be able to make right. History has a way of repeating itself, especially in Autumncrow, but I knew you'd be different. You thwarted the cycle tonight. Keep doing it. Do you hear me? Break the chain. Fight. And if all else fails—"

The ground rumbles again and the music from the radio grows louder, drowning out the footsteps.

"What'll I do with just a photograph to tell my troubles to?"

"If all else fails," Cassandra repeats, *"run.* Don't hang around like I did. You protect what's yours and start running. Don't ever stop. Now go. *Hide!"*

I do as she says. I limp across the room, trying to keep my balance on the shaking floor, and open one of the metal cabinets. One side is made of shelves crammed with landscaping equipment, but the other is long and narrow, a space to hang a jacket. I squeeze inside, and Mrs. Hagen closes the doors behind me. Much like the school lockers, there are small slits in the door at eye level.

Cassandra peers inside the cabinet and whispers, "Thank you for being a friend to my girl," then pulls away and presses her back against the wall beside the open doorway. She holds a sharp object to her chest—the saw from the workbench, the one encrusted with blood.

Suddenly, the rumbling ceases, as does the music. Silence engulfs the room. Complete silence. No more footsteps in the hall. No more grunting.

Where is he? Oh God, where?

I hold my breath, feeling the thrum of my pulse in my temples, the nervous contractions of every muscle in my body. I stifle a gasp as something stirs in the dark doorway. A set of bloodied fingers comes into view, grasping the doorframe. A head peeps around the corner. The light from the furnace reflects off the glistening, mangled features of a man's face, blue eyes scanning the room.

It's him. Kallum Greendale.

Cassandra was right; this boy is Dennis no longer. His demeanor is rough and surly, just like the phantom man who attacked me in my room last night. Dream or not, the threat was real—Kallum Greendale is back.

"Hello?" he rasps. His swollen, scabbed lips crack with the movement. Fresh blood trickles down his chin.

What happened to his face?

"Anyone here?" he asks, leering. His once beautiful teeth—those that remain, at least—are chipped and jagged.

Mrs. Hagen presses harder against the wall, gripping her weapon with shaking hands. Kallum doesn't seem to see her. He waits for a moment, watching, listening, before pulling away from the boiler room and resuming his task.

There it is again—that sliding noise.

He pulls, tugs, yanks a dark mass past the doorway and out of sight, singing to himself, "What'll I do when you are far away and I am blue? What'll I do?"

Cassandra shuts her eyes tight as a tear rolls down her cheek.

Now that Kallum is gone, venturing deeper into the basement's spiderweb of corridors and rooms, I start to open the cabinet door. Cassandra stops me, holding her hands out before her and shaking her head. I pull the door shut and freeze.

"Stay put," she mouths. I watch as she tiptoes to the doorway.

"What'll I do?" Kallum's voice echoes.

Holding out her hand once more, insistent that I stay, Cassandra steps into the hall, swallowed by the darkness. I wait, listening intently, hearing nothing but Kallum's sing-song voice fading into the recesses of the basement before vanishing altogether.

As I stand here watching, listening, time gets away from me. My shoulder muscles cramp in the limited space. Razor blades of pain rip and tear at my wounded leg. I bite down, urging the sting to subside.

Mrs. Hagen, where are you? Please, come back. Let's just leave. We shouldn't be here. Let's go back to the police station, tell them what we know, let them handle it.

I'd laugh at my own idea if I weren't so terrified. *The police won't do anything, Melody. Not a damned thing.* They never do in this town. Come to think of it, Dalton was awfully nonchalant about his own sister's disappearance, despite having just discovered the mangled corpse of one of her classmates. It's like he's under a spell. All the adults are under a spell.

Even Cassandra Hagen.

"Don't stay like I did." She told me. *"You protect what's yours and start running. Don't ever stop."*

I can't run if I'm stuck in this cabinet, I decide.

Slowly, so as not to make a noise, I push open the door

and step into the stuffy room.

That's when a sharp scream rips through the silence.

My heart leaps into my throat. I fall back against the cabinet as my hands rise to my chest. "Mrs. Hagen?" I whisper.

Another scream—long, desolate, and full of anguish.

Full of despair.

CHAPTER 26

NO, NO, NO... PLEASE NO, I pray as I hobble down the corridor toward Cassandra's gut-wrenching screams, toward another open doorway emanating light—a deep red light. Unlike the furnace's fiery glow that tosses and turns like a dreaming child, this light *stays.* It clings, holds tight to every surface as if it means to smother, to drain all other color from anything it touches.

"My girl! My baby girl!" Cassandra's wailing reaches my ears, but I hear it as if deep in slumber. I should react, but rest is easier. It's far too warm. I can't climb the dark slopes into wakefulness.

I don't want to.

A few feet from the door, I drop the ax and fall to my knees. I barely feel the dagger of pain in my leg as my knees

269

hit the ground. The ache in my rib cage is unlike any pain I've ever felt before.

"What'll I do when you are far away . . . ?"

The song is in my head now, filling the space between my ears with those somber lyrics. The stone in my throat sinks into my gut, weighing me down.

"My girl! My baby girl!" Cassandra's words turn into another guttural wail of agony.

My head is fuzzy and light, my body heavy. So heavy. I lean my head against the damp wall.

I'll rest for a minute. I just need a little rest.

I'm about to close my eyes when I feel the skitter of spider legs on my cheek. I slap at it, but my hand comes back wet with tears. No spider.

"What'll I do with just a photograph to tell my troubles to?"

Looking past my damp fingers, I see a trail of smeared blood on the ground below, reminding me of whatever— or whomever—Kallum had been dragging down the hall before the screaming started. The trail travels the entire length of the corridor, past the door of the boiler room, and curves into the red room—where a Bailey-shaped shadow now hovers in the doorway. She stares listlessly into the red light, spine curved, head hanging sideways, right arm missing—exactly as she appeared last night in my bedroom window.

Translucent in the gloom, she listens to her mother cry, watching quietly until at last she speaks, addressing the red light in a hollow whisper: "I don't think I'm here anymore."

With that, she turns and joins the shadows of the basement, leaving me alone on the cold dirt floor, my hands reaching out to her . . . reaching . . . reaching . . .

"When I'm alone with only dreams of you that won't come true, what'll I do?"

CHAPTER 27

I CRAWL TO THE DOORWAY, into the eerie red light, sliding my injured leg behind me, gripping the wooden handle of the ax like my life depends on it. I'm blinded at first by the harsh burning glow, unable to see anything else. I squint, shielding my eyes with one arm until I can see two silhouettes in the center of the room, one kneeling and holding on to the other. Clinging. Crying.

The light doesn't have a source. It's as if death itself has spilled over and taken on a color of its own.

Red. The purest red.

Circling Bailey's lifeless body are candles, dribbling wax—also red—onto the earthen floor. Beside the circle of candles is a long object concealed by a dirty cloth.

Cassandra rocks back and forth, cradling Bailey, running her fingers through her hair, whispering in a low, quivering tone. "I've got you, my girl. I've got you. I'll make it right. I promise, I'll make it right."

"I knew you'd be here, Cassie."

Mrs. Hagen starts at the sound of the raspy voice and stands, letting Bailey's head drop limply to the floor like a ragdoll. I want to reach out and touch her, to close her unblinking eyes so she can sleep. But I can't without being noticed, so instead I say, "I'm here, Bailey," in a whisper that barely leaves my lips.

"*You!*" Cassandra growls, holding the saw before her, the sadness in her voice eclipsed by pure, seething rage.

Kallum leans back into a corner of the room, seemingly relaxed despite the ruined state of his face. He calmly points a finger at the saw. "That's mine."

"*She* was mine!" Cassandra shouts through gritted teeth, directing a firm finger at her daughter's body. Tears of rage flow from her eyes.

"Wrong." Kallum's calm posture shifts. He pushes away from the corner and leans forward. His crystalline eyes bore into Cassandra's. "She was never yours. You gave her away. She belongs to Autumn. Just as you do."

"Liar!" She pounces, swinging the blade at him in a crisscross motion.

Kallum dodges her attack and rolls past her, dragging a shiny object across her shin. Cassandra unleashes a howl of pain and doubles over, covering the blood gushing from her sliced leg.

I smother a gasp with my hand.

She needs my help. I have to get up. I have to help her.

But I'm so tired—so weak. I feel imaginary.

Kallum laughs gleefully and wriggles a switchblade in front of his face. "Remember this? I'll bet you do. Summer 1958. We carved our names into the big tree in the town square, the one where they used to hang people." He wipes the bloody blade clean on the hem of his tattered letterman jacket. "I got you home late that night and had to make up that story about a flat tire."

Cassandra gives him a venomous glare. "Tell Autumn to bring her back."

"I'm afraid I can't do that."

"She brought you back. Tell her to do the same for Bailey. I'll do anything."

Kallum places the blade of the knife on his bloody chin and ponders this. "Anything?"

"Yes, anything!" She's sobbing again. Desperate tears. "Tell Autumn to take me." She presses her hands to her chest. "Me! That's what she's always wanted, right? A vessel." Cassandra winces in pain as blood spurts from her cut. "I know Autumn and I are connected. The ritual Macy and I performed as kids . . . it did something to me."

"Those pesky bad dreams," Kallum says with a dark grin.

"The water from the well . . ." Mrs. Hagen's eyes find me. I sense the panic in her stare—a look that says, *"I told you to stay!"*

Doing all I can to fight the fatigue, I stand, using the ax as leverage. *I'll do it,* I tell her silently.

She quickly looks away from me. "Tell Autumn she can have me . . . but she has to bring my daughter back."

"I think you're forgetting something," Kallum says, kneeling and pushing the strings of hair from Bailey's face.

"Don't you dare lay another finger on my girl!" Cassandra orders. Then she turns to me and mouths, *"Wait."*

I nod and hang back in the hall, out of sight.

Kallum smiles and withdraws his fingers. "As you wish." He reaches for the covered object beside her and pulls a skeletal limb into the light.

"What is that?" Cassandra is unable to hide her fear.

"Funny you should ask. I paid a visit to a crypt in Kilgore last night. In this new flesh, you see, I'm free to roam wherever I please. This," Kallum declares, "is Autumn Crow's right arm. Her left was 'bound in holy matrimony' and unfit for our purposes tonight, but fortunately this one will be more than adequate."

He places the arm beneath Bailey's severed elbow. "Do you recall pledging your firstborn daughter to Autumn Crow?"

"I was a child!" Cassandra booms.

"Doesn't matter. Autumn heard you. A promise is a promise."

"NO!" Cassandra strikes again, flinging herself at Kallum and slashing furiously. He dodges and makes a clean cut across Cassandra's cheek with the switchblade, just below her right eye. Blood trickles down her face like the red wax of the burning candles.

"I have to say," Kallum sneers, motioning to his own face, "your daughter put up a much better fight."

I took down at Bailey, at her bloodless face, her muted eyes ... There is still power in those eyes—an undying power.

"You did fight, didn't you?" I want to say. *"You fought*

275

hard. So, so hard. You never stopped."

Cassandra ignores the gushing cut in her cheek. "What do you stand to gain from all this, Kallum?" she asks. "Don't you see that Autumn is using you? She kept you alive just to see you stripped of everything that ever mattered to you, trapped in the place you hate most, surrounded by constant reminders of the glory days you squandered and lost. She made you into a soulless monster, her own little henchman. You sacrificed your own son for her—and what do you get out of it? A second chance at some delusional teenage fantasy you never outgrew? You've already turned yourself into roadkill! You're nothing but a pathetic worm. Mark my words, Kallum: once you've outlived your usefulness, she'll kill you too."

"Shut up!" Kallum barrels at Cassandra, tackling her around the midriff and collapsing with her to the floor. They scuffle—a blur of limbs, cold metal, and fury.

But I stay enraptured in Bailey's stare.

"Run." Her lips don't move, but it's her voice. I'd know it anywhere.

I lift the ax blade from the floor and place it on my shoulder.

"No," I say. "You never ran, Bailey. Not once."

I step into the harsh light of the room. My heart is suddenly calm for the first time all evening. "You never ran. I won't either."

Kallum is on top of Cassandra, pinning her hands to the ground, loosening the saw from her grip. He leers down at her. "Give it up, bitch. It's over."

Cassandra glances past his shoulder, watching as I lift the ax above my head, but the expression in her eyes is not one of relief—it's defeat.

"Yes. I'm afraid it really is over," she whispers.

I let the ax fall, bringing it down, sinking the sharp, heavy blade into Kallum's spine with a sickening crack.

Kallum gasps. He freezes, staring down at Cassandra in shock. Then he moves a hand to his back, feeling the cold steel lodged between his shoulder blades.

Cassandra uses her newly freed hand to shove him away. He drops onto his side as his body spasms, arms and legs twitching as though electricity were surging through his entire body. And then nothing. Quiet. Stillness. His unblinking eyes glaze over as blood dribbles from the corner of his mouth, adding to the ever-growing puddle on the bare floor.

Dead. He's dead.

I killed him.

I look down at my hands, at the curves of my fingers, the lines in my palms. They look the same, but they don't feel like my hands anymore.

"It's over," Cassandra says. "It's done."

I lower my hands and search for my voice, but it comes out soft and childlike: "We stopped him."

"No, Melody. We didn't stop anything." Cassandra rolls onto her side, away from Kallum, and utters a sharp gasp as she reaches—stretching out her hand until she finds Bailey's. She squeezes it tightly and closes her eyes, holding fast to her daughter's icy fingers. "Now I understand—this was her design all along. Autumn found a way."

"What do you mean?"

Cassandra doesn't answer.

"Mrs. Hagen?"

Silence. She doesn't move. Doesn't open her eyes. It's like she's fallen asleep.

That's when I notice the blood. It blossoms across her chest, away from the hilt of Kallum's switchblade, pooling around her and seeping into the ground.

"Oh my God!" I crouch and shake Cassandra's shoulders. I lightly slap her cheek. "Mrs. Hagen! Mrs. Hagen, wake up!"

She doesn't respond.

My chin quivers. "Mrs. Hagen, please. I can go get help. I'll call an ambulance. Just please wake up. Please—"

I pause.

What was that? I look at Cassandra's hand, the one grasping Bailey's. *Is it moving? Are her fingers really moving?*

No. Not *her* hand—Bailey's.

"Bailey? Oh my God, *Bailey!*"

My dead friend's fingers squeeze and contract, releasing her mother's hold. I slosh through the puddle of blood on the hard floor, relief flooding my heart. *Please be okay. Please!* I'm about to grab Bailey's shoulders and shake her awake—when I notice her right hand is moving too.

But that can't be . . . Bailey's arm had been severed. And in its place, Kallum put—

"Oh God . . . No."

Cassandra's last words replay in my head: *"Autumn found a way."*

Autumn's dry, brittle bones have become flesh, melding with Bailey's arm at the elbow. I cover my mouth, smothering a gasp of horror as I watch the muscles in Autumn's hand ripple under the skin, flexing as the fingers twitch.

And Bailey's body . . . it's beginning to rise. It lifts off the floor into the air, her arms and legs dangling beneath her like dead weight.

A puppet on strings.

I sit back, gaping in terror at Bailey's levitating body as the ground begins to rumble again. All the while, the red light glows brighter and brighter around me. I squint and cover my eyes until, at last, the ground stills and the light finally fades—fades into nothingness.

I'm in darkness now. I can barely see the blue smoke wafting from the extinguished candle wicks, can barely discern the dark figure standing where Bailey's body once lay, peering down at me with glowing red embers where her eyes should be.

"Autumn found a way."

Terror grips my body as the dark figure saunters toward me, those evil red orbs floating closer and closer.

That's not Bailey anymore . . . Bailey is gone.

Autumn Crow got her wish.

I crawl backward, aiming for the doorway but hitting a wall. "No, no, no!" I'm scrambling sideways now, hugging the wall, feeling for the doorway.

I need to get out of here!

A hand shoots out of the blackness, stopping me in my tracks. Icy cold fingers wrap around my jaw, jolting the back of my head against the cement wall. Pain clouds my senses, but I fight my attacker's hold, punching and kicking . . . hitting nothing but air—air as cold as the grave.

As those terrible red eyes glow just inches from my face, burning into me, another hand latches onto my leg and presses into my wound. I let loose a sharp cry of agony, but

I'm cut short when the figure slams the back of my skull against the wall once more. My eyes roll back in my spinning head.

As my mind surrenders to unconsciousness, those frightening red eyes give me one last hateful look. Then, out of the darkness, comes a foreboding message, spoken in a dry, gravely tone: "I'll be seeing you."

CHAPTER 28

WHEN I COME AROUND, I am alone with two bodies. Bailey is gone.

The red light has vanished too, exchanged for the soft glow of candlelight. The candles are burning again, as though they'd never been snuffed. Everything is back to normal—or so it appears.

No . . . nothing will ever be normal again.

My throbbing head feels as if it weighs a hundred pounds, but nothing is heavier than the forlorn ache in my chest.

I stare at Cassandra's body and wonder how long she'd known what Autumn intended for her baby girl? Was it only now that she finally grasped it, or had the possibility plagued her before Bailey was even born? She couldn't have understood as a child what it meant to pledge her daughter to the witch, but at some point she must have begun to fear what she might have set into motion. Had she ever tried to warn Bailey?

It isn't fair. Why did it have to be her and not her mother, even after Cassandra offered to take her place?

Was Bailey different somehow? Special?

She was special to me.

I bring my knees to my chest, hugging them, wishing to go home to my bed but not wanting to move from where I am.

"I'm sorry," I say. "I'm so sorry I didn't listen to you."

"M-Mel . . . Melody?"

I scramble to my feet in panic.

Kallum is moving. He lifts his head from the pool of blood around him and looks right at me, reaching out his hands. "Melody?"

I snatch the pruning saw off the floor and hold it up in defense. "Stay right there," I bark at him.

"Melody, it's me," he says. "Me."

I lower the saw. "What?"

"You have to destroy the jacket." His eyelids droop, but beyond them—where there was blue earlier—are those sweet brown eyes I remember falling for the day we met.

"Dennis?"

"The jacket," he whispers. "Burn it, shred it—I don't care how you do it."

I drop the saw and kneel at his side. "Is it you? Is it really you?"

He nods.

"I'll—I'll get help."

"No, it's too late. I'm a goner. Always was." Dennis coughs. Blood erupts from his throat, spattering my face, my jacket, my hands. "Sorry," he mutters.

My face contorts in sadness. "Shh. It's okay."

"It must be cursed or something. He meant for me to find it. He lured me here, got in my head somehow. There was a voice that called out to me in those dreams I'd been having, dreams of this place. Once I got to town, I heard it all the time. 'Come, Dennis. Follow me in.' I thought I was going crazy. It sounded just like my—" He begins to cough again, uncontrollably.

"Like your dad?" I ask, stroking his blood-soaked hair.

"No, it sounded like my mom," he says with a whimper. "She died last year after my eighteenth birthday. I lied to you, Melody. I lied about a lot of things. I wasn't really—" More choking.

"I know. I understand," I tell him. And I do. What else would he have told me—that he was hiding out in the school basement, searching for the source of a voice calling his name? I would've had him committed.

"I didn't mean to fall for you, Melody. I never meant to cause any trouble," he says. "I've just been alone for so long. And when I heard Mom's voice, I thought—" He pauses and stares at the ceiling for a long time.

"Dennis?"

He looks at me again with doleful eyes. "I thought she came back for me. I missed her so much. I thought she came back . . ."

He doesn't stir after that. Doesn't blink or breathe.

With shaking hands, I place my fingertips on his eyelids and close them.

"I'll do it, Dennis," I whisper. "Don't worry. I'll burn it."

I pull the jacket off Dennis's body, struggling to free it of his limp arms, struggling even more to work around the ax protruding from his back. I don't want to remove the blade. I don't even want to look at it . . . don't want to see what I did.

If I'd burned the jacket before killing Kallum, would Dennis still be with me?

It's an impossible question, and I may never know the answer. Perhaps that's for the best.

At long last, I have the jacket in hand and carry it down the hall.

I enter the boiler room and wrap the jacket around my hand, using it to open the sizzling grate of the furnace. The hungry flames toss and churn, reaching out as though they mean to lick my flesh. I pull back and toss the jacket inside, letting the flames engulf it, singe the embroidered lettering, devour every thread until there is nothing left but embers and ashes. My mind turns to Bailey, Tommy, Cassandra, Dennis . . . all those I lost today.

And those who may be next.

CHAPTER 29

"WHAT'LL I DO when you are far away and I am blue? What'll I do?"

The haunting melody rolls down the empty halls like a dense fog, calling me out of the basement, taking me by the hand and guiding me through the school into the main hall. The music is louder here. It blares behind the doors of the gymnasium bordering the cafeteria a few yards away, daring me to enter.

The front doors of the school are open too, all the way at the end of the hall—so close, yet so far away. It's as though they're saying, *"You may leave now."*

I'm not so trusting anymore.

Cautiously, I limp to the closed doors of the gymnasium

and peer through one of the narrow windows. The vast room is dark and empty, the bleachers tucked away against the wall—but the music continues to ooze from the stereo system inside, serenading me.

"What'll I do when I am wond'ring who is kissing you? What'll I do?"

"I can see you."

I twirl at the sound of Bailey's voice and find her broken body standing in the center of the hall. At first, my mind tells me this is Autumn Crow come back to finish me off, to rip me from this world the way she has so many others. Perhaps I'd let her. I may even beg her to.

But when I see those pale olive eyes staring back at me, body translucent in the moonlight filtering through the stained glass windows of the main hall, I realize this is the real Bailey. *My* Bailey.

"I can see you," she repeats, shambling toward me.

I whimper. It seems she's trying to stand straighter but can't. I part my lips to speak, to apologize and hug her and find some way to bring her back to me, but I can't find the words or the ability to move. I watch with tear-stricken eyes as she walks, coming closer and closer—and then passes me by, pushing through the gymnasium doors.

"I can see you now."

I watch in confusion as she enters the gymnasium like a baby taking its first clumsy steps, her broken body caressed and embraced by the multicolored lights that bathe the room in pastel tones. A sea of baby-blue and pink balloons swarm at her feet as she makes her way onto the dance floor.

She is surrounded by smiling faces, young souls from another time dressed to the nines for what I can only surmise was supposed to have been the best night of their lives—a night that ended up being their last.

The crowd creates a path for Bailey, parting like the Red Sea to reveal a tall, slender man in a tuxedo standing in the center of the floor. A smile lights up his face, a twinkle in his eyes.

Mr. Hagen.

The doors ease shut behind Bailey, separating us. I peer through the windows as the crowd offers kind smiles and a round of applause for Bailey. The music swells around her, carrying her onward, carrying her closer to the waiting arms of her father.

"What'll I do with just a photograph to tell my troubles to?"

I smile through my tears, wanting to clap for Bailey too, wanting to cheer for my best friend having received what she's longed for all summer—to see her dad again.

But I freeze when notice a reflection in the window glass that isn't my own, a face looking over my shoulder.

Macy.

I don't have time to turn around. Her reflection evaporates before I can react, but not before leaving me with a single whispered word: "Watchdog."

I feel the floor fall out from under me.

Grabbing the door, I peer through the window as goosebumps stand on my arms. Felix Hagen is no longer awaiting his daughter on the dance floor. Instead, *it* is there. Naked and covered in fur. Holding its inky hands out to Bailey.

"Here, sweet girl. Let me fix you," it rasps.

"No!" I throw myself against the doors, but they hold

fast. *"No, no, no!"*

Bailey continues to walk, her outstretched hands trembling.

She doesn't see it, I realize. *She still sees her dad.*

I throw all my weight against the doors again and again, shouting at the top of my lungs, "Bailey! Stop! Come back!"

SLAM! SLAM! SLAM!

She doesn't hear me. She doesn't—

"See me!" I cry as Bailey draws nearer to the sinister beast. "SEE ME!"

Finally, the doors buckle. I fall onto the gymnasium floor, regain my footing, and bolt, sprinting through the crowd. As I rush past the raptured students, their smiles melt away. Their eyes darken and sink into their sockets as they reach out for me, grabbing me with oily fingers, pulling me back.

"Help us?" they say. "Help us?"

"No! Let go!"

I fight their hold, looking ahead to see Bailey reaching for the watchdog's daggerlike fingers.

Yards away. She's only yards away from it.

There's no time.

"Let go!" I scream. "Bailey, *STOP!*"

I don't know what will happen if Bailey falls into the watchdog's arms, but I fear it may be the end of whatever is left of Bailey's soul. I need to get to her. I have to stop her.

With one last fleeting effort, I pull away from the desperate, clinging hands and find myself running again.

"I've got you," I say under heaving breaths, dashing, reaching for Bailey. "I've got you."

With Bailey's fingertips just inches from the beast's, I throw myself at her, diving through the air, my arms outstretched.

"I've got you!" I close my arms around Bailey—and collapse onto the floor, clinging to nothing but air. Breathless, I scan my surroundings, finding myself on my knees in the middle of a dark, empty void with nothing but the gymnasium floor beneath me. The crowd is gone. The beast, the balloons, the streamers, the lights, the music—all gone.

Bailey.

Gone.

A scream tears out of my chest. It reaches into the unsung emptiness, vibrating the wooden floorboards around me, and crawls to a whimper. I hug my shoulders, rocking back and forth as the sadness washes me away.

"Come back," I plead quietly. "Come back."

The words return to me sealed and unreceived. Bailey is gone. Really gone. A part of her was here, and now it's not. It's as though someone reached inside my chest and ripped out my beating heart—or left me without my right hand.

"Come back," I sob. "Come back. Come back. Come back."

The words bounce off the cavernous walls and ceiling, making me feel like the smallest creature in the world. I stay down here at the bottom, weeping at the feet of oblivion, crying and calling out, falling deeper, spiraling down—until another voice calls me out of the depths and wrenches me free, a voice that says, *"Make it right."*

I recognize the voice as my own.

Lifting my bleary eyes, I realize I'm not in a dark chasm at all: it's the darkened school gymnasium, a space I've frequented many times over the past few years. I stand, bracing my feet on the solid floorboards.

Just the gym.

Behind me, the doors hang open, and farther away, tucked in a corner, is Cassandra Hagen. She stands stark still, blood staining the front of her outfit, just as death stains the irises of her watery eyes. She stares into nothing and cries in silence, her shoulders heaving, tears rolling down her cheeks in an endless stream.

"I'll make it right," I promise her.

She doesn't seem to hear or see me—just stares blankly ahead, tears falling as though she's been crying forever and will cry forevermore.

"I'll make it right," I repeat as I walk to the exit. Cassandra's spirit fades into the darkness. "I promise."

CHAPTER 30

I STEP OUT of the school into the cold nighttime air, descending the front steps, walking the well-trodden path onto Black Lane.

I look back at Autumncrow High. It puts on a mask, gleaming at me with an evil jack-o'-lantern leer, but I pretend I don't see it until, eventually, I don't.

Just a building.

I continue on, passing through the rural moonlit streets until the properties become smaller, the houses more densely packed. The golden glow of streetlights soon appears, offering a false sense of security.

I know I'm not safe though. I'll never be safe in this town.

From the corners of my eyes, I detect movement. All

around me, shapes drift in and out of the shadows—dark, blurry figures that dance and parade about. Fiendish ghouls. Toil-and-trouble witches. Pumpkin-headed cornfield stalkers. Eight-legged beasties.

I do my best to ignore them, but I see them ... sometimes. They seem to flicker in and out, here one moment and gone the next. I can hear them sometimes too, chanting and singing like they're at a jamboree, but only if I listen very closely.

They look like trick-or-treaters from another time and place, wearing masks and costumes that seem a part of them, far more than just latex and plastic. I recall Rae's dream. She was right—they do resemble children.

But they're not.

A dark mass drops from the branches of a dead tree in a nearby yard and glides toward me like a storm cloud that has lost its way. I keep my eyes trained on the lights of downtown twinkling ahead as the mass catches up and keeps pace beside me. In my periphery, I see it take the shape of a small child dressed in a witch's costume. Pointed black hat. Long, crooked nose.

"Trick or treat?" The words are spoken in a deep rasp that sizzles and pops. The smell of charred flesh burns the insides of my nostrils.

Keep walking, I say to myself. *It isn't really there.*

But I'm not so sure about that. Part of me—a very scared part—tells me these things, while blurry and indistinct, are quite real.

The sinister being lingers beside me, then it changes form again, becoming taller—*much* taller. Several feet taller than me. Its bones crackle and snap. Its fingers elongate, dragging on the weathered blacktop as it drifts along. Its face swells until its skin splits, discharging a creamy pus the color of regurgitated candy corn. Its mouth drops open as an ashy, white tongue flops out.

The urge to run is strong, but I hold my ground and keep walking, ignoring the giant creature until it finally glides away from me and finds another tree to inhabit, climbing its trunk and camouflaging into its dark branches.

A manic giggle dances on my lips. Then a tear falls from my eye.

As I approach downtown, the chorus of evil little things in the shadows grows louder and stronger.

"Autumn lives!" they chant. "Autumn lives!"

EPILOGUE

WHILE THE HEART of the town is alive with the bustle of shoppers, Autumncrow Cemetery is as deathly silent as its inhabitants. I stroll along its lonesome trails, ignoring the dull ache in my shin. The doctor suggested I lay off my injured leg for a couple of weeks until the stitches could be removed. And I was happy to follow her orders, but then she couldn't resist quipping about my two-week suspension from school and its "convenient timing," at which point I decided to take up jogging. Not just to spite her, but to keep an eye on things around town. As hard as I've tried, though, I've seen no trace of the fiendish creatures that marched through Autumncrow's streets that night almost two weeks ago.

Climbing to the top of the steepest hill in the cemetery,

I pause, taking a moment to catch my breath and soak in the vast landscape with its forlorn crypts floating in a sea of concrete and spidery brambles. From up here, I feel as though thousands of eyes are peering at me from the colorful trees peppering the view. A specter-like gust of wind weaves through the tombstones and whispers in my ear: *"You can't see us, but we can see you."*

I shiver and zip up my windbreaker to my chin as I descend the hill. They're still out there somewhere. For all I know, those evil beings have always been here, watching me—watching all of us—and I just couldn't see them until they decided to reveal themselves, to show me it's all over: Autumn Crow is back, lurking somewhere in the rolling hills and valleys of this doomed town, dwelling in a body that isn't hers.

I dig my fingernails into my palms as my body shudders with rage, fear, and grief. Wherever Autumn Crow is, whatever she's planning, I need to be ready.

All hell is about to break loose.

I take deep, trembling breaths, trying to calm my nerves as I make my way to the back of the cemetery where the newer graves are added. Where the Hagen family plot is located.

"Hi, Mr. and Mrs. Hagen," I say as I approach, even though only Bailey's mom is buried here. Her dad's whereabouts remain unknown, and now I understand that he'll never be found. Still, Felix's name is engraved on the tombstone he shares with Cassandra, and it comforts me to imagine them reunited in the afterlife.

Beside their grave is Bailey's memorial, where I kneel and, with hands that won't stop shaking, replace the dead rose lying at the base of her portrait with the fresh stem I picked at the flower shop in town.

"Hey, Bailey." I wait a moment as I always do, giving her the opportunity to reply. *Even just a whisper,* I silently beg. *Please. I need to hear from you.*

Nothing.

I close my eyes and bite back tears. *Please, please, please...*

Last year, after Grammy passed away, Dad took me to the cemetery every weekend, stepping away to give the two of us a few moments alone together. "Talk to her as if she's standing right in front of you," he suggested. And I did. I shared everything that was on my mind during those visits—from homework, to boys, to how desperately I missed her. And each time, I felt Grammy's soothing presence, her hand on my shoulder, guiding me through the sadness and confusion.

But it's different with Bailey. Because Bailey isn't here. There was no body to bury, no casket to fill, no soul to usher through the pearly gates. Everything that Bailey ever was has been ripped away from me. Where she went, I wish I knew. I wish it more than anything in the world.

I hang my head and attempt to swallow the stone in my throat. "Bailey," I say, "wherever you are, I'm going to find you, okay? I promise. I'm going to find you and set you free."

No response. No warmth in my bones. No sensation of inner peace.

"I'll make it right," I try again.

Nothing.

I tuck a loose strand of greasy blond hair behind my ear,

reminding myself that I should really shower at some point. "I probably look like a mess. I guess I am a bit of a mess," I say. "It's just so weird here without you. Last night, I picked up the phone to call you. Obviously, I didn't get very far before I remembered you weren't going to answer."

I bury my hands in my pockets and roll a piece of lint between my fingertips. "There are so many things I wish I could ask you now. We were always so close, but now that you're gone . . . Jeez, Bailey, I'm realizing what a lousy friend I was. I guess I took for granted that you'd always be there, that our friendship would endure no matter how our paths diverged after high school, that we had all the time in the world. But I never even bothered to ask you about your plans. What did you want out of life? What were your ambitions? What were your hopes and dreams? I talked about mine all the time, but you . . . you never did. Why?"

I think I know. It all goes back to the first day we met, when Bailey handed me that sketch of a ghost under a sheet. "It's me," she said, and truer words were never spoken. Like a lonely ghost, Bailey was always one to listen quietly and watch life from the sidelines, taking in every experience as an outsider. A stranger in a foreign land. An innocent. Maybe she struggled to imagine a future for herself, or maybe she felt it wasn't worth putting into words. Maybe she didn't think I'd understand. I know she felt out of place, out of time, like she didn't belong here. But she did. She belonged here. She belonged with me.

"You belonged."

I stare the makeshift memorial, feeling utterly alone—like I, too, am fading away. Bailey's framed portrait stands on an easel amid all the flowers and ribbons, photos, and other tokens of remembrance people have left for her. Beneath the portrait hangs a plaque that I had engraved for her myself: "Bailey Alexandra Hagen. Daughter, sister, friend, dreamer."

Sister . . . Poor Rae.

The last time I saw her was at the funeral. She didn't cry; didn't show any emotion at all. She just stared at her mom's casket as it was lowered into the ground. When I gave her a hug afterward, she looked at me with eyes full of hope and said, "It's okay, Melody. No one's ever really gone in Autumncrow." But then *she* was, carted across the state to live with her Uncle Pete.

I stare at Bailey's portrait now in hopes that Rae is right.

"Hey, did I tell you Bill Macklin came to your vigil?" I ask Bailey, praying a switch in tone might bring her to me somehow. "He was real eaten up. He said he always thought you were super cute."

The first part is true; he did look eaten up.

"He said he'd been to five funerals already this year. I guess the university isn't much better than Autumncrow High. So much death . . ."

The branches of a nearby oak rustle as though a large animal is scrambling about, hidden in the leaves. I cast a quick glance in its direction, and the movement stops. I do my best to ignore the chill creeping up my spine.

"You know, the school graveyard isn't nearly as pretty as this place. Tommy—" The name catches in my throat; I still can't say it aloud without feeling like I'm going to burst into tears. "Um . . . he's buried at school, under the oak. I'm still not allowed on school property to visit him since I'm suspended. I could sneak in a visit, I suppose, but I'm not ready to go back there just yet."

A crow sails through the air and lands on a tombstone a few yards away. It squawks at me, and I squawk back, scaring it off.

I shake my head at myself. "Maybe I really am cracking up. My mom certainly thinks so. This morning, she said jogging is just a way of running from my problems. I told her I'm not running from anything or anyone. That may be what most people in Autumncrow end up doing, but not me. The way I see it, unless you're ready to face your fears head-on, running isn't much different from standing still, and I'm not about to do that anymore either. You know what I mean?"

I toss my bag beside Bailey's memorial and sit in the dry grass. "I know you told me to run, but I can't. Autumn Crow is back, and I'm the only one left alive who was there to witness it. Which is why I need to warn everyone I can."

I unzip my bag and pull out a sealed envelope and pen. *"To Agatha and Jerry, for the front page,"* I scribble on the face of the envelope. *"I owe you guys."* Then I set it at the foot of the memorial along with a Polaroid I recently found in Bailey's bookbag—a picture of her and me as kids, posing happily in front of the Ferris wheel at the Halloween Carnival.

"I'm leaving these for Agatha to pick up after school," I say, setting a pebble on top of the envelope and photograph so they won't blow away. "She spends a lot of time here in the cemetery. You would've liked her. Jerry is great too, especially once you get to know him. Kind of cute, in a dorky way." I blush. "I guess some things never change, huh?"

I stand and muster a tiny smile. "I just hope Monique

doesn't suspect anything before the paper goes to print. Her parents decided not to press charges, by the way, but once my leg heals, I'm required to pass out caramel apples for the entire length of the Halloween Carnival. I guess it's not so bad. The rides wouldn't be the same without you anyway."

I throw my bag over my shoulder. "Well. I should get going. I'll see you tomorrow. And the day after that."

I wait in silence a moment, not really wanting to leave. I touch my fingertips to Bailey's portrait and trace the outline of her red hair, wishing I could feel even a glimmer of her warm presence instead of the cold frame glass.

Sadness rises from my heart and into my throat. "I loved you with all my heart, Bailey," I utter. I close my eyes as I quietly weep, my shoulders rising and falling. "I don't know how I'll ever make it without you, but I'll do my best to make you proud. Thank you for being my best friend."

Another chilly gust stirs a cloud of dead leaves and twirls them in my direction. As usual, a few of them get stuck in my hair, but I'm too consumed with grief to care like I once did. I offer the Hagens a farewell wave, then I step away from their plot—and freeze.

What was that?

I look down and watch as a red leaf cascades to the ground.

And then there it is again—the feeling of someone lightly tugging the leaves from my hair. More continue to fall, creating a small, colorful pile at my feet. I turn, fully expecting there to be someone behind me, but all I see is Bailey's memorial, her portrait on the easel standing firm in the breeze.

And just like that, there it is—the comforting warmth

I felt while talking to Grammy after she died. It spreads over my body, carrying with it a fond remembrance of happier times: I'm walking to school on the first day of senior year with Bailey at my side, pausing just long enough for her to pick the leaves from my hair one by one.

I smile as I lose myself in the memory, reliving it again and again.

Oh Bailey . . . maybe you aren't so far away after all.

To be continued in the next installment of
AUTUMNCROW HIGH

About the Author

Cameron Chaney was born and raised in a small Ohio town you've never heard of. He spent his childhood roaming his family's six-acre property and devouring one spooky book after another. He now enjoys writing spooky stories of his own in his home library and talking about all things spooky on his YouTube show, *Library Macabre*. Cameron also works as a youth services librarian aboard his local bookmobile. He currently resides in yet another small Ohio town you've never heard of. Don't feed him after midnight . . .

HORROR STORIES
BY HORRORTUBERS

Local Haunts
Served Cold
Lurking in the Dark

AVAILABLE NOW
in paperback & e-book

Printed in Great Britain
by Amazon

28131034R00178